PLAGUE

A Medical Thriller by

VICTOR METHOS

There are maladies we must not seek to cure because they alone protect us from others that are more serious.

-Marcel Proust

Think of the earth as a living organism that is being attacked by billions of bacteria whose numbers double every forty years. Either the host dies, or the virus dies, or both die.

-Gore Vidal

CHAPTER 1

It began with a cough.

Michael Pettrioli sat on a large stone near the Amazon River, sipping warm water out of a plastic bottle. The river churned its brownish contents into white foam and though he was only a few feet away from his adventure guide, who was convincing a local tribesman that they were not here to steal their women, he couldn't hear anything but the river.

It'd been two days since he'd felt feverish and last night he'd been up at least half a dozen times either vomiting or with diarrhea. For several days before, he was unable to sleep from the blanket of insects that would attack him at night as he lay in a hammock a couple feet off the ground. Even with nets and repellent he seemed helpless to fight them. They ranged from harmless pests to life-threatening monsters. There was one type of biting fly that sought the fleshy part of the lip and injected her eggs there. One person in the group had already become a host and the guide had said they'd need to wait until the eggs are larger and cut them out with a hot scalpel.

The adventure guide, a tall Australian man by the name of Clifford, finished speaking with the local villager and then came over and leaned down in front of Michael. He placed his hand on his head and then his neck.

"You don't look so hot, mate. Feeling warm."

"Just a little fever," Michael said. "It's nothin'."

"Well, isn't nothing out here nothing. I think I need to send you back to the village to see a doc."

"No way. I blew ten Gs for this trip and I ain't goin' back to spend the next week in some filthy hospital bed. I'm fine, seriously. I think I caught a stomach bug or somethin'. I'm sure I'll be cool in another day or two."

Clifford shrugged and stood up. "If you say so. Stay hydrated best you can. If we're moving too fast, you let me know."

"Thanks."

It wasn't long until Clifford gave the word that it was time to move out. They had at least a six-hour trek ahead of them before nightfall and much of the terrain they needed to cover was either dense vegetation that needed to be cut through or muddy ground that would come up to their ankles. It was tough going for the most experienced of guides and Michael knew for an amateur like him, feeling like he did, it was going to be hell.

But this wasn't the first time he'd experienced hell.

He grabbed his backpack and followed the group of seven into the dense jungle canopy. They didn't speak or laugh or crack jokes as they did the first few days. Everyone was dehydrated and tired, a few of them sick, most of them hungry, and none of them having a good time.

Michael kept his eyes on the ground, watching his feet as he pushed one foot and then the other in front of him. That was how he had climbed Everest and how he crossed half the continent of Africa. One step at a time. But this was much harder. With each step he felt his strength leaving him and his mind turning to mush. He couldn't think clearly and after about an hour his vision began to blur.

He kept this to himself. The girl in front of him was ten feet away and he kept his eyes on her boots, a magnet to draw him forward. But as his vision grew worse, so did his nausea. He felt bile in his throat and tried to swallow it down but could only do so much before it burst out of his mouth.

Considering there was nothing in his stomach but crackers and water, hardly anything came up. But it was so violent that it brought him to his knees. He felt the soft, wet dirt underneath him, against his skin. It felt welcoming, much more so than the humid air and the insects burrowing into him. He collapsed onto his back, certain he would just take a quick nap and then catch up to the group.

When Michael awoke he was in a hospital bed, staring up at dirty ceiling. He glanced next to him and saw a nurse wiping a needle that she had just removed from the arm of the patient in the bed next to him. She then placed it in a bottle, withdrawing fluid before sticking it into his arm. Michael looked away and saw Clifford sitting in a chair by the bed.

"Where are we?" Michael said, his voice raspy.

"Hospital in Iquitos. How ya feeling?"

"Like I got hit by a truck. You drive me back here?"

"Came in by plane."

"Man," he said, turning his face up to the ceiling, "don't remember that plane ride. How long it take?"

"'Bout twenty minutes."

"You don't have to sit here with me, Cliff. You need to go with the group."

"Nah, I ain't never left a fella behind yet. Group's good. I got someone to cover for me. I just wanted to make sure you're feeling right as rain before I go on my way."

Michael took a deep breath. "Ten grand down the crapper."

"Well, we'll give you a discount next time. Cheer up and get better. There are more adventures yet for a young bloke like you."

The nurse jabbed a needle in his arm again and Michael flinched. "Ouch. What is that?"

"Chloroquine. They think you got yourself a bad case'a malaria."

"Shit," he said, shaking his head, "can she at least get a new needle?"

"Don't work that way here." Clifford rose to his feet. "Well, I leave you in good hands. I got some things to do in town and I'll be back to check on you tomorrow before I head out."

"Thanks. Sorry about all this."

Clifford put his hand on Michael's shoulder. "No worries."

Ten minutes after Clifford had left, the nurse gave Michael a shot of morphine. That feeling he knew. He drifted off into his memories, remembering playing with his grandfather in the garden by his house. He was smiling and relaxed when he felt a wet sensation on his chin and chest. He looked down to see black blood spreading in a large pool. Lazily, he brought his hand up to his mouth and came away with dark ooze on his hand. It was coming out of his mouth, nose, and eyes and he was choking.

He tried to scream and it came out a gurgling wet mess. He began coughing violently, spatters of the black liquid flying over the hospital room. The nurse was shouting something and a doctor came in. They held him down as he thrashed violently, the pain rising from his stomach to his throat and out of his mouth. The morphine didn't touch it.

He gurgled one final scream before he lay back on the bed, his lungs filled with blood, and life began to leave him.

CHAPTER 2

Dr. Jose Cabero sat in his office on the second floor of the Health Administration Building in Lima and wondered why he had been sent a file about a death from over 629 miles away. This was something the locals should have dealt with. He sighed as he opened the folder, looked at the photo of the patient, and saw his nationality: American. That was the reason. The death of an American in a high tourist locale had to be addressed immediately. Americans were prone to panic and tourism was the lifeblood of many of the small villages. Without the guided tours and photo safaris and sightseers, many would starve.

He read the autopsy report of the treating physician, Dr. Alvarez, and reread the cause of death: DEATH BY MISADVENTURE. It was a way of saying they had no idea how he died without saying it officially.

Cabero looked at the autopsy photos and saw the young man covered in a thick, black liquid. It appeared like blood from a liver wound. He had seen many abdominal gunshot-wound victims with similar-looking blood. But underneath the skin was a thick, purple coloring giving him the appearance of being charred in a fire. That, he had not seen before. At the end of the file was a note from Dr. Alvarez: "Call me right away."

Cabero picked up the phone and dialed the number to the Hermana de la Misericordia Clinic. A nurse picked up and he asked for Alvarez. He got on the phone. "I've been waiting two days."

"Sorry," Cabero said. "Busy."

"Did you read the file?"

"Yes."

"What do you think?"

"About what?"

"You didn't read the file, did you?"

"I just told you I did."

"I want to send a sample of his blood and have it tested with you. We don't have the laboratories for it here."

"Fine. Send whatever you like."

"Have I done something to upset you, Jose?"

"I'm sick of these tourists coming here with dreams of finding lost cities and ending up dead. Then it's my mess to clean and I get yelled at by every bureaucrat who sees tourism drying up. I'm just sick of the whole thing."

"Sick of it or not this American is going to cause problems. We have over ten tours a day with each person paying thousands of dollars."

"I know," Cabero said dismissively. "Send the blood. I'll have someone look at it. What are we looking for?"

"Unknown pathogen."

CHAPTER 3

Clifford Lane finished the tour near the Jutai River and thanked the five remaining guests, taking a moment to answer questions and exchange emails. A few of them told him they'd like to stay in touch and talk about another tour next year.

When he was done he gathered up his supplies, rolling his tent and strapping it to his backpack, which lay on the ground. He went to stand on the edge of the river and dialed a number on his cell phone. There was still no reception. He turned the phone off and heaved the backpack on before taking a deep breath and starting the two-mile hike to the village and the Jeep that awaited him. From there, it was on to a plane headed for Brazil for a few days of relaxation before going back home to Honolulu.

As he trekked through the vegetation he felt an enormous amount of sweat pouring down his forehead. It made his shirt cling to his back and he had to stop every few minutes and guzzle down as much water as he could. His legs began to feel weak from the dehydration and he stopped underneath a large capirona tree and lay down, putting his arm over his face to shield it from the sun that was beating down through the canopy. He felt hot and faint and remembered that he hadn't eaten since this morning. He pulled out a granola bar and some jerky and ate them slowly with a bottle of water. Waiting another few minutes, he felt better, rose, and began to walk.

Clifford climbed aboard the 747 bound for Rio de Janeiro and collapsed into his seat. It seemed he couldn't get the sweat to stop pouring out of him no matter how much water he drank. The fever had increased to the point that he couldn't sleep and the previous night, which he'd spent in a hotel, he'd lain in bed with an icepack on his head, rubbing furiously at a rash that was developing on his chest.

He reached up and turned on the air conditioning, pointing the fan over his face. Leaning his head back, he closed his eyes and his eyeballs felt hot against his lids. He debated just getting a sooner flight back home to Honolulu where his girlfriend, a nurse, could get him in to a good doctor at a good hospital right away.

"You doin' okay, buddy?" the guy next to him asked.

"Fine," he said without opening his eyes.

Clifford felt vomit rising in his throat. It came in waves, up and down his esophagus. He unbuckled his belt to go to the bathroom and the motion exhausted him.

"Holy shit!"

Clifford opened his eyes. The man next to him was staring at him liked he'd fallen out of the sky. He was about to ask what was wrong when he noticed the backs of his hands. They were turning a deep black just underneath the skin. Drops of blood fell on them from his nose. The blood was bright red, almost comically red; he'd never seen a red quite that color. He stood up to run to the bathroom when the man next to him screamed. Clifford looked down and saw the blood that had dripped over the man's face.

“Sorry,” he said to no one as he stumbled out into the aisle. He leaned on the seats and pulled himself forward though his legs were not responding. It was like they were moving in slow motion; heavy, weighed down by something he couldn’t see.

Clifford reached for the doorknob of the bathroom as people on the plane were alerting the stewardess. He grabbed the doorknob, felt its warmth in his palm, and then the world went black as he fell forward into the door.

CHAPTER 4

Dr. Samantha Bower looked up from her textbook and at the clock on the wall of the cafeteria at the Centers for Disease Control in Atlanta. It was nearly one in the morning and her back was beginning to ache from an old soccer injury she'd incurred in high school. The fact that she had gone skydiving earlier that morning and landed hard on a steeply inclined hill didn't help the old injury.

She stretched from side to side and checked her iPhone. Her boss, the director of the National Center for Emerging and Zoonotic Diseases within the CDC, had decided to take a three-week European vacation. The task of finishing the report on a rare strand of influenza infections in Mongolia—that the deputy director of Infectious Diseases wanted right away for no reason at all—fell on her shoulders. It'd been ten days of eight hours in her actual work, fielding calls, drafting research memos, and filing reports, and then eight hours on her own time, fielding calls, drafting research memos, and filing reports.

She decided she'd had enough for today and stood up, picking up her book, Kann's *DNA Virus Replication*, and headed out the doors to the parking lot. It was warm and the moon was up in the dark sky. The lighting over the lot was dim, as many of the bulbs were out. Few things in the building were maintained well but no one that worked there seemed to mind. As the director had said in a recent speech, they were at the forefront of medicine and microbiology. Using theories to predict outcomes in real-life scenarios. It was, as far as she could tell, the most exciting place for a physician or microbiologist to work, though few of her colleagues from medical school would think so.

She hopped onto Interstate 75 and headed home in her silver Jeep Grand Cherokee. She rolled down the windows and let the air flow over her face and through the car, rustling some papers in the back. Atlanta at this time of night was no place for her to be out but she had never been afraid. Her father had warned her that Atlanta had more car-jackings per capita than any other major American city. But she saw instances, like car-jackings, as statistical probabilities not real threats. By driving at night she had increased her probability of being car-jacked but the chance was still so remote that she wasn't worried. Then again, lightning had to strike somewhere.

It took her thirty-five minutes to reach her brownstone in a quiet suburb just near Sandy Springs. She parked in the driveway, too tired to open the garage, and set the alarm to her car before deactivating the alarm to her house.

The house was cool and the air conditioner clicked off as she entered. It was decorated modestly with little extravagance other than a few photographs and paintings related to music, a career as a violinist being her first choice since she was a child. Sam kicked off her shoes, set her alarm, and crawled into bed without brushing her teeth or changing.

Sam awoke at ten in the morning. It was Saturday and the sun was streaming through the windows, lighting up the open spaces in her home. She considered calling her sister Jane in San Francisco and then decided to shower first.

After showering and changing into denim shorts and a black Calvin Klein shirt, she turned on her iPhone and grabbed a protein shake out of the fridge. She stepped outside and wondered whether she should take a quick walk around the park that was located a few minutes up the block.

Jane didn't answer and Sam left a message asking her to give her a call back when she got up. Three houses down was a small bungalow with an American flag up over the porch, a carving up on the door of marines putting up the flag at Iwo Jima. Sam took out a key and unlocked the door before entering.

The house was decorated in a style that belonged to decades past; she had always guessed the sixties but had no evidence for that other than a black velvet painting of Elvis. She walked through the house and shouted, "Hello?" There was no reply.

Making her way to the north side of the house, she entered the master bedroom. An elderly woman lay in bed, staring at a television that had the sound turned down all the way. Sam pulled up a stool and sat down next to her.

"How are you, Ma?"

"Your uncle Johnny needs to get into the house. Don't forget to leave your key above the door frame."

Sam reached over and began to straighten her sheets. "Uncle Johnny's been dead for over twenty years, Ma. Remember, we talked about this yesterday."

"He needs the key so that he can get his albums. Oh, him and those albums. I swear he loves those things more than he loves me."

Sam looked at her a moment; the innocence in her eyes penetrated her. "No, he loves you more than anything." Sam cleared her throat, choking back the emotion that bubbled inside her. "Where's your nurse, Ma?"

"Oh that one, that's another one. The Mexican."

"Rosa's very nice. She really likes working here."

Her mother shrugged. It was confusing for Sam at first: the moments of lucidness coupled with the immediate comment or question that revealed her mother did not know where she was or what time she was in. But Sam was used to it now, as much as someone could be, and she tried to ignore it as much as possible.

"Do you know where Rosa is?"

"She went out for some milk of magnesia. We're all out. She's a nice girl to get my milk of magnesia."

Samantha saw a bowl of cereal on the side table. "Let's finish the cereal," she said, taking the bowl and spooning some cereal gently into her mother's mouth.

She stayed with her mother, rubbing her head until she fell asleep. Rosa got home shortly after. Sam spoke a few minutes with her about the medication situation and told her she would be back tonight to take her mother on a walk in her wheelchair.

Sam stepped outside and had to lean against the door for a moment. She remembered when her mother stood at the oven, stirring delicious stews or baking cakes with generic ingredients bought in bulk because they could only afford to get groceries every other week. Though Sam could afford expensive restaurants now, somehow the cheap cupcakes and beef stroganoff her mother made were the best things she had ever eaten.

After her father's death late in life, her mother seemed invincible raising four children on her own. To see her shrink away to nearly nothing and not even know who Sam was most of the time tore her guts out, but she couldn't stop coming. Her mother had been there when she needed her and she was going to return the favor no matter what.

Sam called her sister again but again there was no answer. As she pulled the phone away from her ear, she saw that the voicemail icon had a one next to it. She clicked on it and listened to the message:

This is Gale with CDC dispatch. Please call Dr. Ralph Wilson immediately.

The time display on the message said she had received it at 3:17 a.m.

Sam called the CDC mainline as she leisurely strolled down the sidewalk. It was going to be hot today but for now the temperature was perfect in a cloudless sky. She could see the park no more than two blocks away and throngs of children were already there. Occasionally, she would sit on the benches and watch them for long periods of time.

"CDC dispatch, this is Monique."

"Hi, Monique, this is Samantha."

"Oh, hi, Dr. Bower. How are you?"

"Good. I got a message from Gale that Ralph needed to speak to me."

"Yup. I'll put you through."

After a click, Dr. Ralph Wilson, one of the most influential men in public health, sneezed, swore under his breath, and said, "My wife doesn't return my calls either," by way of greeting.

"Sorry, I was up until one in the morning working on something for Nancy."

"Yeah, she'll do that to you. What was it for?"

"The report you wanted on the influenza outbreak in Khovd."

"Shelve that. I got something I want you to look in to."

"What is it?"

"Could be nothing, but could be something. I know it's Saturday but you're the agent on call right now I think."

"I am. We alternate weeks."

"It's an emergency room physician in Honolulu. Gerald Amoy. Goes by Jerry. Do you have a pen?"

"No."

"I'll text you his information. Give him a call. He's put in a request for help so I took the liberty of booking your flight for two this afternoon. You okay with that?"

"Sure, I didn't have any plans for today," she said calmly, hiding her excitement for a free trip to Hawaii.

"I figured you wouldn't mind. I'll send his information over now."

Sam got to the park and sat on a bench in front of the swing set. A young girl was being pushed by her mother and Sam watched the young girl's smile and the way she would squeal when she got pushed just a bit too high. Sam didn't notice that her phone had vibrated with an incoming text and when she glanced down at it she saw that ten minutes had passed.

She clicked on the number displayed in the text.

"Queen's Medical Center Emergency."

"Hi, this is Dr. Samantha Bower with the Centers for Disease Control. I need to speak with a Dr. Gerald Amoy. I'm returning his call."

"Let me page him."

She was put on hold and heard a ukulele with a soft voice singing over it. The lyrics were in Hawaiian and it excited her even more. She hadn't been on a real vacation…well, ever. She had worked her way through medical school at the University of Arizona and had no time off during her surgical residency.

Just thinking of the hours she put into her residency in a busy hospital in the suburbs of Chicago sent a chill up her back. As a matter of course she would be in the hospital over a hundred hours a week, leaving no more than six hours a day to eat, sleep, drive, shower, spend time exercising, reading, talking with her family, and anything else she might have had to do. Within the first two weeks, she knew she no longer wanted to be a surgeon.

Luckily, she had met the chief of infectious disease research at the University of Chicago's Department of Biology at a CME course for physicians. He'd shown up half-drunk and hit on her and then, seemingly to impress her, indicated he was looking to replace one of the physicians on his staff that was leaving the program due to substance abuse issues. She jumped at the opportunity. She applied and got the position after just one interview. The fact that it paid half what the average medical school graduate could expect to earn didn't hurt, as there were only seven other applicants.

The nine-to-five research schedule made her feel as if she had been freed from prison. She completed three years and was going to take a position with a prestigious clinic in her hometown of San Francisco when she discovered the world of epidemiology on the job, and, almost without any effort, received an offer from the CDC through her connections at the University of Chicago.

"This is Amoy."

"This is Samantha Bower from the Centers for Disease Control. I'm just responding to a request we received."

"Oh, I'm glad you called. Just a second." There was some shuffling and she could hear him give instructions to somebody. "Sorry about that."

"No problem. So what can we do for you, Dr. Amoy?"

"I have two patients here that are displaying symptoms of an unknown viral infection. One of them is in critical care—I don't think he's going to last much longer. The other has just started displaying symptoms. We have them both in isolation here in the hospital."

"What are their symptoms?"

"The first victim had a rash that's now displaying on the second. The first victim is hemorrhaging sub-dermally. In the last ten hours or so the skin has begun falling off in sheets. There's been dark hemorrhaging from the eyes, ears, penis, and anus. We've had him on almost constant blood transfusion but it's not affecting him anymore. Infection is spreading through his body on the portions where the skin has come off. I called because I didn't think he'd survive more than another day or two and thought you might want to look at him."

"I won't be there until tonight. Can I call you when I land?"

"Sure, I'm heading out right now but I'm on a twenty-four-hour shift starting at eleven. Just leave a message if I don't answer right away."

"Okay, thanks, Doctor."

"No, thank you."

Sam hung up and took a deep breath as she put her phone away. The symptomology of the victims indicated a severe viral infection. There were any number of known viruses that could cause those symptoms, and many more that science hadn't discovered yet. Of course, she'd seen similar symptoms before and it had been a false alarm. The patient displayed Marburg virus type symptoms and it turned out that they had smoked a bad batch of methamphetamine, cut with dozens of poisonous substances, over the course of a week. An actual unknown viral infection that could cause those symptoms was extremely rare and the likelihood was that this was something else.

Still, her belly tingled with excitement and anticipation, and also fear. This was why she had gone into epidemiology in the first place. She looked at the young girl and smiled at her before rising and heading back to her house to pack.

CHAPTER 5

The layover at LAX took two hours and Sam perused the magazines and books in the gift shop. She had her iPad with her and refused to read any book in paper form that could be found electronically, but there was something relaxing about the actual feel of a book in her hands, the smell of the pages as she flipped through them.

She got a salad with extra cheese and an apple juice from a café at the airport and spent her time reading the *New England Journal of Medicine* near a window, glancing over occasionally as a plane landed or took off. They called her flight and then delayed it another twenty minutes before she was finally let on the plane.

It wasn't until past midnight that she stepped onto the tarmac of Honolulu International. Traveling over the ocean at night had been an experience she hadn't expected. The moon lit the water a dim white and it looked like a flashlight shining in a pool of black oil. A ship was on the sea underneath the plane and she watched it until it disappeared into the murk of the Pacific at night.

She grabbed her two bags and went to the curb to hail a cab. Rather than finding a hotel, she went straight to the hospital.

Honolulu struck her as a resort town created specifically to cater to tourists. The restaurants, bars, shopping malls, and even convenience stores looked uniquely islander. The air had the salty taste of the ocean and it was humid, but pleasant. She kept her window rolled down on the cab ride over and tipped the driver well before getting out.

She stood, staring up at Queen's Medical Center. It too appeared like a resort rather than a hospital. The valet area was lit with the soft glow of tiki torches and the building itself resembled an upscale hotel. She had read about it on the plane and knew that, with over five hundred rooms, it was the largest hospital in the state.

As she walked through the ER's sliding glass doors, she was struck by the familiar smell of hospital antiseptic. Rather than a nostalgic, warm feeling as many physicians had upon entering a hospital when they had not been practicing in the profession, it brought up images of being so exhausted she couldn't keep her eyes open and would fall asleep at a cafeteria table. Or of being yelled at by the attending or the chief for minor errors brought about by the exhaustion, or of turning down dates because there simply wasn't enough time to sit down for dinner at a restaurant without being called in.

She went to the reception and asked for Dr. Amoy. While waiting, she set her bags down on one of the waiting room chairs and stretched her arms over her head and rolled her neck. She had missed her run today and it was a ritual that, if ignored, would throw off her entire rhythm and cause insomnia at night.

"Dr. Bower?"

She turned to see a man in blue scrubs and a white coat approach her. He was tall and lean. Clearly of Hawaiian descent but with light skin and sandy hair. They shook hands and she picked up her bags.

"I'm Jerry. Nice to meet you."

"Nice to meet you," she said.

"I take it you haven't checked into a hotel yet?"

"No, not yet."

"You can leave your bags behind the reception desk. The first patient isn't doing well. We'd better head up there as soon as we can."

She dropped her bags off but took out a legal pad and pen. It was what she always used for notes on field assignments because she could copy them into her iPad before leaving the scene and then throw away the notebook in case it had been exposed to any pathogens. Such a risk was minimal but it helped her feel better and was certainly worth the two-dollar price tag for a pack of legal pads every few months.

Dr. Amoy took her up the plush elevators to the third floor where there were women's locker rooms. She changed into scrubs and was given a facemask, gloves, and booties. After changing, she looked at herself in the mirror. Sometimes it struck her how odd a job she really had. She was like a fireman that ran into a burning building when everyone else was running out. It was counter-intuitive and certainly anti-evolutionary. Biologically, humans were not set up to expose themselves willingly to disease. If she didn't control her thoughts and her breathing, panic could strike her as easily as it would anyone.

When she came out of the locker room she saw Dr. Amoy speaking on his cell phone. "I have to go…love you too." He looked to her. "Ready?"

"I'd like to see their charts first if I could."

"Certainly."

They went back to the elevators and up to the top floor. They walked down a long corridor where there was only one reception desk, which was left unattended. She noticed more offices than hospital rooms and also a kitchen and lounge area.

"They're converting this floor but this used to be our psychiatric unit," Amoy said.

"I gotta tell you, this is one of the nicest hospitals I've ever been in."

"You're preaching to the choir. My residency was done in St. Catherine's in Detroit. You ever been?"

"No."

"It's like a cheap office building with an OR. We'd get a dozen gunshot victims a weekend and it would take the staff days just to clean up the blood. We were underfunded and they contracted the janitors out—it's just up here to the right."

They turned down another empty corridor and walked past some construction that was taking place. No workers were there at this hour but Sam saw half-empty Gatorade bottles and burrito wrappers lying out.

Once they were in a small conference room with a fridge, Amoy went in and pulled two charts off a wall hanger. He sat down at the table and Sam did the same.

"Clifford Lane, resident of Honolulu, twenty-nine and in perfect health before this. Second victim is an Erin Simon from Los Angeles. She was here on vacation."

He passed the charts to her and she began reading. She took notes on her pad of the patients' statistics: height, weight, occupation, marital status, sexual orientation, etc.

"I'll need their medical records," she said.

"We can get that afterward when you've signed the HIPAA release. I really think we should see them now and do the paperwork later."

They rose and Sam checked her gloves and mask for any tears or holes. Amoy did the same and they walked out to the corridor and down to the room at the end of the hall. Two adjoining rooms were connected by a thick door and Sam saw a woman of thirty-six lying on her back, her eyes closed, a morphine drip attached to her arm.

"Hello, Erin," Amoy said, approaching the bed. "How we feeling today?"

Sam stood by the foot of the bed, bending as close as she dared to get a good look at her exposed arms and neck. Her skin appeared smooth, no pustules, but splotches of black and dark purple appeared underneath. It didn't cover her entirely but it occurred frequently enough that she could tell instantly it wasn't bruising. It was blood that was flooding out of her body just underneath the skin.

Sam looked to the woman's mouth. Crusted, dried blood lined her nostrils and her lips. Her teeth were stained with it and her mouth was completely dry and hanging open as if she were struggling to suck in air.

She heard something out of the patient that sounded like a groan but caused Dr. Amoy to respond and Sam realized the woman was speaking.

"I want to go for a walk," she gasped. "I've been in this bed for five days. I want to go for a walk."

"Soon," Amoy said, checking the morphine. "We just gotta make sure we're dotting our I's and crossing our T's before we take you for a spin. We want to get you home to your family as soon as we can, darling. Would you like anything else right now?"

There was no response and Sam saw that the woman had dazed off into sleep or unconsciousness. Amoy lightly touched the bed, running his fingers over the sheets. Sam could tell he wished to touch the patient; human contact was important to the best doctors, the ones that went into medicine to actually heal patients rather than for money or prestige. Instead, he had to settle for the sheets behind a rubber glove.

"I'd like to see the first patient," she said, not taking her eyes off Erin.

Amoy walked to the door and opened it to reveal another room identical to the first but set up diametrically opposite. The bed was against the wall, facing them, and Sam stopped at the doorway when she saw the patient.

He looked as if he'd been burned in a fire. His skin was black and large portions of it were covered with antiseptic gel used for burn patients when the skin had peeled off. Bandages covered his legs. He opened his eyes briefly, flashing a feverish anger from confusion, and she could see a bright red conjunctivitis, the whites of his eyes soaked in blood. His eyes closed and he let out a long, raspy whisper.

"He's unresponsive at this point," Amoy whispered so the patient couldn't hear. "We've spoken with the family and they're upset that they can't see him but I figured I'd wait for the OK from you guys first, in case this is something serious and dangerous to the public health."

"We shouldn't be in this room," Sam said. "We need to set up full-barrier nursing for both of them. You need to make sure no one has access to this room except nurses who know how to handle the barrier and won't have a problem with it."

"Why would they have a problem?"

"Nurses can get brave around illness over time. They may feel it's not a big deal."

Amoy took a deep breath. "You're right. I should have done that from the beginning."

"I understand why you didn't. I'll need tissue and blood samples to send to the labs in Atlanta. Until we find out what this is, nobody can be up here."

CHAPTER 6

On a quiet stretch of land in Fort Detrick, Maryland, Duncan Adams pushed on his brakes as he arrived at the United States Army Medical Research Institute of Infectious Diseases, the most advanced research facility in the world dealing with bioterrorism and home to over eight hundred scientists, both military and civilian.

At the entrance of the unassuming building, which could have easily passed for a community college or an antiquated office building, Duncan showed his identification to the guard and parked in a stall reserved for civilian employees. He took out his notepad—a small pad bound by looped wires that he carried around in his pocket—and wrote "19%" on the front page underneath today's date. The percentage was what he thought the probability was that he would catch a fatal disease that day.

It was morbid, childish, immature, and completely unscientific. The number, after all, was based on nothing more than what he felt as he parked and turned off his car every morning. It wasn't based on any reports or conversations or historical data. It was just a gut hunch. Despite this, he stuck to it with religious fervor. If the number he wrote down on any given morning was higher than 40%, he would take a vacation day and not go in. It had happened twice in the four years he'd worked at the Institute.

Duncan went inside, preparing his badge to show the layers of security set up at the site. He went to the fourth floor and rode the elevator with what he guessed was a colonel and they both stepped off and went in separate directions.

Housed at USAMRIID were some of the deadliest diseases Mother Nature had ever produced. He needed a top-secret clearance just to enter the offices he was entering and log in to the computer he was logging in to.

Most of the organisms didn't concern him. Four levels were set up, corresponding to the safety required when handling a biological agent. Biosafety Level 1 were viruses, such as canine hepatitis, thought not to be dangerous to humans. Biosafety Level 2 were viruses and bacterium, such as Lyme disease, thought dangerous though not typically deadly to humans. Level 3 contained potentially deadly viruses, bacterium, and parasites, such as SARS and anthrax. It was reserved for a select few within the military and civilian workforce that had the experience, education, and guts to work with such agents day in and day out.

Duncan was a researcher in Biosafety Level 4.

Level 4 was, by his estimation, one of the most dangerous spaces on the planet earth. There were obviously better candidates for deadliest environment—such as the bottom of the Marianas Trench in the Pacific where a screw becoming loose in your helmet could result in your head imploding from the pressure—but to a person not seeking out extreme environments, no place could bring about such a thrill, and at the same time paralyze you with fear like Biosafety Level 4.

It was where nightmares lay dormant, frozen in liquid nitrogen. Marburg, Ebola, Congo Hemorrhagic Fever…and numerous other viruses referred to as "hot agents." A section of the laboratory was devoted to what were termed X Agents: viruses that had yet to be identified. This was the area Duncan most liked to spend his time. The Age of Exploration had ended and his generation and every generation after would not have anywhere on earth to explore and declare discovered. Most people believed space was the next great landscape of discovery. But in this building was a storage unit that housed ancient beings as strange as anything science fiction had dreamed up. When he was there, surrounded by unknown agents, he felt like he was on a different planet, like an explorer observing things that no one before had known existed.

He saw Dr. Janice Robinson working in another part of the lab and she came over and sat on his desk, sipping coffee out of a mug that said, WORLD'S GREATEST MOM.

"What'd we get today?" Duncan said, opening his email.

"Reporter coming to watch a blood extraction."

"I thought that was next Friday?"

"Nope, today."

"Who's he with?"

"*LA Times.*"

"Oh, I kinda like the Times actually. Maybe I'll decide not to hate him."

"Any big plans for the weekend?"

"Racquetball with my pops and then back here for some good old-fashioned thesis research."

"When's that damn degree gonna be done anyway?"

"This summer, I hope. My bioinformatics professor is giving me some grief but he's a raging alcoholic. I think once he has a lucid spell I can get what I want out of him."

She finished her coffee and took a deep breath. "You ready?"

He closed all the windows on his mac and stood up. "Let's do it."

Duncan followed Janice up to the BSL 4 area and to the locker rooms where he changed into scrubs. He thoroughly washed himself and put on latex gloves, rubber gloves over those, and Kevlar gloves over those. Then he did the same for his feet with different booties. In the waiting area leading to the labs, he found his blue suit and began to prepare.

The suits were essentially space suits. They held positive pressure and inflated with a hose that connected to the back and made the scientists appear like they had tails. There were ports in various rooms where they would hook up and fresh air would circulate in the suits.

Over their heads they placed thick plastic helmets with clear faceplates. They connected with the suits and prevented any sort of penetration by airborne pathogens. Except of course if the zipper that ran down from your neck to your crotch ever opened up, which it did all the time because the suits were only replaced when absolutely necessary. There was a mirror up near where he was dressing, and Duncan looked at it every day, wondering what the hell he was doing here exactly. He had a master's in microbiology and epidemiology and soon would have a doctorate. He had also finished his MD a long time ago and only needed to complete a residency he had begun and abandoned. He could work at a lab as a director and have a plush office and a well-endowed secretary. Instead, he was putting on an old space suit and about to handle some of the most dangerous substances on earth.

He and Janice moved from the dressing area to a negatively pressurized chamber. That meant air was being sucked into the room rather than being allowed to escape. Only one door could be opened at a time and to enter they locked the heavy steel door behind them and unlocked the one in front leading to the first room, which contained a chemical bath.

They made their way to the exterior door of the laboratory and hooked up their blue suits using their hose attachments. They roared to life. The sound in the helmets was so loud you couldn't hear without shouting. They opened the final door, and entered the laboratory.

Standing over a microscope were two men in blue suits. The first was explaining something about protein synthesis to the second who tried to angle his faceplate so he was able to see into the microscope.

"FIND ANYTHING GOOD?" Duncan shouted.

Dr. Taylor Nielson looked at him and smiled. "THAT TWENTY BUCKS YOU OWE ME."

"I PAID THAT BACK."

"NO YOU DIDN'T."

"YES I DID. WE WERE AT THE DODO EATING BURGERS AND I PAID AND YOU SAID WE WERE EVEN."

Taylor thought a moment. "ALL RIGHT FINE, BE THAT WAY." He turned to the man seated at the microscope. "THIS IS ALEJANDRO NEVAL. CALL HIM ALEX."

"ALEX," Janice shouted, "HOW DO YOU LIKE OUR LITTLE LABORATORY?"

"IT'S AMAZING. I CAN'T BELIEVE HOW MUCH NORMAL STUFF IS IN HERE."

Duncan knew what he meant. When he had first come to the labs, he was amazed that a laptop sat on one of the counters. Some of the scientists had been taking notes on Teflon treated plastic that could be decontaminated in the intensely hot decontamination process that all inanimate objects leaving the BSL 4 labs went through. There were also the standard instruments, cleaning products, and other items you might find in any laboratory.

"YOU READY TO SEE OUR SPECIMEN?" Duncan asked.

Alex nodded and rose from the microscope. Another sealed door led to what appeared like an autopsy room one might find in a pathology department at a small hospital. They unhooked their hoses, stepped into the room, shut the door, and hooked their suits back up to the outlets there.

On a metal gurney at the far side of the small room lay a monkey. It was a howler monkey, its eyes frozen in the last expression it had in life. Duncan walked to it and ran his thickly gloved hand over the fur. The monkey's blood contained a level 4 hot agent, one of the deadliest in the world: the Ebola virus. Though Ebola habituated some unknown host somewhere in the jungles of Africa—perhaps a bat or a fly—when it performed an inter-species jump to primates, it was absolutely devastating.

Janice got the surgical instruments out of a container. They gleamed in the harsh lights of the lab as she set them one by one on a tray next to the gurney. Taylor approached; he was the zoologist of the group and would be performing the extraction. A vial of the liver would be taken for analysis at the labs in the Centers for Disease Control in Atlanta: the only other laboratory in the United States capable of handling BSL 4 hot agents.

As Taylor readied the instruments, Alex stood behind him, attempting to take notes on one of the Teflon tabs provided. Taylor began lecturing Alex about the process of tissue extraction and how the monkey had ended up at USAMRIID. Janice stood next to him in case he needed anything and Duncan stood behind them near the door, wondering exactly why three people were required for any visit from a reporter.

Taylor began with an incision in the monkey's belly. He was shouting to Alex the whole time, impressing him with his knowledge of primate physiology, and Alex was leaning in close so he could actually hear over the endless air pumping through his suit. Duncan had always thought it sounded like a vacuum cleaner pushed up against each ear. He was about to tell Alex not to get too close and give Taylor some breathing space when Alex leaned just a little too far forward. The awkward shaped suit created enough forward momentum that he bumped Taylor's arm.

There was a moment when nobody moved. Duncan thought that perhaps some delicate procedure was happening. Tissue extractions on a liver that was an inch across were difficult enough. Throw the space suits and thick gloves on top of that and you would have to be a skilled surgeon to get the proper samples.

But that wasn't what had occurred.

Duncan, in a moment that seemed to slow down time, saw that a thick, black liquid was dripping off Alex's faceplate and onto the floor. The elbow bump had caused Taylor to nick the heart, causing blood to spray over the three people and the ceiling.

Duncan's first thought was that he should grab one of the disposable towels on a metal rack in the corner and clean the blood before taking Alex to a chemical shower and beginning the decontamination process. Before he could move, he heard the muffled scream and saw Alex raise his hands to his helmet.

"No!" Duncan yelled.

But it was too late. Alex ripped off the helmet in panic and began tearing at the spacesuit. He tried to run to the door and Taylor had to tackle him at the waist and pin him to the floor. Janice stood frozen, staring at the scene in wild-eyed amazement.

Duncan jumped on top of Alex and held his arms down. He was screaming and spitting and biting. He had drifted away on a cloud of terror and was not responding to any commands. The two men each grabbed an arm and looked to each other. "UP," Taylor yelled.

They lifted the man and began to drag him to the door. Janice ran over and unlocked it. He was dragged across the lab and to the first of the chemical showers. The chemicals washed down his head and into the opening of the space suit at the neck. Duncan tried to shield Alex's eyes with his gloved hand. He was now calming down, embarrassment and horror coming into his eyes in equal parts.

"COME ON," Taylor said, taking the man by the arm and into the next chamber.

Duncan stepped into the shower next as Janice stepped out of the laboratory. They glanced at each other and a moment passed between them where they didn't say anything. They both understood that Alex was to be placed in quarantine for double the length of the incubation period of the Ebola virus. It would be a type of solitary confinement and it would be Duncan and Janice's job to ensure he didn't go insane.

Janice leaned against the wall. They both wanted to say something, but the only thing Janice thought of was, "SHIT."

Duncan couldn't think of anything to add to that.

CHAPTER 7

Samantha Bower sat on the white sand beach and absorbed the sun. She had been in the hospital collecting blood samples for two hours and figured she had earned this. Collecting blood samples for a viral infection that was suspected to be unknown was not an easy task.

She had to find vacu-containers in the supply closet with a nurse that had no intention of making her job easy. Then she needed anticoagulants and sodium hypochlorite. The hypochlorite was to wash the outside of the plastic bags the blood would be contained in. The risk of even a droplet of blood on the outside of the bags typically made the extraction of blood the most dangerous part of her job.

She had also taken throat swabs from both Erin and Clifford. Everything had been sent back to the labs at the CDC and would be analyzed by one of the most brilliant men she had ever met: Stephen W. Pushkin.

Stephen had begun work at the CDC as an undergraduate and returned every summer while completing his degree in biological engineering and microbiology at Harvard. He worked briefly at New Day Systems, designing heart valves and artificial limbs and whatever else caught his fancy, the company recognizing his brilliance and giving him free reign. He soon grew bored designing limbs and became obsessed with disease after being present in Guadalajara, Mexico, after a particularly brutal strand of dysentery killed over thirty people. That, and his background as an intern at the CDC, made him an ideal candidate for work in the laboratory.

Sam lay back on her towel and let the sun wash the stress out of her. She still felt the knots in her belly but the heat, at least, made her muscles relax. She was drifting off to sleep when she felt her iPhone buzz next to her. She picked it up, her eyes still closed behind her sunglasses.

"This is Sam."

"Dr. Bower, it's Jerry Amoy. From Queen's."

"Yes, hi."

"Um, hi. I was calling because two more patients exhibiting symptoms came into the ER in the past hour."

"What symptoms?"

"Fever, a rash, vomiting blood. One of the patients is having bloody diarrhea. He doesn't seem to be able to control it. I noticed some dark splotches on his back that resembled the other two patients'."

"Okay, I'll be right down."

Samantha changed and was at the hospital in less than twenty minutes. She went directly to the ER and had Amoy paged. He arrived a short while later and said, "They're upstairs."

The two of them rode the elevator up together and went through the procedure of cleaning and scrubbing themselves. Sam wasn't as nervous this time and she couldn't decide whether that was a good thing or a bad thing. Barricade nursing had been put in place and there was little chance of an exchange of body fluids. Samantha remembered another field agent at the CDC named Melissa who had been leaning over a patient with a suspected Marburg infection in Washington, DC, some three years ago. The man had suddenly vomited blood into her eyes. Luckily—or miraculously, Sam thought—the woman had not been infected with the virus, and the patient had survived.

The two new patients were set up in rooms across the hall from each other. Sam chose the one on the right and went in. He was a young man, no older than thirty, and was reading a paperback novel as he lay in bed. He looked up and she could see the discoloration in the conjunctiva of his eyes. The whites of his eyes had turned a dark red. A clear plastic sheet hung over his bed like a canopy except that it went all the way underneath the bed and wrapped around. The man was running his toes along it near the bottom.

Sam glanced down at the chart that Dr. Amoy had placed in her hand. She flipped through a few pages and said, "How are you doing, Jake?"

"Not so good."

"What's going on?"

"I've been throwing up blood."

"When did it start?"

"Yesterday. It comes in waves, like, it'll come every half hour and then stop for a few hours and then come again."

"It says here you had a fever. When did you notice that?"

"Like two days ago. It wasn't bad, though. I got headaches then too."

"Jake, have you been to Africa or South America recently?"

"No."

"Have you had any interactions with animals in the past few weeks?"

"Like what kinda animals?"

"Wild animals. Monkeys, birds, swine…"

"No, nothing like that. I got a dog. But that's it."

Sam noticed a handwritten note on the edge of a sheet of paper on his chart. It said, "Patient does not know Erin or Clifford."

Sam read through the rest of the chart. It had been thrown together hastily by the nurse and Amoy. It was subtle, and unless you had read several hundred charts, you wouldn't have noticed it. But fear was creeping in. The nurses did not take the time to fill out the chart properly and ask all the questions that needed to be asked. They wanted less and less to do with these patients.

"Would you mind sitting up?" Sam said. "I'd like to take a look at the rashes on your back."

Amoy helped her as she lifted Jake up to a sitting position on the bed. She saw his abdominal muscles and the striations in his shoulders and concluded that he was perhaps some sort of athlete or at the very least a gym rat. But she could already see the gray, sagging skin on his face and body, and the way it took two people to even help him sit up indicated that the disease, whatever it was, was multiplying at an enormously quick pace. He had displayed symptoms and almost immediately had to be admitted to the ER. Sam ran through a list of viral infections that could cause such a quick change. She could think of several, along with a host of their mutations: smallpox, influenza, meningitis, and Ebola…the list could go on and on.

The rash on his back was fading and she didn't notice any pustules, but she did see a slight discoloration just over the lungs. His skin appeared shiny and black in jagged splotches. It seemed like a dark purple bruise covered his whole body. It was blood, just underneath the skin. His lungs were bleeding.

"Okay," she said, gently helping him back down. "You let us know if you need anything. We're gonna have someone come take your blood in a minute and run some tests."

"What is it, you think?"

"Viral infection of some sort. Did Dr. Amoy tell you there're three other patients here with the same symptoms?"

"Yeah."

"Well, we're working as fast as we can to figure it out. In the meantime, you're not going to be going anywhere, so if there's anyone you'd like to call please buzz the nurse and she can do it for you. We have speaker phones and you're free to use them."

"Thanks." He closed his eyes. "I feel like I'm getting hotter."

"We'll get you something cold to drink."

Sam walked out of the room and Amoy followed. He appeared nervous and she wondered whether it was from the disease or the fact that it was his hospital that would be in all the newspapers.

She heard the ding of the elevators and two men in suits stepped off. One of them was pasty white with a slightly pink, balding head and orange hair just above the ears. He turned to Sam and Amoy and began walking toward them as the second man followed.

"Dr. Bower," he said, stopping before her as she removed her facemask and gloves and threw them in a biohazard bin. "I'm Dr. Terry Whitman. I'm the director of Queen's Medical."

"Nice to meet you."

He smiled widely. "You as well. Ah, do you mind if we talk for a bit? Maybe grab a soda in the cafeteria?"

"Sure. I just need to change."

It took Sam less than ten minutes to change. She didn't feel she had to, but she took a quick shower and scrubbed herself twice with a bar of soap she had brought.

When she stepped out into the corridor, she saw Whitman turn to the man behind him and nod. He then offered her the elevator first and she got on, noticing that Amoy and the other man stayed behind.

"Have you been to the island before?" he said on the ride down.

"No, first time."

"Well," he said, turning to her, a smile on his face, "it's a fun island…if you have the proper guide. I'd be happy to show you around when we're done with today."

Sam looked down and noticed the wedding ring on his finger. He immediately curled his hand so it was out of view.

"I would appreciate that, Doctor, but I'm on a strict timeline. I don't leave the hospital much."

"Understood," he said, the smile disappearing from his face as he looked forward.

The elevator opened and they walked across the first floor down a long corridor with island art up on the walls. A group of young men and women in green scrubs were standing around, talking, and as they saw Whitman, they straightened up and exchanged a few more words before disbursing. One wasn't quick enough and remained leaning against the wall. Whitman stared him down as they passed.

"Medical students," he said to Sam when they were alone.

"I remember what that was like. I usually looked as terrified as they did when a boss walked by."

"Not me. I figured most of the other students were kiss-asses so I took a different approach and had balls. I always told the attending and the chief what I thought if I ever got the chance."

"Did it work?"

"Not really. That's why I went back and got my MBA and got into management instead. Too much bureaucratic BS in medicine nowadays. Especially with managed care and the government stepping in."

They turned down another corridor and into the hospital cafeteria. It was clean and open with enough seating for at least a hundred people. They were serving Indian food and the smell of broiling chicken and spices filled the air. It reminded Sam that she hadn't eaten today and she made a note to get a plate of Indian food as soon as they were done speaking.

Whitman got two juices out of a cooler and cut in line, paid with a five, and left the change. They sat down at a table by the window. The sun was bright and warmed Sam's cheeks and neck as she opened the juice bottle and took a sip.

"So any word on a culprit?" Whitman said.

"No. I would expect that our labs are growing a culture from the samples right now and that's going to take some time."

"But you have to have some guess as to what it is."

"I do."

Neither of them spoke for a long moment.

"You're not going to make this easy on me, are you?"

"Dr. Whitman, I've been in this situation before. I've been at this table with other chiefs and directors having this same conversation. I know what you want to ask me so just ask me."

"And what exactly do you think I want to ask you?"

"You want to ask me not to get the media involved and to keep this as quiet as possible. No hospital wants to be the epicenter of an epidemic and I don't blame you."

"So?"

"What?"

"So what's your answer?"

"I will try to keep this quiet as long as possible, but not because of the hospital's bottom line. Because a viral epidemic causes panic and people can't think when they're panicked. It just makes things more difficult for us. But I will tell you that eventually word will get out and reporters will be all over this hospital. When it gets near that point, it'll be much better if we control the message and hold a press conference. But that isn't my department."

"Whose department is it?"

"My boss's, Deputy Director Wilson."

He grimaced and took a long swig of the juice. "Then maybe he's the one I should be talking to?"

"When we get the lab results, if it is anything to worry about, I promise you he'll be on the next plane out here."

Whitman leaned forward on his elbows. "You know why I became a doctor? I genuinely thought I could help people. Most people apply to med school for the prestige, but I thought that if I could really pick a good place to practice, somewhere without too many other physicians where I would really be needed, I thought I could make a difference." He sighed. "But's that's just idealism. And idealism has no place in this." He rose. "If word gets out prematurely, we will file a suit against you, the CDC, and the United States government. Make sure that it doesn't."

CHAPTER 8

Samantha finished her lunch of curry chicken and basmati rice and threw away her paper plate and utensils. She went to the second floor near pediatrics to a small couch and table that were placed in a quiet area in the corridor and pulled out her iPad. She opened a document that listed the names of the four patients: Clifford Lane, Erin Simon, Allani Haku, Jacob Ichimora.

One of these might be the index patient: the point of origin. The one that spread it to the others. Unless of course the index patient had not been admitted yet. But they would be so ill that a hospital or clinic would be the only alternative and Amoy had sent out an announcement to all the hospitals and clinics on the island—which were only a handful—to notify them of any patients that were admitted with similar symptoms. There were no hits as yet, so Sam had to go forward on the assumption that one of these four was the index.

Once the index was found, she then had to scour his life and determine where he could have picked up the virus. Its origin would tell them as much about the disease as they would find out in a laboratory.

Logically, the patient with the worst symptoms had the latest stage of a disease, which meant they had carried it the longest. In this instance, that was Clifford Lane.

She opened Clifford's file, which she had scanned as a PDF, and began reading all the information they had about him. But the hospital file was like a resume. Birthday and genetic history wasn't the type of information she was looking for. The best place to search for the information she needed was on a patient's Facebook and Twitter accounts. Clifford Lane could no longer speak or respond to voice commands. She would have to find out the passwords to his accounts another way.

At the back of the file was a list of emergency contacts. The first was his wife, Suzan Lane. There was an address and a phone number. She took out her iPhone and dialed. After three rings she heard Clifford's voice and realized it was his cell number.

Sam walked out of the hospital into the parking lot and hailed a cab from a line of three that were waiting for passengers. While she was thinking about it, she scheduled a time tomorrow on her calendar to go rent a car.

"Where to?" the cabbie said in a thick, Hawaiian accent.

"1572 Kalakaua Avenue."

They pulled away from the hospital and onto the streets. It was overcast today and she usually responded poorly to bad weather. She had been troubled by seasonal affective disorder since she was a child. On snowy or rainy days, she would sometimes get so depressed she couldn't function. Her mother had tried to get her on antidepressants but since it only occurred during bad weather, Sam refused. She figured a better cure was to move somewhere with a temperate climate.

"Where you from?" the cabbie said.

"Montana originally."

"Lotsa cows."

"There are definitely lots of cows, yeah."

"What you doing here?"

"Visiting some patients. I'm a doctor."

"Oh yeah? You know my wife have diabetes and they said that she losing circulation to her foot. Will they have to cut off her foot?"

"Ten years ago I'd say yes. But in this day and age they shouldn't have to do that."

"Yeah, that's what I think. But doctors say they may have to." He chuckled. "She loves cream and butter mochi. You had this yet?"

"No, what is it?"

"Very very good dessert. You have to have it. But don't go to restaurant. On the streets you see, um, merchants, and they sell. Much much better."

"I'll have to try it."

They rode in silence a few minutes and then the cabbie would ask another question about diabetes or about his cousin who's getting migraines or about the thousand other medical concerns she was asked about every day. It often surprised her how much need there was for medical doctors and how few the medical schools were actually training.

She arrived at the address and asked the cabbie to wait for her. He turned off the meter and said it was for answering his questions and then pulled out a magazine and began to read. Sam stepped out of the cab and saw a two-story house with concrete steps leading up to the front porch. The steps and pavement leading to them were cracked and weeds were growing out of them.

Sam walked to the front porch and, as she knocked on the door, noticed the stains on a rocker that was placed outside. From inside she heard some motion, things being moved, and then she heard a toilet flush. A woman came to the door and opened it, peering over the chain that connected the door to the frame.

"Yes?"

Sam could instantly smell the marijuana smoke coming from the home.

"Mrs. Lane?"

"Yes, and who are you?"

"My name is Samantha Bower. I'm a doctor with the Centers for Disease Control. I'm one of your husband's physicians."

"Oh, hang on."

She closed the door and slid open the chain before opening the door all the way. "Is there news?"

"No, I'm sorry. Clifford is about the same, last time I checked. I was just wondering if we could talk for a few minutes."

"Sure, come inside."

The home was messy. Books and dishes and clothes were left out, like they had been too busy to clean up, but the entertainment center with the large screen television and state-of-the-art stereo was spotless. On the walls were posters of rock climbers, snowboarders, explorers, and surfers. A golden retriever sat on the couch, eyeing Sam suspiciously.

Suzan sat on the couch next to the dog and began petting it, running her fingers through his fur as she put her sandaled feet up on the coffee table. Sam sat across from her on the love seat. She saw the burnt remains of a joint in an ashtray. Suzan saw that she had noticed and panic gripped her face for an instance before it faded away.

"You're not gonna call the cops, right? Doctor patient privilege and all."

"Technically you're not my patient, but, no, I don't care."

"It's medicinal. I got a medicinal license from California and the chief of police here don't care if you smoke if you got a medicinal license from another state."

"It's really none of my business, Mrs. Lane. I'm just here to see if there's anything I can do to help your husband."

She looked down, biting her lower lip as she gripped the dog's fur tighter and then let go. "He's a good man. He ain't never hurt anybody in his life."

"I have to ask you some sensitive questions, Mrs. Lane."

"Suzan."

"Suzan, I have to ask some questions that are going to make you uncomfortable. Is that all right?"

"More uncomfortable than my soul mate dyin' in the hospital?" she said, a little annoyed.

"I'm sorry. I didn't mean it that way."

She took a deep breath and leaned her head back on the couch. "I know you didn't, sweetheart. I'm sorry. I'm just beside myself, you know?"

"I can't imagine what you're going through right now but I want you to know, Suzan, that I—we—are doing everything possible to make your husband well again."

"I believe you. So, what're these questions?"

She pulled up a note-taking program in her iPad. "Has Clifford ever had a blood transfusion?"

"No."

"Has he ever done any illegal drugs?" They both smiled and Sam blushed. "I'm sorry. I meant has he ever done any intravenous drugs?"

"No. Well maybe when he was a kid, like sixteen or seventeen. He had some crazy years."

"Did he ever tell you whether he shared needles or anything like that?"

"No."

"How many sexual partners has he had in his life?"

"In his life? I have no idea. I think he said nine or ten, but you know how men lie about that."

"How many sexual partners have you had?"

"Twelve."

"When was the last time you and Clifford had sexual intercourse?"

"Um, some four weeks ago. Somewhere around there."

"Have either of you ever had an extramarital affair?"

There was pain on her face and she glanced away. "Yes. I had an affair about three years ago. With a younger man; nineteen. You're still young and don't think this way, but when you get to be my age, the attention of younger men is very flatterin'. It lasted about a month."

"How old are you if you don't mind my asking?"

"Thirty-nine."

"How many sexual partners do you think the man you had an affair with had?"

"No idea. I don't even remember his last name."

"Have you or Clifford ever had any sexually transmitted diseases?"

"Yes."

She waited a moment but got no response. "What type?" she finally said.

"I had chlamydia twice. He had herpes."

"Right before he got sick, did Clifford begin spending time with anyone new in his life?"

"Why? You think he was having an affair?"

"No, not that. Just curious about new friends or social clubs. Anywhere he might be exposed to new people he wasn't exposed to before."

"No, I don't think there was anythin' like that."

"His chart just said he's self-employed. What does he do for a living?"

"Tour guide."

Sam looked up from her iPad. "Where?"

"South America."

"When was the last time he was there?"

"About a month ago. Peru, I think. An Amazon tour."

"How many people were with him?"

"I don't know. We never talked much about his job unless something weird happened."

"When he came back, did he mention anything? Specifically anything about not feeling well?"

"No. He did say some other guy had gotten sick and he had to leave the tour early."

"Sick with what?"

"Malaria."

Sam took a few quick notes. "This is an unusual request, but is there any way I can look at his electronic data? I'm interested in his Facebook, Twitter, and email. If he had a blog or a Tumblr I'd like to see that too."

"Oh, Clifford hated computers. He didn't have an email address. He said they were corrupting and taking us away from nature."

"Suzan, is there anything else you can tell me that you think could help?"

"He lived a hard life and I know people judge him for it. I can see it on your face. And don't deny it—you nearly pissed your pants when I said he might've had a drug problem. But he's a good man. He takes care of anyone that needs it. Someone broke their leg on one of his tours and he walked over a hundred miles to get help for him. That's the kind of man he is."

"I appreciate you telling me that." She stood up. "I better get going. We'll call you with any news."

"When can I see him? They told me on the phone that I wasn't allowed to see him anymore."

"That's just a precaution," she said. "If it is a virus, we need to expose as few people as possible to it and only those that are necessary."

Suzan rose and began walking toward the front door. The dog followed her, rubbing against Sam's leg. She bent down to pet it and rubbed his ear a moment.

"Please tell him," Suzan said, "that I rescheduled his next two tours. He was worried about that. Tell him they're rescheduled and he has two months to get better before his next one."

Sam realized that no one had told Suzan her husband was unresponsive. Or they had, and she wasn't processing the information. Sam had seen cases of denial so extreme that people had come to the hospital to pick their loved ones up to go home days after they had been informed they had passed away. The mind had many barriers to protect it from harm, and most of them occurred without the conscious part of ourselves even being aware of them.

As she left the house and walked to her car she took out her phone and noticed a message. It was from the hospital. She listened to it and heard Amoy's voice come on the line. It was a simple message; only one sentence:

"Clifford Lane is dead."

CHAPTER 9

Duncan Adams went home directly after work and took a long, hot shower. He let the water run over him until his skin grew water-logged and then he quickly soaped himself, shampooed, and conditioned, and then began his routine of lotions and body creams. His father had died of skin cancer so he had developed a detailed skin-care routine.

After he had finished, he dressed in jeans, a T-shirt, and a sports coat and headed out the door.

He checked his watch as he drove down the interstate and noted that he was twenty minutes late. It would take him ten minutes to get to Circle Lounge Bar and that, he figured, was perfect. A date would be waiting for him there. His friend Hank had set him up in the past to no success but assured him he would fall in love with the woman he was going to meet tonight. However, it was a double date and there wasn't a doubt in Duncan's mind that he was just posing as wingman so Hank could date her friend. But still, a date was a date and he'd had a long dry spell in the romantic arena.

Circle Lounge was located on a busy street near a tattoo shop and a dive restaurant. Surprisingly, the best Indian food in all of Maryland was also located on that same block. When he got to the block he looked at Circle Lounge and saw there wasn't a line out front or even a bouncer and it gave him the impression that is was more of a restaurant than a bar. In fact, the west half of the building was a sushi restaurant that operated until five in the morning.

He parked across the street in paid parking and checked his watch again. He was half an hour late. Most women would tolerate a man that was ten or fifteen minutes late, but half an hour was too much for most. They would complain or make snide comments the entire night. One girl had even thrown her drink in his face.

But it was a trick he had been taught by his father. He had told Duncan that any woman that had the patience and grace not to mention your being half an hour late or let it bother her was one he needed to keep.

Duncan got inside and stood by the entryway to let his eyes adjust to the dim lighting. The restaurant smelled of strong perfume and he guessed trace amounts of scented air were being circulated through the vents to cover the smell of vomit or urine. No matter how classy the bar, over time, they would all stink like bodily fluids from drunks that were unable to make it all the way to the bathroom.

He saw Hank seated at a table on the restaurant side. He had two women with him, one on either side. Hank waved, irritation on his face though he tried to cover it with a smile. Duncan made his way over.

"How are you guys?" Duncan said. He held out his hand to the attractive blonde seated to Hank's right. "You must be Rebecca," he said. Rebecca was whom Hank had said he would bring. Duncan then turned to the other woman.

She was also attractive and wearing a revealing black dress with white stockings. She was dipping a toothpick into her martini, trying to get the second olive.

"And you must be Heather."

She acknowledged him with a quick hello and then went back to the olive in the glass. Duncan sat down next to her.

"Hank's told me a lot about you."

"Oh yeah?" Heather said, not turning to him. "Like what?"

"Like he said you were at Georgetown right now getting your masters. In environmental studies, right?"

"Yup."

Duncan could almost feel her irritation coming off her like an electrical charge. He turned to the menu. Hank sent him a quick glance and then said to Heather, "So, Duncan's a microbiologist."

"Hm," Heather said, nibbling on the olive. "What made you want to do that?" She asked it in a way that let him know she wasn't curious, more disgusted by the ridiculous career choice.

"The Congo," Duncan said.

"What do you mean?"

"I was in the Congo as an intern for the United Nations when I was an undergrad. I was there during the Ebola outbreak in Tuwintu."

"I haven't heard about it."

"No? Few people have. There's so much horror there, an outbreak usually doesn't catch people's attention. But this one was particularly savage."

Duncan glanced to Hank who gave him a look that said, *Please don't tell some gross story and ruin this.* Duncan smiled at him.

"See," Duncan continued, "it infected an entire hospital. The staff, the doctors, the administrators, all the patients…the military was there and not allowing anyone to leave. Anybody that tried was gunned down in front of the exits. The bodies eventually piled so high you couldn't open the doors."

The waitress interrupted them to take Duncan's order and he got a plate of sushi with a sparkling water.

"So," he continued, "you have about two hundred people stuck in the same building, all of them except five shooting blood out of every orifice in their body. Ebola itself doesn't kill you; it causes you to bleed to death. But the blood that comes out of people doesn't look the same as what you see when you get a cut. It's black and it has the consistency of coffee grounds."

"Duncan," Hank interrupted with a grin, "I'm sure the ladies don't want to hear about that while we're about to—"

"The blood doesn't stop," Duncan said, ignoring him as he took an edamame and peeled it. "It comes out of the eyes, the ears, the mouth. But the worst places are the genitals and anus. When you have a bowel movement the blood comes pouring out and doesn't clot. It can actually take pieces of organ with it. The patients were finding long strands of a thick, gelatin substance when they went. I didn't realize until later it was part of their colons and intestines."

Heather had stopped playing with her olive and had a look on her face like someone had just vomited in her purse.

"I have to use the restroom," she said, standing.

"Me too," Rebecca said as she followed her.

When the girls were gone, Hank threw his napkin and hit Duncan in the face. "What the hell are you doing? They're in there right now talking about how to get out of this."

"I never had a shot. The blonde's still going to finish the date with you, though. I wouldn't worry."

"Well, now you really don't have a shot—"

"She's awful, Hank. She's pretentious and feels life owes her something just for existing. Those are some of the most unpleasant people to be around."

"And you can tell all that from five minutes of conversation?"

"I could tell as soon as I said hello and she didn't even look up from her drink."

A couple walked by and the male did a double-take of Hank. He came over and said hello and asked if Hank remembered him from some engineering conference last year. He did, or at least said he did, and they began speaking about people from the conference and what they'd been up to. Duncan could tell Hank didn't know who any of the people were, but was keeping a grin on his face.

When the man left, Hank said, "I have no idea who that was or what conference he was talking about."

"I don't think he picked up on it." Duncan sighed and put his elbows on the table. "I think I'm just gonna go."

"What? No you're not. Rebecca is Heather's ride. If she leaves, Rebecca does too."

"What're you gonna do for me if I stay?"

"What do you want?"

"A new Xbox game."

"You're kidding."

"We all have our weaknesses."

"Fine, if you stay so I can score with Rebecca, I will buy you an Xbox game."

Duncan smiled as the sushi was brought out. The waitress placed it down and asked if they needed anything else. It was another few minutes until the girls came back. Heather seemed in a much better mood and Duncan wondered what they had been doing in there. She was asking about his time in the Congo and Duncan glanced over to Hank who tapped one side of his nose with his finger and nodded.

Duncan was about to say something when his phone buzzed. It was a private number from the USAMRIID dispatch. Duncan had only received a call from that number once before, when he was still an intern in grad school, on September 11, 2001.

"This is Duncan…yes…yes…"

The phone nearly dropped out of his hand. He felt weak and his stomach was queasy. He looked down to the sushi and it suddenly made him feel sick.

"You okay?" Hank said. "You look like you've seen a ghost."

"I need to go," Duncan said, standing up and nearly falling over his chair.

"What? Where you going?" Hank yelled as Duncan made a beeline for the front door.

"To Hawaii."

CHAPTER 10

It was two o'clock in the morning when Samantha received the first call.

It was a nurse from Queen's Medical. Sam didn't get to the phone in time and the nurse left a message stating that Dr. Jerry Amoy had asked that she call him. Six new patients had been admitted, exhibiting symptoms of the "UF": the Unknown Flu. It was what the staff at the hospital had begun to call the disease because they had to call it something and just calling it a flu made it sound less toxic than it was. Even though Samantha knew that influenza was one of the worst serial killers of all time.

Just as she had rolled over and was going back to sleep, her phone rang again. It was a long distance number with an Atlanta area code.

"This is Dr. Bower."

"Sam, glad I caught you. This is Dr. Pushkin, from the lab."

Even though Sam had known him several years, Stephen preferred that everyone call him "Dr. Pushkin" rather than Stephen.

"Doctor, hi. What are you doing up? It's four in the morning there."

"You haven't spoken to Wilson yet?"

"No, why?"

"Sam, we received the results of the lab work. It's black pox. It's fucking black pox."

Samantha sat quietly a while and stared at the floor. "Are you sure?" was all she managed to say.

"Yes. The symptomology matches the cultures. Wilson's on his way down right now. He's going to hold a press conference with a general or secretary of something. The military's involved now too."

"Why?"

"You know damn well why. I don't have time for silly questions. Shake the sleep off and call me back in ten minutes. I'm grabbing the next flight and need to talk to you about our next steps."

Sam was down to her rental car in five minutes. The night sky was glittering with stars. It was clear in a way she had never really seen before, as if a wound had been torn open in the sky and she was allowed to look into the innards of space. Along with the stars were planets, lit up brightly like incandescent bulbs, and farther off, galaxies. Even with the hotel, the light pollution was so minimal it was like looking at the sky from the top of a mountain.

She drove down to Queen's Medical and saw a news van from Channel 4 parked out front. Several Jeeps in basic green and two sedans were all parked illegally. Sam parked in employee parking and walked inside.

At the entrance to the Emergency Room an MP in uniform was checking IDs and turning people away, giving them directions to the Straub Clinic and Hospital. Sam pulled out her CDC identification card.

"One moment, ma'am."

He checked with someone on the radio hooked to his shoulder and they gave the clearance for her to come in.

The hospital looked empty with the exception of the staff. Sam smiled to the receptionist and realized it was the same one from yesterday morning.

"They're all in the conference room down the hall," the nurse offered without being asked.

Sam made her way down and saw the news crew setting up. At least twenty men and women were meandering about in both suits and military uniforms. Bagels had been set out on the table with sodas and coffee. Only one man was sitting at the table. He was young with auburn hair and wearing a Depeche Mode T-shirt with canvas shorts and sandals. He looked more like a surfer than a doctor. Sam sat across from him and he glanced up and smiled as he spread cream cheese on his bagel.

"Hi, I'm Duncan."

"Samantha, nice to meet you."

"Hm, you're a doctor, right?"

"Yes."

"Interesting. You didn't introduce yourself as a doctor. Everyone I've met in this room calls themselves doctor like they don't have names."

"It's ego. That's probably why they went to medical school. Are you a physician as well?"

"Sort of. I got my MD before my PhD but I never took the boards or practiced."

"That seems like a lot of work for nothing."

"I wouldn't say nothing. It taught me that I didn't want to be a doctor."

Ralph Wilson got up and stood at the front of the room. A PowerPoint display was on behind him and he flipped through a few slides and then said, "Ladies and gentleman, I'm Dr. Ralph Wilson of the Centers for Disease Control. I'm the deputy director of Infectious Disease Research for those of you who haven't met me before. I know everyone's been called out here in the middle of the night so let's begin so we can get as much shut-eye as possible. We all have a big day tomorrow and tomorrow'll be here sooner than we think." He adjusted his glasses, and began with the first slide.

It was a black hand with yellow, brittle nails that had fallen off. It appeared to belong to a body that was housed in a crypt.

"This," Ralph said, "is a victim of the plague of Justinian circa 541 AD. It afflicted the Eastern Roman Empire, after Constantine had split the empire and left the Western portion with Rome as its headquarters abandoned. Justinian was the emperor of the time and like with all leadership positions, whatever happens is your fault, so the plague was attributed to him.

"It was, by all accounts—and modern forensics conducted by the University of Tubingen has confirmed this—the worst natural disaster in human history. Responsible for the death of over half the world's population. We believe it had its genesis in China and spread from there. It went through the Middle East, devastated Africa, and was recurring in Europe centuries later. It would disappear and then reappear twenty years later to re-infect a new generation."

The screen shifted to a screenshot from under an electron microscope.

"You can see here that it appears much like common bubonic plague, but with these ridges here on the periphery of the virus. In fact, we believed for a long time that it *was* the bubonic plague, but research conducted on the remains of priests in Constantinople—it was the common practice at the time to bury priests in underground catacombs, making a type of preserve for tissue—shows us that it was in fact some now extinct form of Yersinia pestis.

"If you can imagine the scene in Constantinople, you can see how frightening this particular contagion really was. Bodies were piled so high in the streets that they were like roadblocks at every turn. Justinian eventually ordered the burning of the bodies on the outskirts of the cities and this calmed the contagion until the next iteration. But to be perfectly clear, we don't know why this contagion occurred, or why it went extinct.

"In my research into the plague of Justinian, I developed a coding system, a type of shorthand, for the infectibility of a particular contagion. I did this so that those outside the medical and scientific communities could understand the level of threat they were facing with any disease. I called it the T score and now it is a widely accepted rating model.

"Its theory is simple: T-1 means that the contagion is such that each person infected, on average, will infect one other individual. The common flu is a T-1 contagion. The bubonic plague was a T-3 contagion. The plague of Justinian was a T-4. The scale goes to T-7, which, in effect, would cause the extinction of all mammalian life on earth."

Ralph looked up to the screen as it changed to a shot of the earth. It went through the different iterations of T, showing small red spots that grew as the infectibility rate progressed. At T-5, all human life on earth was extinguished. He looked back to the audience and adjusted his glasses.

"This contagion has been determined to be a strand of smallpox. What strand, we cannot say for sure, though we have our theories that it could be black pox. Smallpox, and its derivative black pox, currently, only exist in two places on the planet earth: the CDC BSL 4 labs in Atlanta, and a remote outpost in the former Soviet Union. Other than that, man has conquered and abolished it. It has, to put it bluntly, come back somehow." He shook his head. "Mother nature always has surprises in store for us it seems.

"Our most important goal for this contagion is determining its T score, containing it, and if possible, destroying it." He adjusted his glasses again. "I see many worried looks in the audience. I myself am not taken to panic and I apologize if I seem too relaxed in discussing this subject. But please do not misinterpret my calm for a lack of concern. To put it bluntly, we are looking at an extinction-level event. At least, for mankind."

CHAPTER 11

Wilson sat down after the Q & A and a general took his place to begin talking about logistics. Sam noticed that there were no reporters asking questions, just a news crew taking video and audio.

When the general was done speaking, everybody stood and mingled a bit before filing out of the room. Duncan remained seated and sipped his drink as he stared off into space.

"You look worried," Sam said.

"About possibly the deadliest disease known to man popping its head up? What's there to worry about?" He wiped his lips with a napkin. "Sorry, that was a smart-ass thing to say. It's actually not so much that. I work with stuff almost as dangerous every day."

"Then what is it?"

"It doesn't make sense. Smallpox is abolished. It doesn't exist except in those two laboratories. Why would nature just 'spring' it on us? And here of all places?"

"I don't think it was here. I've been tracking down the index patient's history and he was a tour guide in South America."

"Even if it originated in South America, it's an extinct organism. We wiped it from the face of the earth. It can't just come back."

"So what do you think's going on?"

"I don't know. I don't even know why I feel uneasy about it. Do you know there's a type of moth that only lives for twenty-four hours? It's born without a mouth so it doesn't eat. It does have a full digestive system and could produce excrement if it could eat. It just doesn't have a mouth. Sometimes nature is random and cruel. Who am I to think this disease wasn't just waiting in the jungle for us somewhere and has decided to come out of hiding now? But still, I'm uneasy about it."

"I think your point is a good one. I thought the same thing when I was told it was black pox. It shouldn't exist. And the region the tour guide was exposed to is a place he's been probably dozens of times before. It doesn't make sense that if the virus were living in some host there that only now we would be seeing the beginnings of an epidemic."

He looked up, his eyes in bewilderment. "Holy crap, is that really what we have now? An epidemic? I never thought I would actually live to see one. I mean a real one, not the swine flu BS. An actual Book of Revelation epidemic."

She bent down and took one of the bagels. "You almost sound excited saying that. I wouldn't be."

Samantha sat in her hotel room through the morning and into the afternoon, running through medical charts for all the patients admitted to Queen's Medical with black pox-like symptoms. There were now over a hundred; forty had been added since last night.

Samantha stretched her neck and stared out the window. In epidemics, like in anything that had an outward spreading force, you would hit a tipping point and there would be no turning back. If every patient infected only one other patient, the disease would actually be in decline. Without hitting that tipping point, it would simply run its course and die out. But if it hit the tipping point, it would grow exponentially, and the point itself is unpredictable. The difference could be a half of one person infectibility rate among the population. If every person infected 1.1 instead of just 1 person, that could cause the epidemic to grow beyond control.

Sam rose from her bed and began pacing the room. The thoughts darting in and out of her mind going back to her CDC training courses. The CDC's procedure in a situation like this was clear: isolate, isolate, isolate. Any patient with even a hint of the disease was not allowed anywhere near the general public. Medical staff never made contact with them and anyone that had direct contact was quarantined. Even those that did not have direct contact were observed closely.

She thought of the families; it was always a painful process for families. They would have to watch loved ones through glass and plastic, and that was if they were lucky. Many times families would be unable to see their loved ones for weeks and then one day Sam or another field agent would call to notify the family of the death. It tore Sam's heart out every time she had to place one of those calls.

A simple flu in 1918 had killed off millions of people. With an agent as deadly as this, Sam truly felt that not just the community, but the species might be teetering on the brink of extinction.

CHAPTER 12

Two men sat in a café and wiped the sweat from their brows with silk handkerchiefs. This time of the season Bangkok was sweltering; it felt like an oven that had been left on too long. It was also the tourist season and the sidewalks and streets were packed to the point that you couldn't walk more than a foot in front of you without bumping into somebody else.

"I fucking hate this place," Conrad Moore said. "It's too hot and the food is awful."

Tyrone Booth finished the last gulp of his Tsing Tao beer and waved to the waitress for another. He took a piece of his spicy chicken and reached below the table, letting his Pomeranian finish it off before licking his fingers.

"I love the food. You never got to liking spicy food. If you did, you wouldn't be knockin' Thai food at all."

"It's spicy 'cause there's not much sanitation here and the spices kill the bacteria. It has nothing to do with flavor."

Conrad sighed and looked out the windows onto the busy street. They were seated in a corner booth away from the rest of the public in the restaurant, a place that was supposed to give them privacy but instead made their waitress ignore them.

He'd been to Bangkok before, at least three or four times. The prostitutes were some of the best in the world in his opinion. Not that he really needed to hire prostitutes. He'd learned that flashing enough cash can get you just about any woman you wanted—at least the type of women that he wanted. He'd go to bars and pick up some nice twenty-three-year-old. They'd take his limo straight to his Gulfstream and fly to the Caribbean or Mexico for a weekend. He would do what he wished however many times he wanted and then drop them back off at the airport.

But prostitutes were much better. They knew they were whores and they would get into what fantasies he wanted for that night. Plus, there was no need for the pretense of telling them he was going to see them again or having to talk about himself. There was a whorehouse not two blocks from here, one of the best in the city, and he wished like hell he was there right now.

"Where's your man?" Conrad said.

"He'll be here."

"He's an hour late."

"So?"

"So I have places to be."

"You're a private contractor, C. Where do you think you gotta be right now?"

"I don't know, maybe getting drunk with some Thai whore instead of watching you slurp down eel soup."

"He'll be here," Tyrone said, remembering the soup in front of him and taking a sip from the bowl before wiping his mouth on his hand. He fed another piece of chicken to his dog.

It was another ten minutes before either of them spoke again. Tyrone finally said, "He's here."

Conrad saw a man in a black suit and a black button-down shirt walk into the restaurant. He wore aviator sunglasses and his hair appeared wind-swept, like he'd ridden a motorcycle here. The man looked over the restaurant before finally spotting Tyrone. He smiled and walked over.

Tyrone stood up and they shook hands. "How you doin', Robert?"

"Good good." The man reached down and petted the dog. "Glorious day, gentlemen. How's business?"

"Good. This is the man I was telling you about, Conrad Moore."

"Pleasure," the man said, shaking hands. "Robert Greyjoy."

"Nice to meet you," Conrad said. "I've heard a lot of good things."

"None of them true, I assure you."

Conrad gave a forced smile and reached for his water. He took a sip, hoping that Robert would speak first, but he just stood there with a pleasant expression on his face and stared at him. Despite the fact that he was impeccably dressed and perfectly pleasant, something about him creeped Conrad out. His calm, Conrad figured. This was a multi-million dollar deal; he should at least be a little nervous.

"I was just watching television in the hotel," Robert said.

"Oh yeah?" Tyrone said. "I don't think this Asian TV is too good. All game shows."

"No, I was watching Sesame Street on satellite."

Conrad looked to Tyrone and then back. "The kids show?"

"Oh yes yes yes," Robert said. "I learn more from Sesame Street than I ever do reading *Foreign Affairs* or the *New York Times.* Sesame Street is a kind of…cultural barometer. In the sixties, they were using research to educate children. The moon landing had just occurred and science was on the forefront of everybody's mind. America had been told we needed more scientists. In the seventies, with Vietnam and Watergate and the recession, Sesame Street became more pessimistic and began teaching practical skills for children to enter into the workfield. The eighties had more businessmen and celebrities than any other era. By the end of the eighties, with the Savings & Loan and the stock market crash, businessmen were replaced by civic heroes likes cops and firefighters.

"You could even break it down by year and see the evolution of America that way. It, like America, became more and more diverse. Now, however, it's a different story. They're teaching extremely basic skills, things that children that age should already know. And the characters are more extravagant but lacking in depth. It's a reflection of ourselves with all this celebrity worship and a disdain for all things intellectual. I think Sesame Street will predict the fall of our nation much better than any media outlet. They'll begin to have characters, as they're starting to now, that are homeless, or socialists, or felons. Then they'll give up and begin teaching children just enough to get by. How to be manual laborers or soldiers or whatever else the dominant profession of a declining society will be."

Conrad stared at him without saying anything and was relieved when the waitress finally came over and Robert ordered a Tonight or Never, one of the strongest mixed drinks there were. Conrad, for whatever reason, felt uneasy with that too.

"So," Conrad began, "Ty was telling me you're in mergers and acquisitions."

"Among other things."

"And you work for who again?"

"I didn't say."

"I'm sorry, I don't understand."

"You ended that sentence with 'again' but I never told you who I work for in the first place."

Tyrone fed some more chicken to his dog and said, "See, I told you he was all secretive."

"Secretive I can appreciate," Conrad said, "but mysterious I can't. Clearly I'll need to know a lot more about you before I broker this deal. We're talking primo government contracts; easily worth ten million. I'm not just handing them over to the first schmuck that Ty refers."

"There's no need to be rude, C."

"I'm not being rude. You want me to give the subcontracts to this 'guy' that you somehow know but you won't tell me how and now he's sitting here telling me he won't tell me what company he works for."

"You don't require the contracts any longer," Robert said. "Within the year you'll be banned from bidding on all government contracts due to ethical violations. That's why you need to get rid of them. It has nothing to do with charity and you're not doing me any favors. If anything, I am doing you and your company a favor by taking them off your hands while they're still worth something."

"How the hell did you know—"

"They say you're not a true arms dealer unless you've sold weapons to the enemies of your own country. Until your bullets and bombs have killed your kin. How many of your kin did your weapon shipments kill, Mr. Moore? A hundred? Two? A thousand?"

Rage bubbled in Conrad's gut and his face turned a bright red. He threw his napkin on the table and rose. "I don't know what kind of information you and this other bastard have, but I never did anything illegal. And I don't appreciate you inferring that I did."

"Implying," Robert said. "I *implied* that you did and you *inferred* that I have inside information about you."

Conrad looked to Tyrone, bewildered. "Who the hell is this guy?"

Tyrone sat, looking from one man to the next. "I've clearly lost control of this meeting so I'd like to start again."

"Tyrone," Robert said, a slight smile on his lips, "you've done well in setting up this little party. But you've no more use to me. I suggest you keep quiet while I calm your friend down."

"Hey," Tyrone said, his brow furrowing in frustration. "I've done everything you asked and not asked a lot in return."

"Oh, right," Robert said, looking to Conrad. "You see, Ty here was going to get a percentage of the contracts. That's why he's pushing so hard for me to receive them. But we weren't supposed to tell you that."

Conrad looked to him, unable to hold back the disgust. "You son of a bitch! I trusted you."

"C, it's me, man. Calm down, all right. That's not how it played out."

"You've been to my house, you cocksucker! You ate my wife's dinner."

"C, I'm telling you, that's not how it played out. Sit down and let me explain."

Robert took a piece of chicken off Conrad's plate and placed it gently in his mouth. "I'd love to stay and see how this plays out but I simply have to be going. I'm catching a flight in thirty minutes and the police will be looking for me."

"Police?" Tyrone said. "For what?"

"Murder."

The spit of the silenced Ruger .22 caliber could barely be heard over the din of the restaurant, even by the men at the table. When Conrad saw the blood pouring from a small wound on Tyrone's chest, he knew what had happened. He thought it odd that it wasn't like in the movies—a ping with a waft of smoke rising in the air. There was no sound, no drama. It had sucked Tyrone's life away quietly and without fuss.

"Oh sh—"

Conrad felt his lungs tighten as if a fist had grabbed them and squeezed. He couldn't speak and he couldn't suck in air. There was just this horrible nothingness as his mind raced and he stared wide-eyed into the face of the man who had just shot him.

He watched as Robert stood up, calmly put on his glasses, and looked to the dog under the table. He bent down to where Conrad couldn't see and after a yelp from the dog followed by silence, Robert stood and walked out of the restaurant.

Conrad looked over to his waitress who was helping another table. He tried to gasp, but nothing came. Instead, he fell to the floor, pulling the tablecloth and all their dishes with them. As the floor rushed toward his face, he felt the sweet release of his soul lifting from his body and he wished he'd had time to tell his wife goodbye.

CHAPTER 13

Samantha sat in the corridor of Queen's Medical and watched journalists from every newspaper, magazine, blog, and website stream into the hospital and go straight to the media room that had been set up in another building just behind the ER. The hospital's main floor had been cleared with the exception of the staff. They had been asked, politely, to remain on hospital premises for a short period of time to see if any of them had been infected. When they were asked, national guardsmen with rifles stood behind their supervisors. There wasn't a lot of room for debate.

Samantha was one of the few people allowed to move freely. Technically, she would by right be under observation as well. But in an emergency situation when they faced a hot agent as deadly as black pox, it was all hands on deck.

She noticed the man from the prior meeting in the Depeche Mode T-shirt walking by with a Diet Coke in his hand and he smiled to her and came over.

"Hey," he said.

"Hey."

"Are you going to the press conference?"

"Yes."

"So what lab are you with again?"

"I'm with the CDC."

"Oh, man. So this is your press conference. Are you going to be sitting up there?"

"They like to fill the long tables during these things so if there's space they'll ask me."

"That's so cool."

"Not really."

He shrugged. "It is to me. I'm stuck in a nine-by-nine room twelve hours a day and when I do anything important my supervisor takes the credit."

"The CDC can always use good field agents."

"Maybe I'll take you up on that." He took a sip of his drink and she could tell he was thinking of what to say next. "If that guy you mentioned, the index patient, if he did pick it up in South America, that probably means someone's going to have to go down there and snoop around, right?"

"It'll take time to clear it with our two governments, but yes. We'll send down a team to all the locations he visited."

"And try and hunt down a virus. Man, I'm telling you, your job puts mine to shame."

"It's rewarding work. But it's hard to have time for everything that you want. I travel so much I sometimes feel like a stranger in my home town."

"That's not necessarily a bad thing if your home town sucks." He sat next to her on a chair, removing an old issue of *Sports Illustrated* that was open on the cushion. "So what does somebody need to do to be on that expedition to South America?"

"You wouldn't want to go, trust me."

"Why?"

"It's government travel. That means charters and the cheapest lodging and food available. They're rarely fun."

"Well if I wanted to, what would I have to do?"

She stood up. "You'd have to work for the CDC. You ready?"

"Um hm."

They walked down the corridor together, Duncan asking her about how she began with the CDC and why she remained there when she was clearly qualified to work anywhere in the world she wished. They left through the back entrance and came to the second building, which was crowded with military vehicles, police cruisers, and news vans.

"Man, must be a slow news day," Duncan said.

"You don't think this is deserving of attention?"

"You kidding me? Do you have, well, yeah you do, but do you think the general population has any idea how many deadly epidemics are just at their doorstep? Every day in Africa, somewhere, there's an Ebola outbreak. It infects one or two people, spreads to a few dozen or one or two hundred and then disappears. Some people are in the same room with an Ebola infected patient and they contract the disease and others get blood coughed into their mouths and don't get it. That's what creeps me out about it. It seems like the viruses almost *choose* who they want to infect and who they don't."

"They can't choose anything," Sam said.

They worked their way through the cords from the cameras and sound mics that coiled on the ground like thin, black snakes. They showed identification to the MPs at the entrance and went inside.

Everyone seemed to be going in one direction down a hallway so they followed. This building was much different than the hospital proper. The floors were carpeted and clean and there were no fingerprint marks on the glass doors or the walls from children. Samantha guessed this was probably an administration building.

They finally came to a small auditorium and took seats in the back, Duncan sitting next to her. Samantha took out her phone and began reviewing notes of the three patients that had been admitted during the night. Two women and a fifteen-year-old boy. They were all displaying fevers, rashes, vomiting, and diarrhea. The boy had developed what had become the telltale sign of the illness: a spreading, smooth black surface just underneath the skin.

"I guess you lost your seat," Duncan said.

At the table set up at the front of the room sat a man Samantha recognized from long nights in cramped laboratories. In front of him, a nameplate with her name had been pushed to the side and replaced with one that said, DR. PUSHKIN.

The reporters filed in and took their places as Wilson, Pushkin, the director of the hospital, and a man in a military uniform with three stars pinned to his chest took their places at the long table before the cameras.

Wilson took out two pills in a cellophane wrapper and popped them before taking a sip of water. Samantha knew them to be beta-blockers to calm his nerves and remove any performance anxiety.

A man in a suit with a nametag came up to Wilson and made a few adjustments to the papers in front of him. Samantha heard him say, "Ready when you are" and the reporters took out iPads and notebooks.

"Ladies and gentlemen," Wilson began, "I don't need to explain to you exactly what we're facing. However you did it, many of you knew about this before many of us sitting up here did. It's extremely important that we not cause a panic. When people panic, they get aggressive, they make mistakes, and they sometimes lose all sense of morality. I would ask that when you report on this story, you not exaggerate the seriousness of the infection. No one in Kansas or Miami is going to get this agent. It's confined solely to this city. In fact, there has not been one confirmed case more than five miles from this hospital and, since yesterday, we have not received any new patients with the symptomology we're looking for.

"This is, as far as I can tell," Wilson continued, "a fluke. In nature things come out of hiding every few centuries or so, rear their head, and go back to where they came. Once these patients are treated, I have a feeling we won't have any more reported cases."

Duncan leaned over to Sam. "What's he doing? Why the hell would he say that? He has no idea."

Sam shook her head. "I don't know."

Wilson cleared his throat and said, "Now, I thought we would just open it up to questions."

One reporter, an overweight man in a Hawaiian shirt, stood up. "Doctor, can you confirm that there have been twelve infections in the past seventy-two hours, and if you can, how is it that you can assert that you don't think there will be more?"

"I can confirm that there have been twelve cases reported in the last seventy-two hours. Obviously, we cannot discuss the details of these cases due to patient confidentiality, but what I can tell you is that we now believe, thanks to the fine work of our field agent, Dr. Samantha Bower, that the initial infection occurred in South America and was brought here via a carrier who resided in Honolulu. And the reason I can state with confidence that I don't think there will be more infections is that this type of agent has an exponential growth factor. It hits its tipping point quickly and reaches a critical mass in a matter of days rather than weeks or months. That has not happened here. Which means one of two things: it's either not the agent we think it is, or it's dying out. I believe it to be the latter."

Another reporter, a woman in a short skirt and a white button-down shirt stood up. Wilson called her by name and she smiled at him before speaking.

"Doctor, my understanding is that black pox is a mutation of the smallpox virus. And that smallpox, since being eradicated through vaccinations, only exists in two places in the world. One is in the former Soviet Union and one is here at the Centers for Disease Control in Atlanta. Is that correct?"

"Yes."

"Is it possible then that there's been some sort of release of this agent from one of these two labs? Either on purpose or by accident?"

"Absolutely not. The first thing I did was check with our laboratories and with Moscow. All smallpox agents are accounted for. They are stored in a frozen state using liquid nitrogen. The only way they could be released is if they thaw, infect someone, and have that person leave the lab and infect others. But there have been no reported cases in either our labs or the Russian's."

"Is it possible then that perhaps this virus has been manufactured by another entity. Perhaps a rogue nation like North Korea or Iran?"

Wilson grew noticeably uncomfortable. He shifted in his seat and adjusted his glasses. He looked hopefully to the military officer seated next to him.

"Perhaps General Lancaster would be better suited to answer that question."

The general looked at the reporter sternly, unblinking, and said, "There's no evidence of that. And until there is I don't think speculation helps anyone."

The woman was about to ask something else when she was drowned out by a reporter from Fox News who yelled from a seated position, "Is it true that a high ranking member of al Qaida has taken responsibility for the outbreak?"

Before the general could answer, Wilson said, "Lots of people are going to take responsibility. Being the United States means we are the richest, most powerful nation on earth. When that role was held by Babylon, then Egypt, then Rome, and the French, the English, and so forth, they were all hated. They were all attacked. I have no doubt that several groups will take responsibility for this. But that's not what the evidence suggests; it suggests this is a naturally occurring phenomena.

"Terrorist organizations attack clusters of people, like the sarin poisoning in the subways of Tokyo. Or the September 11 attacks. They don't attack a single individual. They would want to maximize exposure to the agent as much as possible. The evidence strongly favors our theory that a single individual returned home from a trip to the jungle and carried this virus with him. Period."

More questions were thrown at the panel and Wilson fielded almost all of them. Sam saw that Dr. Pushkin was checking his watch. She guessed that he wished he was alone in his lab right now.

There were around twenty or twenty-five more questions before they closed the press conference. Once the cameras were off, Sam saw Wilson and his assistant going from reporter to reporter and having a whispered conversation. Probably reminding them that causing a panic unnecessarily would be extremely detrimental.

Sam stood and made her way down to the long table just as Pushkin rose to leave.

"You didn't speak much," she said.

"Ralph seemed to have that particular function covered. You look tired."

"I'm okay. How was the flight?"

"Awful. But this is one beautiful damned island. Let's get lunch or breakfast, or whatever the hell mealtime it is."

They were walking out when Duncan appeared in front of them. He thrust out his hand and Pushkin shook.

"Dr. Pushkin, I'm Duncan Adams."

"Oh, yes. From USAMRIID, right?"

"Yeah."

"You two know each other?" Sam asked.

Pushkin said, "Their laboratories are much more secure than ours even though we have a BSL 4 clearance. I've had them perform a few diagnoses when I require. Duncan here is a brilliant research scientist. When he wants to be."

"Which is rarely," Duncan said. "So where you guys off to now?"

"Breakfast. Join us. I think we may need to do some brainstorming on this."

CHAPTER 14

Benjamin Cornell's heart raced as he walked into the California Department of Health. He glanced around to make sure no one had noticed him though he was sure they hadn't. He'd dressed as normally as possible: Polo shirt, jeans, and sandals. Just an average white guy walking into a public building. He wore glasses and had his sun-bleached blond hair covered in an Oakland A's baseball cap.

The corridor he walked down was long and there was a receptionist at a booth on his right side. He took a deep breath and walked to her.

"Hi," he said, putting on his best smile. "I'm here to see Dr. Wharton, please."

"Fifth floor, two doors on your left."

"Thank you."

He walked to the elevators and hit the button for the third floor, his actual destination. If anyone asked the receptionist later, he wanted her to only remember that someone had asked about Dr. Wharton.

The elevator dinged and he stepped on. There were six other people crammed on and he thought of an email joke he had received. Something about being on a crowded elevator and saying, "You're probably all wondering why I gathered you here today."

He smirked to himself as the doors opened on the third floor. Ben leaned against the wall and waited until the two other passengers that wanted this floor stepped off. He thought it best not to step off on the same floor as anyone else. Instead, he rode the elevator up to the fourth floor and got off.

There was a Workforce Services suite and he walked toward it until he heard the elevator doors close behind him and then he spun and ran over to the stairs leading down. He took two at a time before he stood in front of the door leading into the third floor and then took a deep breath to compose himself.

He opened the doors and stepped through.

The third floor was better taken care of than the fourth. The carpets didn't have any stains and the walls were free of clutter. He walked past a set of double doors that had a black sign emblazoned on the glass that took up half the door: MEDICAL RECORDS.

Ben checked the watch on his phone. It was 11:51 a.m. He had four minutes.

He walked down the hallway to a drinking fountain and took a sip of water but his throat was nearly closed up from the amount of adrenaline coursing through him. There were restrooms just around the corner and down a small corridor and he walked to them and went into a stall. He sat on the toilet seat.

Occasionally, not often, but occasionally, it hit him just what an awkward turn his life had taken. He had graduated first in his class from Berkley's Haas School of Business with his MBA when he was just twenty-one and the world had been his oyster. He'd been offered a consulting job in Manhattan making a hundred and sixty thousand a year and had accepted.

But that felt like a different life now. That was before his son Matthew had developed autism. Before the twenty-four-hour care and the crying and the strained marriage. Before it felt like his soul had been ripped out of his body and crushed. He had to leave the position in Manhattan and he and his wife and Matthew moved back to Northern California. He accepted a job at a non-profit as assistant director, making a quarter of his previous salary. But the job had flexibility so that he could spend more time with Matthew.

He checked his watch: 11:54 a.m. He had one minute.

Ben stood up and walked out into the corridor. He had never done anything like this before. He was not a criminal. The last time he had gotten in trouble that he could remember was when he received a speeding ticket rushing his wife to the hospital when she was in labor.

He took a deep breath, and continued down the corridor to the medical records room.

Ben opened the door, expecting to see a receptionist. He fiddled with the credentials in his pocket that had been forged by a counterfeiter that made fake identifications for illegal aliens and then withdrew his hand. Instead of a receptionist or a security guard or a police officer, there was a sign, handwritten with marker on a piece of paper, that had been pinned up on a small board: PLEASE DIAL 9 FOR OPERATOR IF YOU NEED HELP.

He smiled to himself. You had to love the way government operated.

Ben walked around the counter and past the large stacks of periodicals and folders and papers. What he was looking for wouldn't be here. There was an adjoining room and he opened the door onto a world he couldn't begin to fathom.

Manila folders were stacked on shelves from floor to ceiling. The Department of Health was slowly going digital, but they could not destroy the paper copies until the subjects passed away or moved out of state. The rows of shelves seemed to go on forever like an infinite library of people's personal information. He didn't want to spend the time running through here and he scanned the room for something that...there it was. In the corner was a computer with a barstool in front of it.

He went to it and sat down, typing in several names. He wrote the call numbers on his palm with a pen that was on the counter next to the computer and the writing got past his wrist before he was done.

Ben jumped to his feet, and began running down the rows of shelves. They were arranged by number, rather than alphabetically, and it took a few minutes for him to adjust. But once he did, it was just like scanning through the Dewey decimal system at any library. He found the first two files he needed but the third wasn't where it was supposed to be. He read the name again: it was a female. He wondered whether it was under her maiden name and went back to the computer and found a number for her maiden name and got the file.

He nabbed seven more files and was about to head back to the computer and run the remainder of his names when he heard voices in the room next door. The door opened.

Ben jumped behind one of the shelves, kneeling down with the files in his arms. Two people, a male and a female, were discussing a retirement party that had been thrown for someone at the office. They stopped near the shelves, about ten feet from where Ben was. His heart was pounding so hard it was causing him to be breathless. Sweat was beginning to trickle down his neck and back and it tickled his skin.

Slowly, he began to crawl away from them. He got another twenty or thirty feet before he heard them say goodbye. The male continued down toward him and the female went back to the main office.

Ben was frozen as he heard the footsteps approach him. The man was in another row, just to the right, but he was bound to see him when he walked by. Ben thought about dumping the files and acting as if he had just mistakenly walked into the wrong office. But that couldn't happen. These files were valuable and they wouldn't get another chance: the office of medical records was moving to a secure location a hundred and eighty miles away. If he wanted the files, this was his only shot.

He stood to his feet. There were over four hundred employees in this building alone. What were the chances that this guy had met every single one?

Ben turned the corner and began walking toward the man.

The man was tall and black with a potbelly. He wore a short-sleeve shirt and a tie and he eyed Ben but didn't say anything.

Ben smiled and said hello as he walked past him. Relief washed over him; his heart felt like it had fallen into his stomach and his knees were weak.

"Excuse me," the man said from behind him, "can I help you with something?"

Ben looked to him. "Me?"

"Yes, you."

"Oh, I'm Timothy. From Dr. Wharton's office upstairs. Cami called about these records yesterday and no one was here when I came down."

"What records are those?"

"For the smoking study that Dr. Wharton's doing. They told me everything's cleared up."

“No one ran it past me, but I wasn’t here yesterday.”

“Well I’ll wait if you like and you can call up there and verify.”

The man looked him up and down, running his eyes over the names on the files he was holding. “Nah, just make sure you sign out for ‘em at the front desk.”

“Thanks.”

Ben walked out the door to the reception area where the woman was sitting. He smiled as he signed a fake name to a sheet that was sitting on the counter and then went out the front door, having to lean against the wall a moment because he felt like he was about to faint.

CHAPTER 15

The Center for Anti-Vaccination Studies was a five-room suite in an office building occupied by middle-income lawyers and dentists. The first floor always smelled like popcorn and massage oil from a parlor that took up the first suite. They claimed to be licensed massage therapists, but Ben had never seen one degree or certificate on the wall. Plus, the men coming out of there seemed just a bit too happy.

He walked past it now and smiled to the receptionist at the front desk, a stack of files under his arm as he hit the up button on the elevator.

The fifth and top floor was much like the first except that it smelled a bit better. The CAVS's five rooms were better decorated than most, with glass walls on the interior and exposed brick in the offices. The floor was a slick hardwood donated to CAVS from a contractor whose daughter had developed autism after a routine vaccination at the age of two.

Ben went through the office space, wondering where everybody was until he checked his phone: it was five in the afternoon on a Friday. He went straight to his office and shut the door. He placed the files down on his desk and sat in front of them a long time, just staring. There was a knock.

"Come in."

Tate Buhler walked in, sipping a Mountain Dew Code Red. He saw the files on the desk and nearly spit up his drink. He shut the door. "You got them?"

"Yeah."

"How?"

"You don't want to know."

Tate sat down across from him at the desk and they both stared at the files. There were fifteen total. Fifteen medical records of research physicians that specialized in vaccinations. One of these physicians had recanted everything they had ever written about the safety of vaccination after one of their children developed a severe learning disability days after the MMR vaccine.

"You think it's real?" Tate said. "I mean, I know the government does some crazy shit, but firing a doctor and then suing to keep him quiet just 'cause he's against vaccinations sounds extreme."

Ben smirked. "Do you remember the serial killer from the eighties who supposedly poisoned bottles of Tylenol and half a dozen people died?"

"Yeah, that was in Chicago or somewhere."

"Well one of the people that died bought their Tylenol from a pharmacy. The public doesn't have access to medications in a pharmacy. That means the Tylenol was tainted when it left the factory and so Johnson & Johnson and the dim-witted law enforcement who investigated the case came up with this serial killer story. They dodged lawsuits, criminal liability, any repercussions at all just because money can buy you whatever you want. If they can cover up the murders of innocent people, they can certainly cover up firing one person."

Tate shook his head. "What're we even gonna do when we find this doctor? I mean he can't talk about it, right? What good is he gonna be?"

Ben's phone began to ring. He picked it up. "He's a symbol, Tate. He's a symbol of what we're trying to do here. He doesn't need to open his mouth at all. If he sits next to me on a stage with a name tag, that's enough. People will Google him and find out the rest…Hello, this is Benjamin Cornell…yes…where?…when?…who else knows about this…okay…okay."

Ben hung up the phone and sat quietly a few moments, staring at the desk.

"You okay?"

"I'm going to be gone for a while," he said, standing up and heading out the door.

"How long?"

"I don't know."

"Well where you going?" Tate yelled as Ben headed toward the elevators.

"Hawaii."

CHAPTER 16

Ele Henano sat in the back of Queen's Medical Center with Tiffany Leath and smoked pot from a joint. The weed was freshly picked from his grandmother's backyard and it had a purple tinge that you could see in the fading sunlight.

They smoked half the joint and then leaned back on the old lawn chairs they'd taken out of a patio storage closet. He'd found that if he smoked more than half a joint with another person, people could usually tell something was wrong. He'd been fired from one job previously because his boss, the head nurse, could instantly tell he was high. The smell, the red eyes, the greenish tongue, he could hide all of those. But he couldn't hide his goofy personality or the giggles that pot gave him.

"What'd you do this weekend?" he said, passing a Gatorade to her.

"I met some guy at a bar and hung out with him."

"Just hung out."

"We fucked around, but nothin' too hot. He got all limp 'cause we smoked too much weed."

Ele giggled. "That's why you need a real man."

"I don't mess around with people I work with," she said, taking a swig of the drink and handing it back. "I got fired from my last job doing that."

"Where at?"

"It was a psychiatric hospital on the mainland. It was pretty fucked up. This one patient was a soldier in World War Two and he had a head injury. So to change his diaper, you had to play the national anthem 'cause he would stand up and salute. And then you just had to hurry and change it 'cause otherwise he'd fight you. Then there was this one dude that thought cats had filled his room. He thought he had like thirty cats in there and you had to be careful where you walked 'cause if you stepped on one of his cats he'd attack you."

"Man. That sounds fucked up, yo."

"It wasn't fun. But they paid good. 'Cause you got your hair pulled and got gassed and shit. You know what gassing is?"

He shook his head.

"It's where they shit or piss or both and then throw it at your face. Some a the patients gassed the staff all the time so with some of 'em you had to wear gasmasks. If I ever get old, just fucking shoot me."

Ele took a deep breath. "Ready to go back?"

"Yeah, I guess."

They went inside and up to the locker rooms. Ele went into the men's and changed into a fresh pair of scrubs. He brushed his teeth, used eyedrops, and washed his hands and his face. He ran some cold water through his hair—he knew the hair could hold the scent of marijuana as good as anything—and then dried off with some paper towels and headed into the corridor. Tiffany was already waiting for him.

He had hit her up at a party once when they first started hanging out, but she didn't show any interest. She said it was because she didn't date people she worked with but Ele didn't believe that. She only dated white guys, never islanders. He wondered why she would move to Hawaii if she didn't like Hawaiians but people were like that he guessed. They came out here for all sorts of reasons and few of them made any sense to him. Hawaii was expensive, you made less money, many of the locals didn't like whites, and it was difficult to get all the conveniences of the mainland. But the grass was always greener. While people were trying to move in, he was desperately trying to move out, but money was always an issue.

"Where you gotta go?" Tiffany asked.

"Up to six."

"Nuh uh. I thought no one was supposed to go up there?"

"Nah, they got barriers set up. You just can't touch the people. What you think they're sick with?"

"I heard it was AIDS."

"That don't make sense 'cause I heard Dr. Hennessey saying that patients were getting infected faster than they thought they would. So AIDS wouldn't do that."

"Yeah, I don't know. I don't really care. I just wanna get outta here and chill with a bottle a wine at my house."

They passed the elevators and Ele said goodbye and hopped on. He headed to six, where the patients were quarantined, and when he stepped off the elevator he grabbed some rubber gloves that were hanging in a box on the wall. Several nurses were up here but they wore facemasks and plastic suits over their scrubs. He didn't get any of that because he was only here to empty the trash.

He went from room to room, trying to catch a glimpse of the patients. No one told the orderlies anything and there were a lot of rumors about what exactly was wrong with them. In one room was a young woman who lay back with her eyes open, staring at the ceiling. He would've thought that she was dead but her chest kept moving. It creeped him out and he left and went into the room next door.

This one had an older man with a bald head and a big pot belly. He was laughing with one of the nurses who was preparing a meal for him and he smiled to Ele when he walked in.

The man's name was Phillip Bourde and he'd been committed to level six yesterday when he had vomited blood and displayed a rash over his chest and arms.

"How you doin' today, Ele?"

"Good, boss. You?"

"Oh hangin' in there. Did you see the Chargers play last night?"

"Nah I was with my girl and she hates football," Ele said as he began emptying the trash.

The nurse said a few things to the man about relaxing and not stressing himself and then left as Ele went into the small bathroom that was off to the side of the room and emptied the trash there. Water had splashed onto the sink and he began to clean it with supplies that he carried with him on a belt.

"What's your girl like?" Phil yelled.

"She just one a my girls. She cool. Big fake tits."

Philip laughed. "Thatta boy. You get 'em while you can. When you hit my age if a woman even smiles at you, you think it's your lucky day."

Ele stepped out of the bathroom. "So how's everythin' lookin'? Doctor got good news?"

"They haven't talked to me since last night except to tell me I can't have any visitors and they gotta put this plastic sheet over my bed. But I guess no news is good news."

"Well you look good. I'm sure it's just the flu or somethin'."

"I hope so. I've been feelin' stronger today so hopefully it was just a bug. Hey, do me a favor, will ya, Ele? My phone's in my pants pocket over there. Can you hand it to me?"

"Yeah."

Ele walked to the stack of clothes on a shelf and pulled down the jeans. He took off his gloves and ruffled through the pockets until he found a Blackberry. He walked over to the bed.

A chart and a set of instructions hung on a clipboard next to the bed. Ele noticed that notes were scribbled in on a few lines near the bottom of the page. One note said, MEETING LAST NIGHT ABOUT HANDLING PROCEDURES. He wondered what that was about. He'd found that meetings for nurses, doctors, and staff were frequent but that usually they forgot to notify the orderlies and custodians to attend. Or, it was done on purpose.

He moved the clipboard so he could open the plastic canopy hanging from the ceiling over the bed.

"Thanks," Philip said, taking it from him.

"I gotta run. You take care, boss."

"You too. Get some T and A for the both of us."

As Ele left the room to head down the corridor, he checked his cell phone for messages and emails. He had an itch on the corner of his eye and he rubbed it with his finger, and put the phone away.

CHAPTER 17

Samantha Bower stood on the beach and stared out over the water. Her thoughts were racing and she felt anxiety that she hadn't felt since taking medical school exams. Thirteen more patients had been admitted in the last three days with black pox symptoms and they were averaging one admittance per four hours.

Dr. Wilson planned another press conference, as the news programs kept playing the video clip of him saying he didn't believe there would be any more cases. In the end, as the numbers started to climb, he cancelled the press conference. He had been incommunicado for the last ten hours.

Sam looked back to the Ducati bullet bike she had traded in the car for. It was yellow and gleamed in the bright Hawaiian sun. Eventually, she would have to go back to the hospital, but for now, there was a highway in front of her with few cars on it this early in the morning.

Sam hopped on the bike and it roared to life. Riding motorcycles was something quite routine in her family until her uncle had died on a highway when he hit a stone and careened into a semi. After that, her father refused to let her ride but when she turned eighteen, he didn't stop her.

She turned into traffic and sped through a yellow light as she took the onramp onto interstate H1. She raced up the onramp and slid two lanes over before easing off the throttle. Her helmet was shiny and black with a tinted shield. She knew that many people thought she was a man when they saw her speed by.

The interstate snaked around the island and she would occasionally glance at the bright green vegetation that surrounded her like a closing army. The jungle seemed to envelope everything and the city and its inhabitants were only fighting it off in short bursts. It felt like with one relatively short absence or time of neglect, the jungle could take the city back.

She pulled off on an exit near another beach and came to a stop in front of a roach-coach that was selling Hawaiian sandwiches. She ordered a pulled pork sandwich with French fries and an apple juice before sitting on one of the benches and watching the surfers gliding on the waves. Her cell phone buzzed and she didn't recognize the number.

"This is Sam."

"Oh, hey, didn't expect you to answer on the first ring. This is Duncan. Um, from the hospital."

"I remember, Duncan. What can I do for you?"

"Um well, I was just, I mean um, I was looking at and wondering if maybe…you know, I don't know anyone here and I wanted to maybe grab some dinner."

"Are you asking me out?"

"Yes and it's going terribly, isn't it?"

"Not the best I've been pitched. But not the worst either. Yeah, I'll have dinner."

"Really? Just like that? I was expecting you to say no."

"Why?"

"You don't strike me as the type of person that needs other people around."

She smirked. "A psychopath doesn't need other people around. I'm going to be at the hospital until about six."

"Great. I'm at the base. I'll pick you up then."

"All right, bye."

"Bye."

Her food was ready and she was surprised the French fries had been put on top of the sandwich along with a tube-full of barbeque sauce and at least half an onion and a tomato. She took a couple bites and realized it was the best sandwich she'd ever had.

When she finished, she thanked the cook and got back on her bike, heading toward the hospital. She'd left a bag there permanently now that contained toiletries and several changes of clothing so that she wouldn't have to bring anything with her when she went.

It still wasn't yet 9:00 a.m. when she parked and went inside the building. She noticed several more guards in uniform standing at all the entrances and exits and she saw Wilson speaking with General Lancaster.

"Hey," she said, "where've you been hiding out?"

"We have a situation. One of the orderlies here called in sick to work. On a hunch, the nurse asked him his symptoms. I don't think I need to tell you what they were."

"I knew those canopies weren't enough."

"The canopies were fine. He reached under them to hand one of the patients his phone. I talked to the kid myself. He was with his girlfriend all last night, at least a few days after he'd been exposed to the agent. We think the girlfriend is infected too. Guess what her profession is? Flight attendant."

"Damn it, Ralph," Sam said, anger in her voice, "I told them I wanted full barrier. He shouldn't have been able to reach under there."

"What's done is done. We need to deal with this situation as it is. We can't find the girlfriend, Yolanda Gonzalez, and her cellphone goes to voicemail. We called the airlines and she has a flight scheduled for noon. We need to make sure she's not on that plane."

"I'll head down there."

Sam didn't wait to hear what else Wilson had to say. He shouted something about letting the police and the military biohazard units take care of it. Wilson had more faith in the government than she did. She'd seen military units willingly expose themselves to hot agents because they thought they were helping the patients. She'd also seen confused patients shot by young police officers because they weren't complying with what they were told, either out of ignorance as to what was going on, or because the disease had taken hold and they couldn't think clearly.

As Sam raced to Honolulu International Airport, only one thought ran through her mind: if she gets on that plane, millions could die.

CHAPTER 18

Robert Greyjoy stepped off the plane in Dubai and immediately wished he hadn't worn a suit. He was in a rush and that just happened to be what he was wearing at the time when he bought his ticket. Now he wished he'd bought some shorts and a shirt at the duty-free shop. But the terrible flower-print shirts they had were so atrocious he couldn't bring himself to wear one. Better to suffer a little heat than feel out of sorts with one's sense of style, he'd thought.

Dubai was one of his favorite cities. They served no alcohol, so he was unable to get one of his beloved Tonight or Nevers, but there were other things to focus his attention on.

Women were certainly not it. Many were covered from head to toe in traditional Muslim attire with chadars covering their hair, leaving only their faces exposed, which in itself was a major advancement for feminine rights in this region of the world. Drugs were difficult to come by as well. The penalties were so severe—the government wanting this to be a place of business rather than a pleasure destination—that most people who could supply the drugs stayed away or were pulled out of their homes in the middle of the night and never heard from again. There was a different view of law in this part of the world; something still medieval, cruel almost. Robert soaked it in and felt refreshed whenever he came here.

He hailed a taxi and the driver was a young man of about twenty. He wore a colorful tank-top, sweats, and stunk of body odor.

"Enlishezia?" Robert said.

"Yes, I speak English. Very good. I go to school."

"Yes, I can see that. Your accent doesn't interfere with comprehension." The man gave him a quizzical look so Robert added, "You speak very good."

The man smiled. "So where you go?"

"The mall please."

Dubai Mall is the largest shopping mall in the world with just over twelve hundred stores. It includes aquariums, fountains, bars—where only juices and sodas are served—an ice rink, and a theme park.

As the cab pulled to a stop in front of the mall on Doha Street, Robert paid and thanked the man before stepping out. The heat was penetrating; something he hadn't noticed in the air-conditioned cab. It sank into his skin and head and it seemed to even heat up his feet. He guessed it was over a hundred and ten degrees right now.

Robert walked in and began strolling down the main promenade, stopping at the Aldo store a moment to glance over a few Italian shoes. A man came up behind him and stood quietly until he was done looking at the shoes. Robert turned to him and they began walking together at an easy pace, taking in the sights and smells.

"I assume it's done," the man said.

"It is."

"Was Thailand agreeable to you?"

"It was."

The man nodded, staring at a group of young girls that were drinking sodas near a fountain. "Thailand is an unusual place. Not entirely civilized, not entirely savage. A place in evolution, though I think it's unclear which way it will evolve."

"Savage. The baser instincts usually win out over all else."

"Not entirely true. Especially when a strong belief in God is present. Do you believe in God, Robert?"

"No."

"You will. Everybody does. People may protest and talk about how unreasonable it is to have faith in an unknowable deity, but when their back is against the wall and they have nowhere else to turn, they always turn to God. It is simply how our psychology is set up."

"I guess I'll have to wait and see when my back is against the wall."

"How is your partner?"

"She's fine."

"I noticed you spent a couple of extra days in Thailand. Sightseeing?"

"Something like that."

"Do you love her?"

Robert hesitated. "What do you care?"

"I don't. I was just curious. But I will give you some advice even though you don't want it: love has no place in what we do. You have to have no connections, nothing you care about. That's the only way you'll survive. Love, in our business, will kill you."

"Too late now. Besides, I don't have anyone else to talk to. I think I'd go insane without at least one person I can be honest with."

The man took a deep breath. "Do you ever get sick of this, Robert? Of living on planes, knowing people for days or weeks at a time, no family, no friends…I'm reminded sometimes of the traveling hobos you'd see in comic strips in the fifties. They went from one town to the next on trains, never really knowing where they were going and always forgetting where they'd been as soon as they'd left."

Robert thought quietly a moment before answering. "Do you know how life works in the ocean? The large fish eat the little fish. That's it. There are no laws other than that. No remorse or appeals or complaining. Everybody knows their place and accepts it. That's how it is for us on land too. The ones with power eat the ones without power. We're just not as honest about it with ourselves as the fish are. I don't know about you, but I intend to always be the one doing the eating. Because the alternative is much worse."

"Maybe," he said absently, not looking in his direction. "Regardless, I'm retiring."

"When?"

"Today. Right now. This is my last assignment with the agency."

"Nobody told me."

"Nobody knows. You're the first." The man stopped and sat down on a bench. In front of them was a magnificent fountain that had base lights on the floors and was lighting the water in alternating colors. "When I was going through the application process and I was strapped to the polygraph machine—this was the second day at the end when they ask the twenty questions they actually want answers to rather than just torturing us—they asked if I would kill someone for them. I said yes. Then they asked if I would sleep with another woman other than my wife if they asked me to. I'd done my research on these interrogations and I knew if I answered no they would end the application process and throw me out.

"I couldn't handle that, Robert. I came from a small mining town in Colorado. The mines were the only employment there. Everybody went from high school straight into the mines. Twelve hours a day underground in the dark. I couldn't handle that. So I said yes. Yes I would sleep with another woman if you asked me to. I went home and told my wife that. Two days later, I was accepted for training. My wife told me I could go to training or I could have her, but not both." He exhaled loudly, staring absently at the water as it turned a bright blue. "I've regretted that decision for the past fifty years. She remarried and had two kids. They're in their thirties now. Those were my kids, Robert. That was my life."

"You're serving your country in a way that no one—"

"Country, duty, loyalty—they're all abstractions. Ideas in our minds. They don't keep you company when you're lonely, Robert. They just don't." He was quiet a long time and then said, "You have one more assignment from me." He handed him a flash drive. "Honolulu, Hawaii." He stood up. "Destroy the flash drive when you're done."

The man began to walk away when Robert said, "Wait." The man turned. "We've been meeting for nine years and I don't even know your real name."

The man smirked in a melancholic way. "Jim. My name is Jim."

"Jim," Robert said. "I like that name. That was my father's first name."

"Goodbye, Robert."

"Take care, Jim."

Robert watched as Jim walked away and disappeared into the crowd. He glanced down to the flash drive in his hand. In a way, Jim had been the only friend he had had these past nine years. He was the only one who knew what he really was, what he really did. Briefly, he considered whether it was time for him to leave as well.

He put the flash drive in his pocket and stood up. Not yet, he thought. But soon.

CHAPTER 19

Honolulu International Airport was busy with tourists and conventions that were coming in to enjoy their hot summer months. Sam parked illegally at the curb and noticed only one police cruiser out front.

She raced inside, checking her watch: it was 11:47 a.m.

There were some shops and delis, a restaurant and a bar. She ran past them, sliding through crowds. It suddenly dawned on her that she had no idea what this woman looked like. She texted Wilson and asked for a photo. Thirty seconds later, he sent a photo to her along with the message, "Let the BH team handle this." The fact that he'd sent the photo meant he knew she had no intention of doing that.

Sam came to the TSA checkpoints and saw that the lines were at least forty people deep. They snaked through the waiting areas out into the corridor and around the corner. She got in the back of a line and counted as the next person went through the detectors and was scanned by a handheld device. It took about a minute and a half, which meant she'd be in line for almost an hour.

Sam rushed to the front of the line, pushing past people that began to swear and yell. She got to one of the TSA officers and flashed her CDC credentials.

"I need to get into those terminals right now."

"Ma'am, what you need is to get back to the end of the line."

Sam saw two police officers with several men in slick, plastic smocks walk around the terminal and scan the faces in the crowd. "I need to be with them. Please tell that police officer to come here and they'll verify that—"

"I'm not gonna ask you again, get to the back of the line."

Samantha saw a young woman step out of the bathrooms. She had curly black hair and caramel skin. She was wiping her nose and popped a handful of pills, washing them down with a bottle of water. It was Yolanda. The officers and BH team were standing not twenty feet away from her and didn't recognize her. They were laughing and joking.

"I need to get there, now. This isn't a joke. If you don't let me through, people could die."

The officer shouted behind her and two TSA officers ran up as Sam tried to push past her. The other officers grabbed her by her arms and slammed her down against a table as Sam was shouting to get the attention of the BH team.

Yolanda Gonzalez stared at herself in the bathroom mirror at Honolulu International Airport. She appeared pale and had been coughing all morning. A rash was starting to appear on her chest and she buttoned the top button of her blouse to cover it up. She had a slight fever and had just vomited into the toilet.

"You doin' okay, hon?" Melissa, another stewardess on her airline asked.

"I think I got the flu."

"Maybe you should go home?"

"I can't miss any more work."

"Yeah," Melissa said, washing her hands at the sink, "they used to pay us for sick time but not no more. Used to pay a lot more too. This whole industry's gone to hell. Let me feel you." She placed her hand on Yolanda's forehead. "You're burnin' up, sweetie. You need to go home."

"I'll just do a half day if it gets worse."

"Well, let me give you these. They're Lortab so you gotta be careful. Just take one at a time, four hours apart. It'll get you through the day."

"Thanks, Melissa."

"No problem. If you need someone to cover a flight call me. I'm off at three."

"Thanks."

As Melissa left, Yolanda turned back to the mirror. She took a deep breath, and walked outside into the corridor. She noticed some cops and a few guys dressed in what looked like rain slicks standing around, but they were only there a minute and then walked on. She wondered if there'd been a bomb threat. Since 9-11, they got at least one a week and the cops or FBI or military police would come and look around and then leave. It had become routine and she wondered what it was like before 9-11, when you weren't thinking about terrorists all day.

As she was taking her Lortab, she heard some yelling near the metal detectors and looked over. A woman was shouting and trying to fight her way past TSA. Probably someone pissed that they patted down her kid or something. She watched as three TSA officers pinned the woman down on a table and put handcuffs on her.

Yolanda turned, and headed for her plane.

CHAPTER 20

Samantha Bower sat in a small gray room the TSA used as a holding cell. There were no windows and no decorations. Just a gray table and two gray chairs. No agents from the FBI or the TSA came in however. She guessed she was in there for over an hour before there was a knock on the door and Ralph Wilson appeared with two police officers. He had a knowing grin on his face and said, "Let's go, jail bird. You can get your bike later."

They stayed silent until they were outside and the two officers had returned to their cruiser. A cab waited for them on the curb and they climbed in. Wilson told the driver to take them to Queen's Medical.

"They said you assaulted a TSA agent."

"I didn't assault her. I just tried to push my way past her."

"Pushing is assault." He smiled at her. "I was arrested once in Texas for confining a woman with pneumonic plague to a hospital room and locking the door. Sometimes fighting for the greater good means you're going to get into some hot water."

He leaned back in the seat and pulled out a pipe. He never smoked it, as he had quit years ago, but the feel of it in his mouth, Sam knew from late night conversation, made him feel as if he were in his youth again.

"They won't be pursuing charges," he said.

"Did she make it on the plane?"

"Yes. They're in the air right now. The FBI's agreed to help us and they're grounding the plane. But it's too late for the passengers. Everyone will have to be quarantined." He stared out the window. "We've had forty-one admittees since this morning."

Sam nodded, as if expecting news like that. "The hospital doesn't have any more space. I scouted out a rec center nearby. We can rent the gymnasium and just buy cots. Ralph, we need to ground all the flights coming and going. We need to let the public know this isn't the swine flu or a head cold."

"I know," he said, keeping his eyes glued to the passing buildings. "I never thought I would experience something like this."

They arrived at Queen's Medical and Sam could see there was a heavier military presence than even a few hours ago. Jeeps were parked in most of the handicap and expectant mother spaces and several MPs stood at every entrance and exit.

They walked into a ghost town. The staff was not there anymore. Wilson informed her that several of the receptionists and orderlies had come down with symptoms. Sam immediately went up to the sixth floor. A few nurses were walking around, going from room to room and helping where they could. Now they were in full gear, with facemasks, thick rubber gloves, and booties. The barriers she had asked for were now up and no one was touching any of the patients.

She saw Duncan Adams walk out of a room. He was staring at the floor, lost in thought as he bit his lower lip.

"Hi," he said as he looked up.

"Hi. How's it looking?"

"Incubation period is about seven days, not twelve like it should be. This virus is replicating faster than normal smallpox. I've sent some tissues back to USAMRIID. I need to see what we're dealing with. I'm afraid I'll have to cancel dinner tonight. I'm going to be on a plane back to Maryland."

"To tell you the truth I don't feel much like eating right now."

Sam noticed a nurse near the reception area walk to a large white board. She erased two names and added six others. It was a death board, though it wasn't officially called that. They kept track of the patients and erased the names of those that died. Sam ran down the list: not a single one that had been here when she first came to Hawaii was still alive. A small box in the corner said, SURVIVORS. It was empty.

"I'll be back in a couple days," Duncan said. "I'd like to take you to dinner then."

"I'm sorry, Duncan. I just can't think about that right now."

"You haven't handled too many of these, have you?"

"Too many of what?"

"Outbreaks of hot agents. Most people don't realize that outbreaks like this are quite common in Africa and India, South Asia, places with large numbers of poor that are packed tightly together. In the Congo, Ebola makes an appearance every day. It just appears, out of nowhere. It'll kill a few hundred people, perhaps cause a hospital to be shut down, and then it disappears as the infected population dies off. I'm always sent to those so I may not have the right perspective on this situation. Sorry if I seem insensitive, but I've seen so much of this, I've been a little desensitized."

"You weren't insensitive. I just have a lot taking up my brain's processing power right now. So how many outbreaks have you handled?"

"At least fifty. One of the worst was in Kinshasa. A maternity ward had been infected with bubonic plague. They had no antibiotics so I had to fly them in but it took two weeks to get there. It was the worst two weeks of my life."

"I bet," she said, now purposely averting her gaze from the death board she'd been staring at.

"So what are you going to do now?"

"I'm setting up a new patient center in the rec center a few blocks away. The hospital doesn't have the capacity to hold all these people. Then I'm going to recruit staff from all the hospitals to work it."

"Can I make a recommendation without sounding like an ass? Don't recruit people. If they feel it's part of their job to risk their lives, they won't do it. Ask for volunteers. Once a few of them volunteer, some of the others will be shamed into it."

"Dr. Bower."

Sam turned to see Jerry Amoy run up to her.

"Dr. Bower, I need you to look at something right away. Follow me. Dr. Adams, you should come to. Please suit up first."

They ran to the locker rooms and dressed, grabbing fresh facemasks and booties from stations set up in the corridor. They followed Amoy down the hall to the last room and entered. The man in the hospital bed didn't appear human.

He was covered in maculopapular rashes from head to toe, and blisters had formed on his skin in every inch of available space. The blisters were raised, filled with fluid, and his skin appeared like it had thousands of pebbles jammed underneath it.

"Haven't seen this before," Jerry Amoy said. "He's the first with the blisters. He's also blind. The blisters have formed on his retinas and caused scarring. This isn't the same disease we were seeing; this is classic smallpox."

Sam wanted to step closer but her body didn't allow it. A primordial aversion to sickness and death bubbled within her and prevented her from taking those few steps over to the side of the bed. But will is stronger than instinct. She forced herself over to look at the blisters.

There was no hemorrhaging underneath the dermis causing the characteristic charred appearance of the other patients.

"Is it a mutation in the virus?" Amoy said.

"I doubt it," Sam replied. "We'd be seeing a lot more of it. It might be a new strain, appearing in the population at the same time."

"That's super unlikely," Duncan said. "I've read that some patients are resistant to black pox. His body might have fought it off and just been left with…this."

Samantha leaned down close to the man's face. She felt her heart pounding and her breaths were inadvertently quick and shallow. "Can you hear me?" she said.

The man didn't respond. His mouth was agape and his eyes closed, the lids covered with thick, bubbly blisters.

He suddenly shot up and gasped for breath as he began to writhe. She jumped back, into Duncan, as Amoy called some staff. They held the man down and injected a sedative.

"You okay?" Duncan asked.

Sam pulled away from him and straightened her hair, taking a deep breath. "Just to be on the safe side," she said, "we need smallpox vaccinations."

Duncan said, "We ordered thousands the second we heard. They're not here yet but I'm sure they will be. It may be enough to inoculate against the black pox as well."

Sam walked toward the door and stepped out into the corridor. "That death board has doubled from this morning. If this agent hits its tipping point, there'll be no one left to inoculate. We need to get those vaccinations here as fast as possible."

CHAPTER 21

Robert Greyjoy landed in Honolulu and stepped onto the tarmac a new man. He felt alive and refreshed, as if he'd slept for a week and just woken up to a sunny world that welcomed him with open arms. It was, in his mind, weakness. He was too sensitive to allow weather to affect him like this. He toned down his joyful response and headed into the airport.

The airport was just a simple airfield about twenty miles from Honolulu International. Whenever possible, Robert flew small, independent charters. It wasn't a bad practice; usually it was just him and the pilot. But occasionally he would be seated on a plane with six other people that wanted to talk and he would have to feign interest and tell boring stories. He did everything he could to fit in, to seem so average he would not be remembered should anyone else ask later on.

There was a single cab outside on the curb and he walked to it and put his luggage in the trunk before getting into the backseat. He put on his seatbelt and instructed the driver to take him to Queen's Medical Center.

"Eh," the driver said, "haven't you seen the news? Nobody's allowed in right now."

"I'll be fine. Please go now."

The cabbie pulled away from the curb and quickly made his way to the interstate by running a red light and speeding. When they had climbed the onramp and were cruising at a steady speed, the cabbie turned on a CD and began humming to the music. Robert took out his phone and began reading facts about the island: geography, history, anthropology, political climate, the economy, the most popular television shows and books, and a little about the language.

He was surprised to learn that there was a powerful anti-American movement in the state. Many were not happy with their island achieving unification with the mainland and would have preferred to stay independent. Robert had no doubt if that were so, China would begin making plans to add Hawaii as a colony. It was a little green gem in the sea, too tempting to pass up for larger nations.

The cab stopped at Queen's Medical and he tipped the driver well; after their initial exchange, he had not spoken again. Something Robert preferred. He went around to the back of the hospital and saw two military police officers guarding the only entrance that was not barricaded with tape and plywood signs.

"Hello," he said, pulling out an ID. He had three in his pocket and he took it out based on feel and glanced down quickly to make sure it was the right one. He flashed it and saw the MPs exchange looks.

"You're the first agent from the FBI that's come here, Mr. Donner."

"Please," Robert said, "call me Billy."

"You can go inside and to the left, Billy. They're making everyone suit up. You'll find changing stations on either side of the hallway."

"Thank you."

He entered the hospital and looked down both ends of the corridor. They were empty. He closed his eyes and listened. He could hear someone speaking down the hall to the left. He followed the sound, taking his steps softly so as not to drown it out, and the speaking grew louder as he approached a conference room.

Several men in suits and uniforms sat at a conference table, both military and local police. They all glanced up when they saw him.

He smiled shyly and sat down at the end of the long table. No one said anything at first and the man that had been speaking continued when an older man in a suit stopped him and said, "Excuse me, who are you exactly?"

"Billy Donner. I'm the assistant special agent in charge of this operation for the FBI. I spoke to a Ralph Wilson on the phone."

"Oh, right," the old man said, "yeah, that was me. I'm Dr. Wilson. Thank you for getting out here so quickly, Agent Donner." He looked to the man next to him. "Agent Donner is our liaison with the Feds. Sorry about the interruption, please continue."

As the man resumed speaking, Robert leaned back in his chair. There certainly was an Agent William Donner somewhere, but he wouldn't be making it to Hawaii.

"So in conclusion," the man finally said, "I think the governor's gonna have to declare a state of emergency. We're approaching such a large population of infected that we're risking exposure on the mainland."

Wilson said, "Have there been any reported cases on the other islands?"

The man, who Robert had identified as Dr. Duncan Adams from a nametag on his chest, shook his head. "No, thank heaven. It's completely localized to Oahu for now, with a central point in Honolulu. The initial patients tended to be in their mid to late thirties, healthy and active with above median incomes. That's changing rapidly and we're seeing older and younger people, which means the virus is spreading through the population at an exponentially accelerated rate. It's like compound interest: each infected patient increases the number of patients each patient infects, if that makes sense," Duncan said, looking at the men in uniform.

One of the military men asked, "What's the tipping point? I heard another doctor here discussing that."

"That's the Twilight Zone. That's what we call it as USAMRIID. It's the point when an outbreak becomes a pandemic. It's nothing major; a minor shift is enough to change a simple scare into a disease that kills millions. To give you an example, the flu virus has a one to one ratio, meaning that for each person infected, that person, on average, infects one other person. Should that number go from 1 to 1.3, it would be enough to cause the flu to reach a tipping point and grow exponentially and we'd have a pandemic like the 1918 that killed over a million people."

"Is this disease approaching a tipping point or receding?" someone else asked.

"Hard to tell," Wilson said before Duncan could answer. "Our data is somewhat scattershot right now but we've been compiling it since we got here and we should have some relatively accurate numbers within the next few days or so. Then we'll know which way this disease is going."

Robert said, "Do we know the cause?"

Duncan answered quickly, "Yes, we believe so. We think the index patient was a travel guide in South America that lived here in Honolulu. We think he picked it up in the jungles of Peru."

"How?"

"That we don't know. It could be an interspecies jump or the virus simply could've existed in some hideaway we hadn't discovered yet, like a cave or something."

Robert noticed a young woman walk in. She was beautiful, in an exotic way, and she wore a T-shirt that showed off her muscled arms.

"This is Dr. Samantha Bower from the CDC," Wilson said. "She's been following up on our index patient."

Samantha smiled to the group. "Nice to meet you all."

"What have you found out, dear?"

Samantha cleared her throat. It appeared to Robert that it was involuntary and he realized she had been embarrassed by the use of the word *dear*.

"We located another patient in Iquitos, Peru. It's a small town on the outskirts of the Amazon jungle. We think this patient was one of two people who may have infected our index. The most interesting news we received from hospital personnel there was that the patient is recovering. It's a young woman, named Holly Fenstermac, who was on an expedition. Apparently another member of the same expedition had also fallen ill, Michael Pettrioli. However, he passed some time ago. Holly is a unique case; we don't have any patients here that are showing any signs of a recovery. The CDC is mounting an expedition following our index's route as well as spending time with Holly, running an analysis of the progression of the virus in her body.

"In the meantime, we've received ample shipments of the smallpox vaccine and are ready to begin distributing it to the population."

"Hold on a sec," a man that was tucked away in the corner, taking notes on a laptop, said. "You're telling me we're asking the population to trust us giving them smallpox vaccinations? Isn't it true that a certain percentage of the population actually develops smallpox from the vaccination and becomes a host to the virus, infecting others?"

"That's an extremely small risk consider—"

"During the first round of vaccinations fifty years ago, Dr. Bower, were the patients told that some of them would be developing smallpox from the vaccinations? I mean, did anyone actually tell them they might die?"

Duncan leaned over to Wilson and said, "Who is this guy?" loud enough that everybody could hear.

Wilson replied, "Ben Cornell. He works for the Center for Anti-Vaccination Studies."

"You're kidding me?" Duncan said, glancing back at him. "What the hell is he doing here?"

"I'm representing the people," Ben said, "that may wanna voice some concerns before the government begins filling them with viruses."

Wilson glanced back to him and then forward again. "He is here at the request of the governor's office." He cleared his throat, indicating that was the end of the issue. "Now, when the governor declares a state of emergency, all transportation to and from the island will be halted. We'll be resupplied by cargo plane but because of quarantine procedure, it will be a long and slow process. Some resources are going to be scarce." He turned to what appeared like a captain or chief of police. "Chief, that's where we're going to need a serious police presence. We've had instances like this spiral out of control before anybody even knew what was going on."

"We pulled the greens out of training at the academy," the chief replied, "and we'll be putting them on the streets. I don't think we'll need them but having more police present will have the desired effect. I think we'll be fine."

Wilson nodded. "Grocery stores will run out of food once the governor makes his announcement. We'll need to set up charity organizations and government kitchens to make sure everyone is getting enough to eat. During a state of emergency no one will be allowed public transportation so we'll need to make sure we set up those kitchens as close as possible to population centers."

A man in military uniform said, "The National Guard can help set that up but we'll need men to run 'em. I've got a skeleton crew here. Most a my boys is in Iraq and Afghanistan and we'll have to put in a request for private troops if we want more help."

Robert got a vision in his mind of Hurricane Katrina. He remembered seeing the soldiers in plain clothes with Ray-Ban sunglasses and automatic weapons. Mercenaries that made triple what US Army soldiers made and were better equipped.

"That's fine," Wilson said, "we can work out budgetary concerns with FEMA once they get here."

"I wouldn't hold your breath," someone said. There was muted laughter in the room. Robert knew what he meant: during Katrina people were drowning in the streets waiting for help that never arrived.

Wilson didn't laugh. "Let's keep our humor to ourselves. I don't know how much the families of the people that are dying upstairs would appreciate us down here cracking jokes." He glanced around the table. "Any questions?...okay, let's make sure all agencies are on the same page. The general has asked that we hold bi-weekly meetings at the Ritz-Carlton downtown and I've agreed. Anyone have any problem with that?...didn't think so. Well, ladies and gents, that's all for now. Please remember your protocols. And we are holding a seminar on proper barrier procedures in the auditorium at McKinley High School tonight at seven so please be there if at all possible."

Everyone rose and started filing out. Robert stood and waited until Wilson was done speaking to someone in a doctor's white coat and then approached him.

"You seem to have everything under control," Robert said. "Don't think I'm necessary out here."

"I'm afraid if this goes where we think it will, we'll need every man we've got."

"And where do you think it will go, Dr. Wilson?"

"Hell, Agent Donner. This place will go to hell."

CHAPTER 22

Jimmy Loanoai crouched over his toilet as the thick, black fluid spewed from his mouth and nose. It suffocated him and he began to cough as another fountain burst out of him. He had once been hospitalized for food poisoning from a Circle K convenience store hot dog that he had bought at two in morning, but it was nothing like this. The odd thing was it felt painless. The liquid that came out of him appeared like grape Crystal Light with coffee grounds in it and it tugged at his belly as if his organs were being ripped out, but he didn't feel the pain.

He rose and washed out his mouth and wiped it with a towel. He was nude and he walked into his bedroom and changed into his Honolulu PD uniform, strapping his utility belt and holster to himself. He sat on the bed a long time, his face in his hands, as sweat poured down his face and soaked the collar of his uniform.

He took a few deep breaths and stood up, making his way out of the apartment and to the police cruiser waiting for him outside.

One thing he was grateful for was that the PD had sent a car to pick him up. The kid that drove was a rookie he had met a few times when they went out drinking after shifts but they'd never really talked. Jimmy had gotten the impression he was a fag and didn't really try to be friendly. But now, he had never been happier to see anyone in his life. Jimmy climbed into the car and nodded to him as the car pulled away from the curb.

"You okay, Sarge? You're not looking too good."

"Fine," Jimmy said, mopping up sweat from his forehead with a wad of paper towels. "Even if I wasn't, I gotta go. I can't not be at my own birthday party."

"Well you're gonna be glad you came. I heard Captain Brogan got some strippers."

Jimmy shook his head as he felt a wave of nausea roll through him. "That's the last thing I need."

When they got to the house, they had to park almost a block away, as police cruisers took up most of the free spaces. The party was being held at the captain's house. Since the captain's wife was independently rich—from an inheritance, Jimmy had heard—they owned one of the largest homes on the island and the party was going to be held out back by the pool.

Jimmy climbed out of the car and felt his legs get weak. His head spun and before he could swallow, vomit shot out of his mouth like something had exploded in his stomach. It spewed over the police cruiser and ran down in long, black lines to the pavement below.

"I don't think you're doin' fine, Sarge. Lemme take you home. I'll explain to everyone that you're too sick."

"Let me just get in there and make an appearance. Then I'll leave. Wait for me here."

Jimmy walked up the block and wished he'd told the rookie to just drop him off in front of the house. He got all the way up the driveway before he had to stop for a second and catch his breath. He wondered if he should go to an Instacare and get some antibiotics or whatever it was that he needed to get rid of this damn thing.

Jimmy opened the door without knocking and saw several women in the living room having glasses of white wine. One of the women cheered, walked over, and gave him a big kiss on the cheek. She was the captain's wife, and though she always remembered Jimmy's name, he'd be damned if he could ever remember hers.

She led him poolside and someone shoved a beer in his hand. The pool was filled with men and women, a few of them playing chicken in the shallows. A beach ball flew past his head and he didn't have the energy to duck.

Everyone cheered and yelled happy birthday and someone else shoved another beer in his hand. There was a lounge chair right next to him and he sat down and leaned back.

"You have to try the jungle juice Timothy made," the captain's wife said.

Jimmy sighed and stood up, the blood rushing from his head. He followed her to the table that had all the food laid out and there was a large crystal bowl that contained ice, fruit, and a light red fluid. He stood over the bowl and she took a cup and dipped it into the jungle juice for him. She placed it in his hand and he smiled weakly and took a sip. It stung his throat and he felt nauseated but he managed to catch himself before vomiting.

He began coughing and he tried to cover his mouth but the first couple of coughs escaped him and he hoped nothing had gotten into the jungle juice. He would hate to give everyone else a stomach flu.

"I'm not feeling good," Jimmy said. "I been throwing up all day."

"Oh no! You poor dear, what's wrong?"

"Just the flu. I gotta go home, though. Tell Tim hi for me and that I'm sorry."

"I will. You go home and get better now."

As she watched him go, she took a fresh cup and dipped it into the jungle juice before taking a large gulp.

Amy Greaton stood at the head of her sixth grade classroom and glanced over her students as they finished their exams. She opened a drawer on her desk and took out two ibuprofen, washing them down with orange juice. She glanced down to her chest; the rash was still there. It was red and she saw small bumps beginning to rise in her skin.

Her mother had died of breast cancer and she was worried about anything that affected her chest or breasts. She figured this was some sort of allergic reaction, though. The fact that she had also been vomiting this morning and felt alternating sensations of hot and cold indicated she had probably ingested whatever it was she was allergic to.

She and several other teachers had gone to lunch the previous day and she ran through the entire meal in her mind. She remembered that someone had ordered spinach dip and she had had two bites with tortilla chips.

Then again, she had briefly seen officials from the Department of Health on the news, discussing a new outbreak of some viral infection. She wasn't sure exactly what it had been since she had changed the channel. It seemed like every day some disease affected a sliver of the population and the media blew it out of proportion. Swine flu, avian flu, Korean whooping cough…each time the media called it a pandemic, and each time almost nothing would come of it.

"Mrs. Greaton."

She turned to see a young girl with a long black ponytail and pink sandals standing beside her.

"What is it, Annie?"

"Jacob puked all over the desk."

She looked over to see a young boy who had begun to cry near the back of the room. She rose and walked over to him to make sure he was all right, but stopped when she noticed the color of the vomit: it was black, with what looked like bits of meat or coffee grounds mixed in. She hurried to her desk and grabbed her cell phone, dialing the number to the school nurse.

Dale Baer sat latched to a telephone pole thirty-five feet in the air. He was splicing a wire that had been damaged during last night's rainstorm and he leaned back, letting his lower legs take the brunt of his weight, and pulled out a bottle of water. He mixed in two Alka-Seltzers and drank down a few sips. He had been feeling hot today and a migraine pounded in his head like a drum. But no one else could provide for his family. His wife stayed home and they had six children under the age of ten. Sugar Cane Electric, the company he worked for, which had received a private contract from the utility company for the repair of damaged power lines, allowed only a few days of paid sick time and he had used them already when he had broken a rib playing football with his brothers.

Dale looked down to the street and watched the passing cars. He had a difficult time focusing on the ground and it suddenly dawned on him that he was experiencing something he had never experienced in nineteen years of work: vertigo. For the first time in his life, heights were unmanageable.

He began his slow descent back to the sidewalk, and as he did so, he acutely felt the fatigue that had been nagging him the past few days. It made his limbs feel heavy, like he was moving through water, and his thoughts were muddled and clouded. He would have to go home; he wasn't about to risk a fall. He would just have to figure out a way to work a double some time down the line to make up for it. He got to the ground and unhooked himself from the safety belt.

A few people on the sidewalk were waiting for a bus. Dale smiled at a woman that was listening to an iPod and noticed that she had dropped what looked like a credit card on the ground.

"Excuse me," he said, "I think you dropped this."

He bent down to retrieve it and felt pressure in his head, like it was too heavy to keep up anymore and his neck had lost strength. It was so sudden that it flung him forward onto his stomach on the pavement. He heard someone yell for help.

How odd, he thought. He'd clearly just lost his balance. As he lifted his face from the pavement, he felt the warm slick of blood and saw that it was spewing out of his mouth and nose and pooling in a large puddle around him.

The paramedics did not arrive until eleven minutes later. By that time, Dale Baer had bled to death.

CHAPTER 23

Samantha Bower stood at the entrance to the gymnasium and looked over the patients that were huddled onto cheap gray cots. There were over two hundred with only ten staff to look after them but it was impressive how much that small number of staff could really do.

She glanced over toward the other entrance and saw Duncan Adams interviewing one of the patients. He was wearing a full smock with mask and gloves as all the staff were. But he was still joking around and making the patients laugh. He noticed her looking and waved. She waved back.

The governor was expected to take to the airwaves in about five minutes and a mac had been set up on a desk in one of the other rooms of the rec center. Duncan walked over a few minutes later having already thrown his mask and latex gloves in the trash. He sat down on a stool near the desk.

"We're starting to see a lot of kids."

Samantha was quiet a moment. "I know."

"When's the trip to Peru?"

"I have it booked for five days from now."

"Who else is going?"

"A lot of people it seems. Ralph is coming. He never comes on field assignments like this so I'm guessing he thinks it's either going to be an adventure he can tell stories about at parties or he thinks he can write a book about it. Then some people from the CDC and one guy from the FBI. They seem to think this is a matter of national security."

"It's not totally far fetched. Smallpox could've been sold to the North Koreans or any number of countries. I wouldn't put it past the Russians at this point. They've become a criminal state."

"I really hope you're wrong."

"Why? Because you don't want to believe humanity can be so inhuman? I'll give you a tip: never underestimate how cruel people can be to each other."

There was commotion on the mac's screen and they saw the governor come to the podium among flashes of photography.

"Ladies and gentlemen," he said, "thank you for being here. I would first like to thank the efforts of Police Chief Talona, and our friends from the Army Medical Unit and the Centers for Disease Control. I know each and every one of them is working tirelessly to ensure that our citizens remain protected and that this crisis will soon be a memory.

"As it has been made public, we are facing a public health scare unlike any our state has faced before. I know many of you have been praying and sending contributions or even volunteering on the island to lend a hand to your fellow Hawaiians and I want you to know that I am eternally grateful. None of us should stand alone, and as Darwin once remarked, 'a weakened animal is never alone.' Together, I know we can overcome any tragedy that befalls us.

"We have faced war, we have faced famine, invasion, pestilence, and deadly storms throughout our history. They have been painful episodes, but episodes nonetheless. They, like all things, have passed and we have moved on. Perhaps a little stronger and a little wiser for the wear.

"I know that in times of uncertainty there is fear. You are all worried about your families and friends, as am I. But I can assure you that everything is being done to guarantee that this episode in our history is like every other: evanescent. In the meantime, we must be cautious. As of this moment, all transportation to and from the island of Oahu is halted. Employers on the island have been notified that all businesses are to be closed by tomorrow morning along with public facilities such as schools and other government buildings, parks, and beaches. I know this will be hard. Many of you live in our great state for the sole purpose of being out in wondrous nature. However, we must keep our fellow citizens in mind at this time of need and I ask that you remain home with your families, only traveling out if absolutely necessary.

"All the physicians and biologists and public health experts have assured us that the quickest way for this illness to pass is to end daily public life for a while. We must be vigilant and accept the fact that, for at least the foreseeable future, our lives will be altered. But I have no doubt that we will soon be out on our fine beaches, eating at our wonderful restaurants, and enjoying the natural beauty of our largest island.

"I thank you for your time, for your patience, and for your efforts in helping your fellow citizens. God bless Hawaii, and God bless the United States of America. Thank you."

Samantha looked to Duncan who whistled through his teeth. "All transportation?" he said. "That's pretty crazy."

"There's no other way to keep it from the mainland."

"It's going to get there anyway."

"I think we've done a pretty good job of keeping it out."

"Doesn't matter. This is nature we're talking about. It's fluid, constantly adapting. Viruses are nature in its purest form. They have one purpose, one burning desire and they will do anything to achieve that desire. Nature's ends tend to get accomplished. The virus wants to spread. It'll spread until it can't anymore."

"I think you give viruses too much credit."

He shrugged. "I don't have a girlfriend so I think about viruses all day." She smiled and he grinned. "We never got to have dinner. Have it with me tonight."

"I don't think tonight's a good time."

"It's the perfect time. You heard the gov, they're closing all the businesses tomorrow so I'm assuming they mean restaurants too. Come on, we'll go to the best restaurant on the island and then tomorrow you can start eating Army food and Top Ramen."

She closed her mac and sat down. "All right. Dinner. But it'll have to be a little later. I have a meeting with Ralph."

"No sweat," he said, standing up. "I'll swing by and pick you up from Queen's Medical."

"They meet at the Ritz-Carlton now. Pick me up from there in a couple of hours."

"You got it. I'm gonna go hit the showers."

"Okay. And Duncan? Maybe we shouldn't go anywhere too crowded?"

CHAPTER 24

The Ritz-Carlton sat on three acres of beachfront property and looked like a photo out of a tourist magazine. Normally, crowds swamped the hotel's two pools and half a dozen tennis courts. A restaurant there named Ice served lush Hawaiian inspired cuisine on a large veranda that was open year round.

But that's not what it appeared like now. As Samantha pulled up on her Ducati and parked, she thought it looked like a crime scene. News crews had set up on every inch of property they were legally entitled to and the rest of the space was taken up with military and police vehicles. Sam's parking spot was across the street in a pay lot and she jogged over to the hotel. The concierge informed her that they were not allowed to take any more guests.

"No," she said, "I'm with the CDC; the government. Please call Ralph Wilson and let him know I'm here."

"Certainly. One moment."

Samantha stepped back from reception and watched as a man spoke to another concierge, asking him if there was any way off the island. The concierge said there wasn't and the man began to grow upset and swear at him. The concierge glanced to a group of police officers that were standing by the door and Sam could see him suddenly fill with courage.

"Sir," he told the man, "I really don't give a damn what you think. You can take your attitude and blow it out your ass for all I care. Now either get out of my face or leave my fucking hotel."

Nerves were frazzled, Sam thought. This situation was frustrating enough but throw on top of that a looming food shortage and the closure of all businesses and you had a populace on the verge of violence. Attempting to be a courteous customer service rep for your company at that point was nearly impossible.

"Ma'am?" the concierge said to Sam. She turned and walked back to reception.

"Yes?"

"Dr. Wilson stated that he would like you to meet him at his table inside Ice. It is the restaurant at the end of that hallway and to the right."

"Okay, thank you."

Samantha made her way down the hallway and to the plush restaurant decorated in gold and black. The hostess pointed her right to Wilson's table. He was seated indoors though the veranda looked much more pleasant. The table he was sitting at had views of the parking lot out the windows and his back was against a wall as he ate pasta out of an ornately decorated bowl.

"This place looks nice," she said, sitting down across from him.

"Expensive as all hell. But I figured I wouldn't be getting a decent meal after tomorrow. How's everything at the recreation center?"

"A little over two hundred patients. We seem to average one new admittee per hour."

"I looked over the list. Have you noticed how many were police officers?"

"No, I haven't had time to go through it."

"Honolulu Police have small numbers, around nineteen hundred officers. Over a hundred of them are in your rec center. And those are only the ones that have actually sought medical attention. I'm betting a fair number have stayed home."

"It's something to keep an eye on I suppose."

"It's more than that," Wilson said, taking a sip of the red wine that was on his table. "There are certain professions that a society cannot survive without. The first is maintenance crews. Our infrastructures require constant maintenance. Projections have shown that, without maintenance crews, the city would not be able to function within one month. Within three months, nature will have taken back what we took from it. The city would be in ruins, just like what you'd find in Rome or Constantinople. Just with taller buildings.

"The second profession a society cannot survive without is police officers. If the police force is disabled it'll mean chaos for this island."

"It's just a small percentage now. I'll call the chief and make sure he switches up the crews and has them protected for their shifts."

"That won't be enough. He needs to run on a skeleton crew of volunteers. As the outbreak spreads the police will be more fearful of contact. They'll be as good as on vacation anyway."

"I thought you wanted to maintain order?"

Wilson took a large bite of pasta and finished chewing before speaking again. "There was a fascinating study conducted at UCLA. It was done by graduate students in the sociology department. They wanted to test enticement of crime in minority populations, but that's not what the study became famous for.

"They would park luxury cars in high foot traffic areas and leave the doors ajar. Not wide open, but far enough that anyone walking by would notice. They left Cadillacs and BMWs and Lexuses on this abandoned strip of land next to an empty retail shop with no one around, so that the pedestrians felt that they wouldn't be caught if they felt like rummaging through the cars or taking them. For days, nothing happened. Not a single person even opened the car door to see what was inside. One day some kids were playing outside and they hit a baseball through a window of the retail shop that was about twenty feet away from the car. Within three hours, seven people had rummaged through the car and one tried to steal it. The next day, they had to abandon the experiment because too many people were attempting to steal the car.

"It was perception, Sam; that was the point of the study's findings. Society itself is a perception. When the people saw the broken window they perceived the car as abandoned rather than simply stopped there. They saw chaos and responded appropriately. If the police presence is strong, the perception will be that there are a lot of police officers. If the presence isn't strong and the perception is that there isn't enough police, people will revert to the state of nature and turn into animals.

"What the chief needs to do is have a minimum number of officers driving around the cities, parking in high crime areas. They don't have to do anything, just park there. It will be enough to create the perception we're looking for."

The waiter came by and asked if Sam wanted anything. She asked for a Perrier and fiddled with the fork and napkin that was laid out in front of her. "I can't believe we're even discussing this."

"I know. Lack of order is a difficult thing to grasp when you're accustomed to having order, but that's the way it is. By the way, the governor's orders don't apply to us. You can freely leave the island if you need to but you have to travel by military plane."

"I'm not going anywhere."

He smiled. "The first time we met, you had stayed up for two days straight preparing a report on the contamination of a well in a small town in Oklahoma. Do you remember that? I was so impressed with you that I knew you would be the type of person that would rise in the CDC, if you wanted to. I think one day, Sam, you'll be handed my job. When that day comes, I want you to ask yourself one question: can you handle not having anyone in your life? I have no wife, no children. I'm away from home over two hundred days out of the year. It's not a life everyone can handle. You need to decide if this is the path you want to take. Don't take that decision lightly."

He suddenly appeared melancholy and Samantha didn't follow up with any questions. She figured it was something he would discuss when he felt the urge, although he had once mentioned in an offhanded comment that not having children was the biggest regret of his life.

"Anyway," he said, taking in a large breath, "why don't you stay and have dinner with me? Then decide if you want to stay or leave the island."

"I have plans."

"Oh, that Duncan fellow, correct?"

"How could you tell?"

"His face lights up when you enter a room. I've dealt with him a few times; he's a decent man."

The waiter brought her Perrier and she opened it as Wilson sipped more of his wine. They sat in silence a while, enjoying the calm atmosphere of the restaurant. She couldn't tell if it was really calm or if it was just comparatively calm to the chaos and tension that were building outside of these walls, but it was relaxing nonetheless.

"I better go," she said. "Thanks for the drink."

"Samantha, in a few days, when the data's compiled and digested, I'll have a much better picture of what's going on here. If it turns out to be what I think it is, I'll be having you sent back to Atlanta."

"What? Ralph, I'm fine. I can take care of myself."

"This isn't about that. You don't know what can be unleashed here. This will become a fully military-run operation and there'll be no need for us anyway. But we're not to that point yet. I was hoping you'd go back voluntarily but I had a hunch you wouldn't. I just wanted to tell you so there are no surprises. Now go have fun before they close everything."

Samantha left the restaurant and as she started her bike, she noticed for the first time how empty the streets were. The sun was high though it was late in the evening and there were no clouds.

She wondered how it was that a paradise like this could be harmed by anything.

CHAPTER 25

It was dark by the time Samantha arrived at Niche Café. It was small and cozy with a view of the beach outside. There were only a handful of people inside and most of them were locals having a final meal at the closest restaurant; a sign over the door letting everyone know that the café would be closed tomorrow morning at ten.

Duncan was sitting at a booth, sipping a fruity drink. He smiled and waved when he saw her. Wilson had been right; his face seemed to light up and Sam found it cute.

"How'd the meeting go?" he asked.

Sam sat down and ordered an ice water. "Depressing."

"I'm not there yet. This isn't the most virulent outbreak I've seen, but I haven't seen a pathogen spread so quickly in the population. We're lucky this is an island, so there's that to be grateful for."

"Do you always look on the bright side of everything?"

"That's the only way to live. Whatever thoughts you put out into the universe, that's exactly what the universe gives back to you. It's like some magical genie granting your wishes. But it doesn't know what's a wish and what's just random thought. You have to keep your thoughts positive."

"If one of your loved ones was dying slowly in our cots, I don't know how positive you'd be."

"True. You can never really know until you test it. Luckily, or unluckily, depending on how you look at it, I have no loved ones."

"No family?"

"No, I was adopted by an elderly Mormon couple when I was six. They had some siblings, an aunt somewhere, but no one else. When they passed, that was the end of my family."

"Did you ever try to track down your biological parents?"

"Once, when I was in college. I met my dad actually. He was a trucker in Wyoming. I called and asked if I could come see him. He had a new family now and didn't really want to but I had to see him. I had to see where my genes came from."

"And what'd you find out?"

"That genes are overrated." This made her smile. "What about you?" he said.

"I have a brother and two sisters. My brother's a physician. One of my sisters is a stay at home mom and the other is a physicist. My mom lives in Atlanta."

"What about your dad?"

"He passed away when I was in my twenties. He was a really successful entrepreneur. You remind me a little of him actually. He was really into the positive thinking and self-help movements."

"Sounds like a smart guy. How do you think he would feel about you chasing down the worst diseases in the world for a living?"

"I think he'd be worried about me but he'd understand the odds. Death due to exposure to pathogens is nearly unheard of for CDC employees. We're very careful."

The waitress came and took their order; Sam ordered a pulled pork sandwich and Duncan had chicken nachos.

"Did you see the report by Pushkin?" Duncan asked.

“No? What’d it say?”

“It was just released a few hours ago. He’s termed the pathogen Agent X. Essentially, the report found that the cultures he developed resemble smallpox and Ebola, but are a distinct entity.”

“An unknown hot agent,” she said as she absently played with the straw in her water. “I knew they existed, but I never thought I’d be in the middle of an outbreak for one.”

“There’s a section of USAMRIID’s labs devoted to unknown hot agents.”

“I didn’t know that.”

“Most people don’t. You need top secret clearance just to go in there. See what happens is American—well, don’t really know what to call them—corpses I guess, are shipped to USAMRIID after death when a hot agent is suspected. These are usually CIA operatives, FBI agents on special assignment, military intelligence, people like that. We never learn their identities or even where they picked up the pathogen. We don’t know anything about them other than they’re a body on our slab.

“If we find a hot agent after autopsy and analysis of blood and tissues, and it turns out to be unidentifiable, it’s stored in the unknown agents lab. We have over a hundred unknown agents in there. I’d kill to find out where they came from. We added one several months ago that caused the brain to lose consistency. Didn’t affect any other part of the body. The brain would just melt. It came from the corpse of a woman, but of course that’s all I know about her. It’s fascinating how many ways nature can dream up to kill us.”

"Maybe she doesn't want us here. We are the only species that actively destroys her. This could be her way of fighting back," she said.

"We're her children like anything else. She doesn't strike me as the type to destroy her children."

"I disagree. Look at extinction. Ninety-nine point nine percent of all species that have ever existed have gone extinct. Extinction is the norm on our planet, not longevity. It's that change that allows a new species to rise, have their moment in the sun, and then fade away. It's required somehow, but from our perspective, we're infinite. Like we have to exist forever. It's just not the case."

"We're the most intelligent beings that have ever existed, though. If anyone can find that longevity it's us."

"There's actually some argument to be made that intelligence is counter-evolutionary. It gives us the ability to destroy ourselves at a speed that nature never could. Just look at nuclear weapons. Every time one is ignited there's a small probability the nitrogen in the atmosphere will ignite and burn away all the oxygen. Yet we've still taken that risk over and over again. Eventually, we won't pull our lucky card."

"You know, I think if you want to believe we're helpless cogs in the wheels of nature, then that's how you'll see the world. But if you believe we're luminous beings put on this earth for a purpose, then that's how the universe will appear to you."

"You're religious, aren't you?"

"Mormon, like my parents."

"You don't find it odd that almost all children happen to end up the same religion as their parents but claim they've independently reached the conclusion that their religion is the correct one?"

"Ouch. Going right for the jugular."

"Oh, wow, I'm sorry. I didn't mean to insult you. I just meant—"

"No, I'm totally kidding. It's fine. Well what if children were meant to be part of that faith and that's why they were born into it? But we don't need to talk about that. The French say you should never discuss religion or politics at the dinner table because you'll ruin your appetite."

She grinned. "Have you been to France?"

"Yeah, several times."

"I've always wanted to go."

"Well, maybe I can take you some time."

She smiled and, for the first time since she'd been around him, thought she felt herself blush.

They finished dinner and stayed at the restaurant for over two hours talking, until the wait staff told them they would be closing up for the night. They headed outside and the moon was bright in a cloudless sky. They decided to walk around the block.

Few people were out on the streets and Sam found the quiet peaceful. It was odd how used one could get to the most aggravating sounds: construction, sirens, car horns, shouting…a city was filled with so much noise that it seemed our brains had to go into a trance simply to shut out all the sound so we could function.

They talked about their lives growing up, about why they chose science as the field they wanted to dedicate their lives to. Their reasons were polar opposite: Duncan thought that science, as shown through the recent developments in quantum mechanics and quantum cosmology, ultimately led to God. He believed God had given us the chance to probe his creation and discover secrets that would make our lives better.

Samantha had gone into science because without God, she felt the universe was a cold and lonely place. Science brought order to that loneliness. The fact that the third law of thermodynamics worked on earth the same as it worked on an alien planet a hundred million light years away was comforting. Science showed her that at the core of the chaos was stability.

They came back to where her bike was parked and talked a few more minutes. Duncan came in for a kiss when they heard a man speaking to them. Sam looked over and saw a homeless man sitting with his back against the restaurant's exterior.

"What was that?" she asked him.

"Can you spare some change?"

He began to cough. It sounded wet and he spit a glob of black fluid onto the pavement.

CHAPTER 26

The next day Sam awoke and saw that she had six voicemails on her phone. She had turned it off to try to get a night's rest and didn't think anyone would need her within the five hours of sleep she was going to get. She checked her messages: they were all from a nurse at the rec center. They were running out of space.

She took a quick shower and then headed down there. The streets were completely empty. Every once in a while a car would drive by but that was the only other evidence that anyone inhabited this island at all. Nearly every business was now closed; the only ones she saw open were bars. The grocery stores had already locked their doors.

When she got to the rec center every parking space was taken so she parked her Ducati on the sidewalk next to the building. She went inside, suited up, and went into the gymnasium. She thought she had entered a war zone.

Every cot was taken. The nurses had not turned away anyone and when they'd run out of cots they put patients on blankets in any nook they had available. The sounds were something out of nightmares: a cacophony of vomiting, coughing, groaning…the sounds of people who knew they were dying.

"There you are," one of the nurses, an older woman with thick glasses said. "I've been trying to reach you all night."

"What happened?"

"What happened? All these people got sick is what happened. Many of 'em are just kids."

"How many people did you admit?"

"I don't know, everyone that wanted in."

"We had a specific limit for a reason. You won't be able to take care of all these people."

"I told her it was okay," Duncan said, walking up behind them.

"Have you been here all night?"

"Yeah, I just dropped in to check on them and we started getting an influx of patients. I thought I'd stay and help out. Many of the younger kids," he said, stopping a moment as he choked up, "many of the younger kids don't have the immune systems to fight very long. No more than a few hours after they're ill enough to come here. We're going to need more pain medication to make them comfortable."

Samantha looked out over the sea of cots and the bodies huddled on the floor. "We need a larger space first. I saw a stadium a few days ago; I'll look into getting that for us."

"Okay, I'll speak to Ralph about ordering some more meds."

Sam nodded, not taking her eyes off the patients, their eyes empty, many of their faces caked with dried blood. She took out her cell phone and stepped outside. She felt the urge to take a deep breath and exhale furiously to get everything out of her lungs. It was instinctual, nothing based on reason, and she fought the urge and instead dialed Ralph Wilson's cell.

"What's going on, Sam?" Wilson said, answering on the second ring.

"We need a bigger space than the rec center. We've run out of cots."

"Already? How many patients are there?"

"I don't know, the staff didn't keep track. I would guess somewhere around twelve hundred."

"I'll get some more volunteers down there. What else do you need?"

"Duncan's going to ask you for more pain meds. Just start shipping those now. I saw a stadium on Salt Lake Boulevard."

"Yeah, it's Aloha Stadium. They hold the University of Hawaii football games there."

"We need to take it. I'll call the stadium people. I haven't read Pushkin's report. Is it as bad as I've heard?"

"Well, he basically says this agent doesn't meet the criteria to be identified as any known biological agent. It hit three similarity points for Ebola and four for smallpox, but that's it. Not enough to classify it as either. And it's not black pox like we thought, though it has the same symptomology. This is something we haven't seen before."

Wilson cleared his throat and didn't speak for a moment. Sam knew what that meant. She sat down on the curb and waited for him to speak first, but he didn't.

"What is it, Ralph?"

"The military presented an option last night that is looking more and more viable."

"What is it?"

"There are a lot of smaller islands in the Hawaiian chain. Easy to clear the populations out and put them on the larger islands."

"Don't tell me this is going where I think it's going."

"It may come to that."

"You want to take all the uninfected people to another island and let the infected just die here. Like dogs, Ralph? You're talking about genocide."

"That's a little dramatic, don't you think?"

"And what are you going to do when a mother is infected but her child isn't, Ralph? Are you going to rip a child away from their mother?"

"We're not to that point yet and there's no need for worst case scenarios. It's just an option if this thing gets out of control. But we don't need to talk about it yet. The vaccines have arrived. Pushkin doesn't know whether they'll be effective, but it's worth a shot. I'll need you to set up locations throughout the island to distribute them."

"I'll take care of it right after I get the stadium."

"Okay. Keep safe, Sam."

"I will. Thanks."

She hung up and got on her bike. If she was going to get permission to use an entire stadium to hold thousands of ill patients at no cost, she would have to meet with the owners in person.

CHAPTER 27

Robert Greyjoy checked the clip in his silenced Ruger .22 caliber pistol and waited around the corner of the restaurant. It was an Italian place, red brick with the white and red checkered table cloths in cartoon depictions of Italian restaurants. It had been closed this morning but friends and relatives of the owners had been coming and going all day, stocking up on supplies, as everyone was uncertain of exactly where meals would be coming from over the next few days. People were no longer comforted by government officials telling them food would be shipped in. Robert had had a sense for decades that every successive generation trusted their government less and less.

A car pulled up with four men inside. Three of them exited the vehicle and went inside, leaving the driver alone to bury his head in his phone and ignore the outside world.

Robert waited until the other three men had disappeared inside the restaurant and then he casually walked down the sidewalk, the gun held low by his leg. He opened the passenger side door to the car and got inside, holding the barrel to the man's crotch.

"If you honk the horn or scream I'm going to blow your dick off and then drive the car myself. No, don't talk, just listen. Put the car in drive and start going. Turn right at the intersection that's up ahead."

"Ain't got that much cash, my man. But you can take it."

"I don't want your money and if you don't do what I say, you better hope you've already slept with a lot of women 'cause you're not getting another chance."

"Easy, brother."

The man started the car and pulled away from the curb. Robert ducked down in the car and to anyone watching it would have appeared like only the driver was in the vehicle. The man turned right at the intersection. The streets were empty and he drove slowly, not saying anything.

Robert sat up, the gun still pointed at the man. "You made a delivery two months ago and you were paid quite handsomely for it, Richie."

"Hey, I don't know nothin' about—"

"Don't lie to me. It's very cowardly and if there's one thing I can't stand, it's cowards."

Richie stayed silent a moment and then said, "All right. I remember."

"Did you look inside the package you were delivering?"

"No."

"You sure? You seem uncertain. Maybe I should blow one of your balls off and see if that jogs your memory?"

"No, man. No they told me not to look inside and I didn't look inside."

"Okay, good. You're doing very well, Richie. Now, who did you give the package to?"

"The dude."

"What dude?"

"There was a guy, a Spanish guy. Mexican or something. He came down to where I was and he picked it up and that was it."

"You sure? You didn't lose it? Leave it at the airport or something?"

"Nah, man. I ain't no amateur. I done this before for you guys."

"All right, all right. Here's what we're gonna do; you're going to go—"

Richie twisted the wheel as far to the left as it would go, hitting the curb. Robert's head flew into the passenger side window, cracking it. Richie jumped out of the car while it was still moving and rolled onto the pavement. Robert got off one shot, the sound of the ricocheting slug filling the car as it hit a lamppost.

Robert leapt from the car, holding his head as blood began to flow down and soak his collar. He ran around to the back of the car and saw Richie running down an alley. He aimed his pistol but Richie turned down a side alley and was gone.

"Shit," Robert said, starting a slow jog down the sidewalk.

He saw Richie running down to the intersection a block away. Robert ran back to the car and jumped into the driver's seat. He backed away from the lamppost and then sped down the street, turning at an intersection down to the block Richie was on.

The street, like the rest of the city, was empty. The only other place Robert had seen such desolation had been in Afghanistan last year. Insurgents would send word that they were going to take a town and cut off the heads of anyone that remained. The town, within a few hours, would be nothing but buildings and trails of animal dung leading out of the city from the livestock the residents took with them. Many times, the insurgents never came. When they did, they held true to their promise and by the time Robert came in there would be heads thrust onto pikes along the roadsides.

Robert saw movement to his left. But when he turned his head there was nothing there. To the side of a building were several dumpsters and trash bins. He stepped out of the car.

"Richie," he said, in as kind a voice as he could muster, "come on out, Richie. I'm not going to kill you. But if you make me sift through garbage, I am."

There was no answer, just the breeze blowing bits of debris over the streets. Down the road he could hear a radio playing somewhere but couldn't make out what it was saying.

"Richie," he said, walking close to the trash bins, "I'm going to count to three. If you don't come out I'm going to start firing into the garbage bins. One…two…three."

There was no response. Robert aimed at the first bin and fired two shots. He aimed at the second and did the same, one shot low, one shot high.

"All right!"

After the sound of trash being displaced, Richie crawled out of one of the bins. His clothes already had stains on them and Robert could smell putrid garbage coming off him in wafts.

"Really? Was that worth it, Richie?"

"You were gonna kill me."

"I wasn't going to kill you. If I wanted to kill you I would've walked by when you were sitting in your car and put two slugs into your brain. Now I didn't do that, did I?"

"What'd ya want from me?"

"Information. The man that picked up the package, you said he looked Mexican, right?"

"Yeah."

"Could he possibly have been Middle Eastern?"

"What's that?"

"Wow, our education system is going to be the death of us. From the Middle East, dipshit. Saudi Arabia, Libya, Iran. Did he look like he could be Muslim?"

"Oh. Yeah, yeah I think so."

"Did he have an accent?"

"Yeah."

"Did he sound like Speedy Gonzalez or Apu?"

"What?"

"Nevermind. What did his accent sound like?"

"Um, I don't know, just an accent."

"Richie, you're not thinking hard enough. And if you're not thinking hard enough, you're not helpful to me."

"You don't have to get all crazy, man. I'm tryin'. Um, his accent, I don't know, I guess it didn't sound Mexican."

"Good, good. What exactly did he say to you?"

"He just said he was there to pick up the box. That's what he called it, the box. I gave it to him and he asked if anyone else was with me. I said yes. I said there was two other guys watchin' us. There wasn't but I got a creepy feelin' from this dude and didn't want him to think we was alone."

"Oh, so you do have some brains after all. What happened next?"

He just took it and went back to a Jeep that was waitin' for him. I swear, man. That's all that happened."

Robert stared at him a long while, but Richie didn't look away. "Okay," Robert said, a smile coming over his lips. "Okay, I believe you."

"So can I go now?"

"Here's the problem, my young friend. In the years and years I've been doing this, no one's ever seen my face."

"Whoa, whoa, dude, look I just—"

Robert raised his weapon, pointed at Richie's throat. He took a step forward and Richie screamed.

"You sound like a girl. At least try to have some dignity when you die."

"I'll give the money back," he said frantically, taking a few steps back and realizing he'd pinned himself against the garbage bins. "I'll give all of it back."

"No, no, not enough. What else you got?"

"My girl, yo, my girl is hot yo. I'll let you fuck her, man. I'll let you do it."

"Sex doesn't interest me. You're running out of time."

"Um," he said, panicked, "ah, um, I can find the dude that has the box."

Robert stood frozen, he didn't move and didn't speak for what seemed like a long time. Then he lowered the pistol by his side. "Now you've got my attention. How do you plan to find him?"

"I got his license plate. Just in case I needed it."

"If he had any brains it was a rental or a fake plate."

"No, there was two cars. One of 'em was parked where they thought I couldn't see it. I got the plate to that too and they were Hawaii plates."

Robert smiled. "Richie, you are impressing me more and more every second. Where's the number?"

"First you gotta promise not to kill me."

"If I'm the type of person that can kill you, I probably won't have any problem breaking a promise, but okay, I'll play along. I promise I will not kill you if you give me the plate number."

Richie pulled out his phone. He held it in front of him and Robert took it, noticing that Richie's hands were shaking. Robert memorized the number and letter sequence and then handed the phone back to Richie.

"You've been very helpful, Richie. You're free to go."

"Really?"

"Really."

Robert turned and began walking away down the sidewalk. He heard footsteps fading in the distance behind him.

Robert stopped, and closed his eyes. He listened intensely to the footfalls. They were far apart; Richie was taking long strides. He wasn't zig-zagging and he hadn't run down the alley. He was running directly behind Robert in the opposite direction.

Robert spun, his weapon up, and fired three shots. Two hit their mark and Richie collapsed onto the pavement. If he would've zigged and zagged, Robert may not have been able to hit him.

"Maybe you weren't as smart as I thought," Robert said aloud, putting his weapon away. He began walking back to his hotel, humming to himself.

CHAPTER 28

Samantha awoke and, for a single, terrifying moment, didn't know where she was. The hotel room suddenly didn't look familiar. She had been back in Atlanta only a moment ago, taking care of her mother's funeral arrangements, staring down into the casket at the face of the woman who had raised her. The face appeared as a mask, like it had been painted on. The spirit that had animated it was no longer there and it was no more different, or beautiful, than a table or a chair.

It took a few moments but the events of the previous weeks flooded back into her mind as she watched the sunlight streaming through the windows of her room. She rose and walked to them, looking down on the streets below.

The first thing that struck her was the growth of the vegetation. Lawns were unmowed and hedges untrimmed. Ralph was right: nature was slowly and steadily taking back what was hers.

She took a quick shower and then filled a few buckets she had gotten from a hardware store with water. It was uncertain how long utilities would remain on since maintenance crews were growing slimmer and slimmer.

She went out to her bike and checked her gas gauge; about half a tank left. She decided to walk instead. The gas stations had all been closed as well. Not because of orders, but because no gas shipments were coming in and they had run out of reserves within a week. She didn't know when she would need her bike and it wasn't worth the gas to save the mile and a half walk from the hotel.

There were no clouds today and the sun broiled the city as heat waves bounced off the cement and cooked the streets.

The city appeared like a Hollywood movie set. Without people to animate it there was just cement, steel, and wood. The wind rustled through the streets and bits of trash flew with it. She hadn't noticed it before but the level of trash was increasing every day despite people not being out as much. She couldn't walk more than a couple of feet without some debris on the sidewalk in front of her. Even a week ago, she had been impressed with how clean Honolulu was compared to other American cities.

There was some commotion behind her. She glanced around to see three young men walking in her direction but on the opposite side of the street. They were dressed in normal clothing; they weren't military. Since the majority of the police force was either ill or had quit their jobs so as not to become ill, military were the only ones that were out in public.

Sam faced forward again and continued walking. She had tried to call her mother last night but the nurse had let it go to voicemail. Caring for someone full time was exhausting, both mentally and physically. Sam didn't fault her for sometimes turning the phone off and taking a nap. As long as her mother's needs were looked after, she didn't expect her nurse to be superhuman.

The voices she had heard were closer now and she looked behind her again. The men had crossed over to her side of the street. They were now staring at her and walking at a quick pace. The absence of police presence came barreling at her. Wilson's theory that police simply being in an area would keep crime in check worked for a while, until the mass quitting began. Police officers with families of their own feared infection and so they quit rather than follow orders. There were, as far as she could tell, about fifty police officers left in the entire island of a hundred and thirty-seven square miles, and they were quitting at the pace of about five per day.

She glanced behind her again. The men were closer, their eyes locked on her. She looked forward, pretending not to notice, but her heart was beating as if someone were pounding on her chest. She looked back again. They were closing the distance. She wondered for just a moment if this wasn't all in her head until she saw the knife strapped to the hip of one of the men.

There was an intersection up ahead. As soon as she could, she turned left around a building, and broke into a sprint. She got nearly a quarter of a block up before she heard shouting behind her and saw the men turning the corner and running after her.

Sam saw a convenience store up ahead and tried the doors: they were locked. She thought about going around back but the men were catching up to her now. They were close enough that she could distinguish their shouting.

"Where you running, bitch!"

She ran back to the sidewalk and was in a full sprint, the purse banging against her with each stride. She took her keys and her cell phone out and threw the purse on the ground. A few cars were lined up on the side of the road and she looked in them in hopes that someone had left their keys, but they hadn't.

She could just see a shopping mall up ahead and she ran for it, leaving the sidewalk to run on pavement. Her breathing was labored now, her legs burning like they were dipped in acid. She sprinted as hard as she could, hoping she wouldn't hit a rock or a crack and fly face-first into the pavement.

She got to the parking lot and fell to the ground. She began crawling under the cars. Her knees and elbows quickly scraped and bled but she didn't stop until she heard the footfalls that surrounded her.

"Where the fuck did she go?" one of them said.

"Into the mall."

"Nah," a third one said. "She in one a these cars. Start lookin'."

She could see their feet from underneath the car. They were going slowly up and down the rows, checking each car.

"Look under 'em too," one of the men yelled.

They began glancing underneath the cars as well. They were twenty feet away and on a different row, but they would get to her eventually.

Holding her breath to make as little noise as possible, she began crawling toward the entrance to the mall.

The gravel that was displaced underneath made little scraping noises and to her the sound was as loud as jet engines. She would stop every few seconds and look back to see the sneakers getting closer and closer.

She had moved out from under an SUV when she got to a Prius. It was too low to the ground for her to crawl under and she eased her way back to a different row and underneath a large Toyota truck. She was nearly to the other side when she heard the shoes hit pavement behind her and she froze.

She looked back and saw the sneakers checking the car next to the one she was under. Its door was unlocked and the man opened it and began going through whatever was inside.

Sam, lifting herself off the pavement as far as she could go, which wasn't more than a half an inch, began to crawl to the other side of the truck. She could feel the sunlight on the back of her hand as she made it across. She cleared the truck. Now she would just need to stand, keep low, and make it around to one of the entrances to the mall. She had heard from someone at the hotel that the mall itself was open but the shops were closed. The owner had wanted to give all the shop owners the option of closing or remaining open.

A sound echoed in her head. It was unfamiliar and familiar at the same time. Like something she knew intimately once but had forgotten.

It was her cell phone's ringtone.

She rolled from under the truck as the man in the car next to her jumped out, standing still a moment to find out where the sound was coming from. Samantha was on her feet and at a full sprint toward the mall.

"Right there, you blind motherfucker!"

She kept running, not looking back, feeling the strain in her legs as she pushed herself as hard as she could. She made it across the parking lot and was near the door when she felt an impact against her back. She flew forward into the glass doors and bounced off and onto her back.

A man stood above her, panting. He pulled the knife out from his hip.

"You run…fast bitch. Now we gonna have some fun you and me."

He knelt down and Sam thrust out with her hand, jabbing her fingers into his eyes as far as they would go. He yelped in pain and pulled back. She rolled on the ground and got to her feet as the other two men arrived.

She backed up slowly against the glass doors, feeling for the handles. She felt the grating and tugged. They were locked.

"Fucking cunt!" the man yelled as he rose, his hand pressed to his right eye.

He came at her and then stopped. Her heart was pounding so loud she didn't hear the commotion behind her as two police officers opened the doors. They pushed her out of the way, a shotgun pointed at the man's head.

"Get the fuck outta here, asshole," the cop said.

The men looked to each other and then backed away and walked through the parking lot into the street. The cop turned to her. He lowered his weapon as the other cop behind him did the same.

"You all right?" he asked.

"Yeah," she said, out of breath, "thank you."

"Get inside. There'll be more of 'em."

"More of who?"

"Them. Whatever you wanna call 'em. We been callin' 'em huis. Come on, let's go."

Sam entered the mall behind the officers and they locked the doors. The mall was empty and the lights were off. The two officers kept walking without looking back and got down the hall and to an elevator. Sam didn't feel she had any better options, especially considering that those men were probably outside waiting for her, so she got on the elevator too.

They rode to the second floor and walked to the main offices. A few other people were scattered throughout the space. None of the others wore police uniforms. An older man with a potbelly walked up when he saw them enter.

"Who's this?"

"She was attacked by some huis outside."

The man gave the two officers an awkward glance, like they had done something wrong, and then stuck out his hand. Sam shook.

"Papale Garrett, how ya doin'? Sorry you had to run into trouble out there. Huis is gettin' worse by the day. Huis is just what we call them lawless folks that's out on the streets."

"Are you the police?"

"Well, I guess so. Now. We found them uniforms at the police station an' we help out when we can," he said, looking to one of the men that had helped Samantha. "Well anyway, if you got someone to come get you, you should call them now. Afternoon and night is the worst time to be out, so you should get all your business done in the morning."

Sam looked around the space. There were clothes, food rations, jugs of water, and gasoline along with dishes piled next to a sink.

"Do you live here?"

"Good a place as any," Papale said. "Got water, electricity when we need, we got each other. There's the food court downstairs with enough stock to keep us fed for a year or two. Seemed as good a choice as my own house."

"Food is being given away at aid stations, along with water and anything else you could need."

He chuckled. "Young lady, the day the government does somethin' right is the day I take up ballroom dancin'. There ain't enough food to feed a preschool at them aid stations. The lines go on for blocks and by the time you get there, they outta everythin' but flour and sugar. Soon they'll be outta those too."

"They get resupplied every other day."

"If that's true, I ain't seen it. Once they run outta food, they close and they leave."

"That has to be some kind of mistake."

"Mistake or not, that's what they're doin'. Now if you'll excuse me, I got some work to do thawing some chickens for tonight's dinner. You're welcome to stay as long as you like or you can have someone pick you up."

"Thanks." Samantha pulled out her cell phone. All the men in the office were staring at her and it became apparent that there were no women in the mall with them. She smiled a friendly smile to them and then walked out the doors to the corridor.

"Where have you been?" Wilson's voice said on the other end.

"I was attacked, Ralph. A group of men chased me down the street when I was walking to the hospital."

"Are you all right?"

"Yeah, I ran into the mall and there were other people here."

"Whole damn city's gone to hell. Did you know our vaccine shipments were attacked? They burned the crates. Two guards were injured."

"Maybe they thought it was something valuable."

"Yeah, maybe."

"Ralph, how are the aid stations doing?"

"Fine. Why?"

"I heard that they've been closing and that there's not enough food for everyone."

Wilson was silent a while. "You better get to the hospital. I'm sending down a military escort for you. We need to talk."

CHAPTER 29

Ralph Wilson sat in an administrative office at the Queen's Medical Center and stared out the window at the abandoned streets below. He pictured kids out here, people jogging, teenagers heading down to the bus stop to get to the beach for the day's surfing. But there wasn't any of that. There was fluttering garbage and stray dogs and every once in a while, a group of men out prowling the streets.

It reminded him of Kosovo when he was there supervising, unofficially, a NATO team providing medical assistance to civilians. He was a young man then and too stupid to know that he was expendable.

The Army Rangers had dropped him off without anything but the name of a contact and the clothes on his back, and that was the way he liked it. Or so he thought, until it started raining so hard it was as if the sky had opened a wound and was pouring its lifeblood out onto the crumbling city. He contracted pneumonia and survived only because a family in town took him in and nursed him back to health with soup and tea. Otherwise, he would've died alone underneath a bridge that he was using as shelter.

The family had been Muslim, and he remembered when the soldiers with the harsh Czech accents had come into the home by kicking in the door. They wanted to take the wife and the young daughter. The man of the house had not yet heard of the rape houses where they would be forced into sex acts with dozens, even hundreds of men a day. They would be forced to have sex with other women, including relatives. Mothers and daughters were especially prized.

The Serbs and Croats were no longer human. Ralph had seen their devastation in the mass graves in soccer fields and parks. As the two men were dragging away the wife and daughter, Ralph, still weak from his illness, rose from his bed, pulled out a .45 caliber from its holster, and shot three rounds, two entering one man's head and the other finding its mark in the other man's throat.

The family was grateful but shocked. They would certainly be marked for death now. Ralph helped them gather their belongings and they snuck in the dead of night to a NATO encampment almost a hundred miles away. The route was treacherous. The streets revealed nothing but decaying buildings with decaying souls looking out of them, their eyes blank. The war had taken what was human in them and crushed it.

Now, twenty years later, at night he would occasionally wake up and see the buildings before him. Monsters in the darkness that were slowly collapsing, consuming whatever was around them.

Looking out onto the streets of Honolulu, he saw that same evil here. Whatever it was, it was here. Not fully but a spark. It was beginning to take over and he knew that eventually, there would be nothing left.

"Ralph?"

Ralph looked up from the window and saw Duncan Adams standing by the door. "Yeah, Duncan. What can I do for you?"

"I was calling your name for a good ten seconds. You doin' okay?"

"Yes, yes, I was, um, somewhere else. Have a seat." Duncan sat down across from him and crossed his legs. "So where's your sidekick?" Ralph said.

"Samantha?" Duncan said. "Why would you think she's my sidekick?"

"You guys are always together and when you're not, you're calling each other."

"I wouldn't describe Sam as anybody's sidekick. If anything, I'm hers."

Ralph laughed softly. "She once punched one of her professors when he made a pass at her after class. She tell you that?"

"No."

"Philosophy professor, I think. They're all wackos anyway and this one was an aggressive wacko. I guess she belted him and nearly laid him out. She was almost kicked out of school but her father filed a lawsuit against the university and they backed down."

"That doesn't surprise me. And to answer your question, I'm not sure where she is. I know she's been setting up the aid stations the past couple of days."

"I spoke to her about an hour ago but I thought she would've been here by now. I have some news, Duncan, and eventually you'd hear it anyway so I thought I should share it with you." He pulled out his iPad and passed it Duncan. "That's Pushkin's report on the infectiousness of Agent X."

Duncan read for a moment. "This can't be right."

"It is."

"That's impossible," he said quietly.

"It's not. We're gearing up for—"

The door opened and Ralph's assistant Betty poked her head in. "Sorry, Dr. Wilson, there's someone here to meet with you and I thought you might be interested in meeting with them."

"Who is it?"

"Benjamin Cornell from the anti-vaccination people."

"That son of a bitch. Gimmie a minute, Betty, and then let him back."

"Not happy with him, I take it?"

"He's the one that's been attacking our vaccine shipments. I've dealt with him before. He targeted a meeting at the World Health Organization in Sweden a few years back and he started spraying animal blood on anybody walking in."

The door opened and Betty led Benjamin inside. Ben smiled and nodded hello to both men before sitting down.

"Beautiful day, boys. We should be out enjoying nature, not stuck in an office."

"Nature's trying to kill us right now," Duncan said.

"Cut the shit, Ben," Ralph interjected. "I know you're the one attacking my vaccine shipments."

"They're not your shipments, Ralph. And where's your proof that I was even twenty miles near those shipments? Besides, that's not my style."

"You don't have a style. You're a terrorist."

"I'm a patriot. What I do is no different than what the Founding Fathers did. I stand up to tyranny and arbitrary rules thrown at us from the government. You're too deep in it now to see it, Ralph, but I protect people like you too."

"Protect me from medicine? I don't need your protection. And neither do these people. As far as proof goes, if I had any you'd be sitting in jail right now instead of in my office."

"I don't think there's enough people manning the jails as it is," he said with a grin. "Ralph, we're getting off on the wrong foot. We're really on the same side, you and I. You want to see people healthy and disease free and I want to see them healthy and disease free. Does it really matter that much that our methods of how to achieve those goals are different?"

Ralph stuck a finger near Benjamin's face. "Keep the fuck away from my vaccines or you're gonna be sorry. We're now under martial law. I won't be so inclined to follow procedure if another one of my shipments is attacked. I'll just send some MPs down to arrest you and hold you in a brig until we get back to the mainland."

"Don't you mean if we get back to the mainland?"

Ralph was silent a while. "Who the hell told you?"

"Just an educated guess."

Duncan looked from one man to the other. "What're you two talking about?"

"You haven't told him?" Benjamin said. He chuckled. "I think you should maybe tell the people who've risked their lives coming out here what you plan to do."

"I don't give a damn about what you think. And the only reason I asked you here is to give you one more chance. I have another shipment of vaccines tonight, which I'm sure you know about. They get touched, and you're done."

Benjamin smiled to himself and rose. "Pleasure as always, Ralph. Dr. Adams, nice seeing you as well."

Duncan nodded and waited until he had left before speaking. "What was he talking about, Ralph?"

Ralph exhaled loudly and leaned back in his chair. Exhaustion permeated every muscle, bone, and sinew in his body. Even his skin felt numb and tired. He hadn't slept for thirty-six hours and looked forward to the time when he could be back at his own home and in his own bed.

"Ralph, what was he talking about?"

"What I'm about to tell you doesn't leave this room. Not yet. Understood?"

"Sure."

"You better shut the door then and sit down."

CHAPTER 30

Samantha arrived at the hospital a few hours later. It had taken the MPs nearly two and a half hours to arrive and verify her identity before they allowed her into the Jeep and drove her back to the hospital in silence.

She walked down the main corridor and saw Jerry Amoy sitting in the waiting area. There was an empty plate on the seat next to him and he was sipping a Diet Coke as he watched a DVD of *Friends* on the television that was hooked to the wall. Samantha came and sat down next to him.

"I haven't seen you in a few days," Amoy said.

"I've been setting up the aid stations."

Amoy nodded. "I've heard they've been running out of food."

"I just heard that myself. I don't know how that's possible. They're supposed to be resupplied every night and we have shipments scheduled to come in every week."

"Don't rely too much on the government, Dr. Bower. The government's just people, and unless people have a strong interest, they do just enough to get by."

She nodded, though she didn't agree with him, and they watched television a couple of minutes.

"How are things here?" she asked.

"Same as always. Patients show up at our doors for help and we have no help to offer them. This isn't why I became a doctor: to choose who gets a bed and who doesn't."

"Sometimes we don't get to choose our circumstances. We just have to deal with them the best we can."

"I'm leaving the island."

"When?"

"Day after tomorrow. I can't…it infected a day care for young…" She saw tears well in his eyes and he wiped them with the back of his hand. "It's amazing how evil nature can be. Man's got nothing on it."

"It's not evil, Jerry. It just is." She watched the screen a few moments and then said, "Where are you gonna go?"

"California. I have relatives there. I'll take the licensing exams. This island was a paradise for me, but even when this is all over, it'll be ruined for me. There's nothing left for me here but memories of people dying."

Samantha rose. "You've done good work, Jerry. I wouldn't give up just yet."

As she walked down the corridor, she glanced back to see his face buried in his hands.

Ralph was sitting at his desk when she walked into the administrative offices of the hospital. Other than a few military personnel and the handful of staff volunteers that had stayed to care for the sick, the hospital was empty.

It reminded her of some of the old hospitals from the fifties she'd been given tours of as a medical student. They still had equipment, and many of the rooms were unbearably creepy, as they still had clothing from old patients that had long since passed away. At least here there isn't a thick coating of dust on everything, she thought.

She waited by the door until Ralph looked up from what he was doing and motioned for her to sit down.

"I'm sorry about what happened today. Are you all right?"

"I'm fine. A little shaken up, but I'm grateful someone was in that mall."

He tapped his pen against the desk. "You're going home. Tonight. I've booked a flight for you on a military charter that's dropping off another shipment of vaccines."

"What? Ralph, you need everyone you can get out here."

"I'm leaving too."

"What's going on?"

"Martial law is being declared. The military is fully taking over operations and the World Health Organization is sending infectious disease bio teams to handle the patients. Our work is through."

"What are you talking about? Hundreds of people a day are getting infected. How is our work through?"

"We're containment people, Sam. We deal with the initial stages of a crisis and make sure it doesn't spread. Once it's contained, our job is done and we bring in the disaster handlers. That's the military. It's their show now. Anyway, your flight's at one in the morning. Enjoy your last day in paradise."

"I don't think I should leave."

"Sam, I know we're friends, but I'm also your boss and you need to treat me as such. You're leaving, end of story. There'll be other epidemics and other curious agents. Don't get too hung up on any one."

CHAPTER 31

Robert Greyjoy drove through a quiet suburb near Honolulu in a stolen Range Rover. Well, stolen wasn't the correct word; most cars had been abandoned on the side of the road and he happened to find one that had a half tank of gas left.

The neighborhood was clearly middle to upper class. You could always tell based on the cars parked in the driveway. Some people put themselves in massive lifetime debt over their homes and then had nothing left over for the cars. Cars were much more useful for predicting the socio-economic climate of a neighborhood than any other factor except for the maintenance of the lawns.

A group of men were walking by on the street and they eyed him. One had his shirt off and he had a large tattoo of a shark on his back. He threw up some sort of gang sign and Robert laughed despite himself. He kept driving.

There was a young girl on the corner, perhaps no more than twelve. Another shirtless man with tattoos held her by the arm and was clearly scolding her. He looked over and saw Robert's car and said something to the girl before disappearing into a house.

The girl casually walked in front of Robert's car and he had to slam on his brakes to avoid a collision. She came up to the window. She was lovely, Robert thought. Dark hair with emerald eyes rimmed red from crying. She was wearing a sundress with high-heels that she clearly was not accustomed to.

"Are you looking for sex?" she said.

Robert grinned. "I think what you want to ask is if I'm looking to party or looking for a good time. If you say 'looking for sex' you'll scare most people off."

"Are you looking to party?" she said timidly.

"How old are you?"

"Old enough."

"No, you're not. Why are you out here?"

She looked down to the ground. She seemed somewhere else for a few moments and then looked up again. "Do you want sex or not?"

"No."

She turned and went back to her corner. Robert pulled his Range Rover over to the curb and stepped out. He locked the doors, not that that would really help now, and then walked to the girl.

"That man that was out here with you. Who is he?"

"None of your business."

He leaned down, looking into her eyes. His stare had power. There was a time when he would work on it in the mirror, but that seemed like ages ago. His eyes were reflections of what was inside. Work on the interior, and the exterior will follow.

"Who is he?" he said flatly, menace in his voice.

"My…my mama died and they take care of me."

"How do they take care of you?"

"They gimmie food and I can sleep in the closet. They protect me."

"How many of them are there?" She didn't say anything and Robert grabbed her arm and squeezed gently. "How many?"

"Six, and two other girls."

The man that had been out here before came out again, a cigarette dangling from his lips. "Hey, man, you gonna fuck her or what?"

"How much?" Robert said, beginning to walk toward the man.

"We ain't take no money no more. Ain't no stores open anyway. You gotta come up with somethin' to trade. Last dude gave us a gold watch."

Robert was only a few feet away from him now. "Gold watch? Hm. How's this one?" he said, holding up his watch.

"That don't look like no watch I—"

Robert spun and grabbed his arm, twisting it behind him so violently that the man sucked down his cigarette. He forced the arm up, nearly parallel to the shoulder, using the man's body weight and gravity. There was a snap in his shoulder. The man screamed.

The man reached for a gun that was tucked in the small of his back. Robert grabbed two of his fingers and jerked them to the side, breaking them, and took the gun himself. It was a Beretta.

"Nice gun," Robert said, admiring the weapon. He put the barrel to the back of the man's head near the cerebellum and pulled the trigger. There was no blood at first, just a hole with a bit of gray smoke wafting out.

The man dropped to his knees and Robert pushed him over with the tip of his shoe. He looked to the girl and smiled, before walking up the street into the house.

There was a woman of about forty and a man on the couch smoking something out of a broken lightbulb. Robert put a slug into his left eye. The woman was about to scream and he grabbed her by the hair, using it as a handle, and slammed her face through the glass coffee table. He flipped her back to the couch. Her face looked like bloodied meat and she began to scream.

"No! No, please. I didn't do nothing."

"Exactly," Robert said, leaning over her and picking a few shards of glass out of her face. "God is not passive. He doesn't forgive you simply because you do nothing in the face of evil. Inaction, is action."

She opened her mouth to speak and Robert put his palm against her chin and violently jerked her head with his other hand. After a muted crack, like a cob of corn snapping in half, she went limp. There was still some life in her eyes as Robert leaned her back on the couch and watched her. It would take three minutes for her to faint from lack of oxygen, four minutes for her to fall into a deep unconsciousness and her heart to stop, six minutes for her brain to die. He wondered what those last few seconds before death were like.

The essayist and philosopher Montaigne had been severely injured in a horse riding accident and his lungs slowly filled with blood as he drifted off to death, though he survived by some miracle. He said it was the most pleasant sensation he had ever felt.

In a way, Robert envied this woman. In six minutes the Great Secret would be revealed to her. She would have more knowledge than any scientist or philosopher that had ever lived.

He sighed, and continued through the house.

A man with dreadlocks was in the kitchen with food lying out on the counter in front of him. His earphones were blaring metal. He turned to Robert and gave a quizzical look just as Robert put two holes in his chest.

Robert went upstairs and found another man, who he shot in the back of the head while he was sitting in front of a computer, and then came back downstairs. Including the woman, that was five. Did the girl mean six men or six adults total?

Robert quickly went through the rest of the house. It was in squalor with garbage thrown on the carpets and colonies of ants and cockroaches throughout the various rooms. Robert pulled out a scented handkerchief and kept it to his nose as he walked through the final bedroom. There was no one else here.

He heard a noise outside and instinctively lowered himself to the ground. He duck-walked out to the back door and saw a man working on a car, a cell phone glued to his ear. Robert glanced around and saw no one else. He waited a full minute, and then stepped outside.

"Excuse me," he said, "what's your name?"

"Who the fuck are you?"

A large metal cylinder lay on a small workbench next to the man and Robert grabbed it and bashed it into the man's mouth. He heard teeth crack and the man flew off his feet.

Robert brought the heavy cylinder down onto the man's toes and then his ankles, slamming it into his flesh over and over and over. When he was convinced his feet were too mangled to walk, Robert sat down on a crate that was turned upside down just outside the garage entrance.

"I asked you what your name was."

The man was cursing and shouting and yelping in pain. His mouth was foaming as he spit curses, holding his limp feet in his hands.

"You fuckin' broke my legs!"

"No, I did not. I broke your ankles and your feet. Don't be such a coward. Now, what was your name?"

"Fuck you."

"Fine, then let's avoid pleasantries and get to the only question I actually care about: that girl you're pimping outside, where did you find her?"

"Fuck you!"

Robert picked up the cylinder again and crashed it into his wrist, causing another round of screaming and swearing. He waited until the man had calmed down and then asked him again, "Where did you find her?"

"I don't know, man."

"Oh, you're confused."

Another crash of the cylinder, this one on his other wrist.

"All right! Just stop, fuckin' stop!"

"Where?"

"The school, man, the fuckin' junior high. Lotta their parents died from the coffee lung and they was stayin' there. That's how we get our girls, man. From the school."

"Coffee lung?"

"Yeah, man. The sickness."

Robert remembered reading a report on the plane over to Hawaii stating that victims of Agent X were vomiting blood that had mass in it that resembled coffee grounds.

"Clever name. So how many girls do you have?"

"I don't know, a lot. We got 'em everywhere. We need a lot of 'em."

"Why do you need a lot of them?" Robert asked. The man remained silent and Robert said, "Oh, people with coffee lung have sex with them and then the girls get it too and can't work anymore, is that it?"

He nodded. Unable to hold his feet with his broken wrists, his weary head just tilted to the side.

"Amazing," Robert said, "people that ill, vomiting life out of them, still want to have sex. That's fascinating. I wonder if Freud was right and sex is our primary motivation in all things? We have the power to explore the atom and distant galaxies and we use the majority of our brains to find sex. What a sad little species we would be if that were true." Robert was silent a moment as he thought about this. He decided it was an issue he would consider later and pushed it aside in his mind. "So, the question is, what are we going to do? I'm assuming your operation is larger than the six of you I found here, so if I were to kill you it probably wouldn't stop much."

"I swear, man," he said out of breath and going into shock. "I swear, you let me live and I will never do that shit again. Never."

"Never ever? If we pinky swear?"

"What?"

Robert laughed. "No, you're going to have to do better than that."

"What do you want?"

"What do I want? Hm, well, there's a house not two blocks from here with two Iranian fellows. I want you to knock on their door and when they come out I'm going to shoot them." Robert looked into the garage. "By the way, whoever's back there, I can see your shoes underneath the car. Come on out and join us."

There was a moment of quiet before the shoes shuffled across the cement and a young girl emerged. She was perhaps sixteen and shivering from fear. She stood there looking at the ground, not making eye contact.

"What's your name, sweetheart?"

"Randi."

"Randi, do you want to be here?"

She glanced up and then back down to the ground. "I'm his girl."

"You're his girl, you're his girl." Robert looked down to the man. "So are you going to knock on that door for me?"

"I think you broke my ankles, man. I can't walk. But she could do it. It'll be better 'cause they won't be expectin' nothin' from a girl."

"Hm, not a bad idea. You're right, I will use her." Robert lifted his weapon.

"No!"

He fired one round, the slug entering just to the right of the nose into the corner of the eye. The man fell back as it ricocheted in his skull, having the velocity to enter but not the velocity to exit.

Robert smiled at the girl. "You're not his girl anymore. Do you understand?" She nodded. "Randi, I'm guessing there're a lot of you girls around here, is that right?" She nodded again. "Everyone here is dead. Get the girls and clear out. Find somewhere nicer. There are shelters set up farther in town, go there. Or go to a church. But stay away from men right now. Do you understand?"

"Yes, I understand."

"Good. I'm sure there are guns in this house. After you do what I'm going to ask you to do, come back and carry one or even two with you at all times."

"What do you want me to do?"

"Very simple. We're going to walk to a house two blocks away. You're going to knock on the door and tell whoever answers that you need help and that you need two people to help you. Don't tell them what help you need. Just panic and scream. Scream as loud as you can. As soon as the men come to the door, you jump down onto the ground. Do you think you can do that?"

"Yes."

"Good. Let's go."

"What are you going to do to those men?"

"I'm going to be hiding and then I'm going to shoot them in the heart. Is that something you have a problem with?"

She thought for a moment and then shook her head.

"Good," Robert said with a smile, "then you and I are going to get along just fine."

He held out his hand and she took it.

CHAPTER 32

Samantha waited outside the conference room at the Ritz as two MPs cleared her identification with someone on the other end of a radio. They eventually nodded her in and she saw a room packed with men. She looked over them and recognized only Duncan who was busy at work on an iPad.

"Hey," she said, sitting down next to him.

"Hey. I tried calling you."

"My phone died and there's no power at the hotel anymore."

"They have a generator here. I switched hotels yesterday."

"So I'm being shipped out tonight."

Duncan nodded, glancing at the document he had up on his iPad. "You leaving on the eleven or one o'clock?"

"One. You don't seem too surprised."

"I'm on the one too."

"Duncan, what are you talking about? Ralph told me he chartered a military plane to get me out of here."

He gave her a quizzical look, and then understanding lit up his eyes. "Oh my gosh, he didn't tell you, did he?"

"Tell me what?"

Ralph walked into the room with the general behind him and several men in suits surrounding him. He took his place at the front of the room and waited until there was quiet before speaking.

"Thank you for being here, gentlemen. I don't have much but I do have a few quick items of logistics to go over…"

Duncan leaned over to Samantha and whispered, "Sam, the data came back. Agent X is a T-6—they're shipping out all non-essential personnel tonight. The United Nations and World Health Organization are sending down specialized units."

Samantha comprehended the words but they didn't sink in right away. T-6, T-6…it was something that had only been theoretically possible. Like absolute zero Kelvin or stopping time by traveling the speed of light. T-6 was a thought experiment; how long would it take to wipe out all species with an infectiousness rate of T-6? The answers were always interesting, a quick exercise to warm up the mind before getting down to real work.

"Are they sure?" was all she managed to say.

"I ran the data myself and sent it back to USAMRIID to have my biostats guys run it. It's legit."

Ralph continued speaking and then sat down as the general took to the front of the room. He began by answering questions and issuing orders. Ralph looked to her and had a bittersweet smile on his face, as if apologizing.

When the general had completed his Q and A the room began to clear out. Sam sat quietly until everybody but Ralph and Duncan had left. She noticed the FBI agent from earlier, Billy Donner, standing near the entrance. He smiled to her and she smiled back before he walked out.

"Why didn't you tell me?" Sam said.

Ralph rubbed the bridge of his nose with his thumb and forefinger. His eyes had black circles under them and were rimmed red. "Because you would've wanted to stay."

"I do want to stay."

"Out of the question. You both are on that plane at 1:00 a.m. Don't miss it because there isn't another one for three days."

Ralph stood up without another word and walked out of the room. The door shut behind him and Sam and Duncan were left alone, the sound of vehicles outside as military officers were shuttled to the airport to prepare for the eleven o'clock flight off the island. The room was hot and Sam felt as if she were in an oven that was just beginning to warm. There was no air conditioning, as power was conserved wherever possible.

"I think he should've asked for volunteers," Duncan said.

"T-6. I don't even really know what that means, Duncan. We've never dealt with anything like this. He's just taking every precaution. I don't think it's his fault. Besides, I think the military's calling the shots now. I doubt Ralph could've stopped this if he wanted to."

Duncan shrugged. "So where to for you when you get back?"

"A hot shower and a good meal with my mom. How about you?"

"There's a restaurant in Baltimore called Faustina's. They have a turkey burger that's delicious and you get strawberry bread pudding after the meal. Then after that I'm going to the movies. I really miss going to the movies.

"I used to go every few days. I'd sneak out from work for lunch and just buy a hot dog at the theater. There's something calming about watching movies in a dark theater by yourself. It erases you for a little bit. No one comes to talk to you or ask you questions. All your worries and fears and problems disappear for that little bit." He waited a beat and then said, "Sam, I'd really like it if you came up to Maryland and we went to the movies together."

She laughed.

"What?"

"No, it's nothing. You're just really cute when you don't know what I'm going to say. There's something really 1950s about you. I feel like this is how someone back then would've asked me on a date."

"Would you prefer something more modern? I could send you a tweet."

"No, Duncan. It's very sweet that you asked. But I've been away far too long as it is. I don't think I can take any trips for a while."

"Oh."

"But, why don't you come down to Atlanta? We have movie theaters too."

"Sure, why not?"

They rose and Duncan gathered a few papers. They walked out of the room together and down the hall. The linoleum floors were filthy with black boot prints and dirt that had been brought inside. There was no cleaning crew anymore.

They got outside and past the MPs when a man walked toward them from an awaiting car. Sam recognized him as Ben Cornell. She noticed that Duncan folded his arms and gave him a disapproving look.

"Doctors," Benjamin said, "how we doing tonight?"

"Better once we leave our present company."

"See, that's what I'm talking about. Dr. Adams, you don't know anything about me. We haven't really even been introduced. And for some reason you hate me. And because you hate me, you won't hear anything I have to say, even if I'm right."

"You're not right. Your campaigns against vaccinations kill children. How do you possibly sleep at night?"

"We all have to do what we think is right. I don't know if vaccinations do or don't harm us. But what I do know is that they won't fund any major studies to see if they do. My son has autism, Dr. Adams. He began displaying symptoms right after his vaccinations. Do you know what autism is like? He can't form social bonds. It feels like he doesn't love or care about me or his mother. It's a pain I can't even describe. Some days…some days I think it would be better if he would've just passed away. Or that, maybe, I should be the one to pass away."

"I'm sorry. I didn't know."

"No, you didn't. You just made a judgment without any evidence. Hardly seems fitting a scientist, doesn't it?"

Sam noticed that Duncan was full-on blushing. She considered Benjamin Cornell. He appeared wiry and was shifting his weight from foot to foot. He was clearly anxious about something and it made her worry. But there was also kindness in his eyes. She could see it sparkling through the passion he had for his cause.

"I have no quarrel with you two," Benjamin said. "You both do good work. But you work for monsters. Still, we all have to work for somebody I guess, so I don't blame you for it. But I think what you're doing here is wrong. It's just plain wrong, even evil. I don't know how you, Dr. Adams, can sleep at night doing what you're doing."

"What exactly do you think I'm doing?"

"Government evasion is cowardly, Doctor. Let's at least be honest with each other, even in the lies."

"Ben, I don't know what you're talking about."

Benjamin stared at him quizzically a moment and then recognition dawned on him and his face lit up as a grin came over his lips. "They haven't told you, have they?" he said in almost a whisper.

"Told us what?"

"You're leaving the island."

"We knew that."

"No, not just you. Everyone. The military, the CDC, everyone. This island will be quarantined and the people on it will not be allowed to leave. They didn't tell you that?"

Sam and Duncan looked to each other and Sam said, "He's lying."

"Call Ralph and ask yourself if you don't believe me. They're pulling everybody out and cutting the supplies. These people are supposed to survive on their own."

Sam turned around and went back into the building, Duncan following behind her. She rode the elevator up to the top floor and found Ralph's suite. She knocked but he wasn't in. They went back down to the restaurant near the lobby and saw Ralph sitting by himself, sipping a beer. They sat across from him.

"Tell me it isn't true," Sam said.

"You're leaving, Sam. That's all there is to it."

"Not that."

He glared at her a moment. "Then I don't know what you're talking about."

"Ralph, we've known each other a long time. I can tell when you're bullshitting me."

He nodded, looking down to his beer and absently peeling off the label. "Who told you?"

"Benjamin Cornell."

"Little prick. If I find out who leaked it to him I'll have their asses."

"I don't believe this is happening. And you're so calm about it. Like it just happens every day."

"How would you like me to be, Sam? We're talking about the deadliest virus in history coming out of the jungle and infecting this island. Thank God it was an island and not Los Angeles or Seattle. This is an extinction event. Agent X is the meteor that wiped out the dinosaurs. We can't risk its release no matter the cost."

"This is…I can't believe we're even talking about this. Ralph there are hundreds of thousands of people on this island that aren't infected."

"And I feel for them, I really do. But there's nothing that can be done." He leaned back, taking a sip of his beer. "Besides, I couldn't stop it if I wanted to. The military's taken over. They think it's a national security threat, which it is. This is the official decision."

Sam shook her head. "We're the monsters Cornell thinks we are."

Ralph laughed. "Don't be so dramatic. What did you think this job was, Dr. Bower? As a physician you make life and death calls. What does it matter if it's over one person in an ER or on the scale of an island?"

"Ralph, please, don't do this."

Duncan jumped in, "There are alternatives. We can request volunteers, not just from here, from all over."

"And what happens if one of those volunteers gets infected and we don't catch it when they decide to come home? Do you have any idea what a virus like this could do in a major city? Pushkin's run the numbers. Within ten days, fourteen percent of the population of the United States would be infected. Within twenty-five days, it would be sixty percent. Within a month, ninety-eight percent would be infected. We're not talking H1N1, we're talking Armageddon."

Samantha rose. "There are some things you don't do, even at the risk of your own life. You're giving these people a death sentence. And I can't be a part of it."

"You want to quit? Quit. It won't change anything. You're still on that plane."

"I'm going to stop this."

"Feel free. I think it's probably time for you to learn that there are things beyond your influence."

Duncan gently put his hand on her arm. "Let's go, Sam. There's nothing we can do here."

As they walked out of the restaurant, Sam kicked over the trashcan outside and began to pace.

"Feel better?" Duncan said.

"What can we do, Duncan? These people are all going to die. They asked for help from their government and we're going to abandon them."

"Sometimes there is nothing you can do. You just have to do the best you can and hope it works out."

She shook her head, her thumbnail in her mouth as she paced back and forth across the hotel's entrance. "There's got to be something…we're not helpless in this."

Benjamin Cornell was waiting on the hood of a car and he hopped off and came over to them. "So?"

They didn't respond and he grinned. It wasn't a happy grin; it was filled with melancholy. As if he were sad he had been proved right.

"I thought so," Benjamin said.

Duncan was about to grab Sam and leave when Benjamin heard her say, "There has to be something we can do."

"There is," Benjamin said.

"Sam, we're ending this conversation. We're not helping *him* do anything."

Sam ignored Duncan. "What?" she said to Benjamin.

"Iquitos, Peru," he said. "The woman that survived. They've cancelled the expedition to find her. Only one known survivor of this thing and they're going to completely ignore her." He glanced around and saw Ralph Wilson leaving the building, surrounded with men in suits, discussing something. Ralph saw them and shook his head before entering a Jeep. "I'm not going to ignore her," Benjamin said. "Why don't you come with me and meet some of our people to talk this over?"

"No," Duncan said. "Sam, this guy is a borderline terrorist."

"Why, because I don't accept everything my government tells me? My father fought in Vietnam, young kid of seventeen. He was so patriotic he lied about his age to fight. He got sprayed with Agent Orange by his own government and died of cancer nine years later. That's the government you work for, Dr. Adams. So don't you dare tell me I'm the terrorist."

"Stop it, you two," Sam said. "Duncan, I'm going to go with him. Are you coming with me or not?"

"Sam—"

"No, I'm not sitting by and watching these people die. I have to do something."

"Why? You don't even believe in a God; what does it matter to you if these people die?"

"It matters to me because I've devoted my life to helping people. God or not, I couldn't live with myself if I just went back to Atlanta and pretended like these people didn't exist." She turned to Benjamin. "Be honest with me: why do you want me to come?"

"An honest question, and I have an honest answer: This woman may not come back with us. She may not even want to talk to us. But I think I can convince her to give us some blood and tissue samples, or maybe the hospital still has some. But I need a laboratory, a very advanced laboratory in a BSL 4 environment to analyze them."

"Okay, I'll see what I can do. Let's go."

As Sam was climbing into Benjamin's car, Duncan ran over and got into the backseat. "I'm coming, but I'd like to make it official that I think this is a mistake."

"Duly noted," Benjamin said, starting the car and pulling away.

CHAPTER 33

They pulled to a stop in front of what had been a massive grocery store, something like Wal-Mart but with a name Sam had never heard before, and parked near the front in handicap parking. Benjamin stepped out without saying anything.

"You sure you want to do this?" Duncan said when they were alone in the car.

"Rather than just sit at home and read about what's going on on Twitter? Yes."

They got out and followed Benjamin inside through the automatic doors. The grocery store had been rearranged in a way that all the goods were up against the walls. The floors were cluttered with desks and cubicles but they weren't staffed with more than half a dozen people. Samantha recognized one of them as the FBI agent she had met earlier.

"You know he's with the FBI, right?"

"Who, Billy? Yeah we know. He's one of the good ones, though. He's been helping out now here and there. Damn good at everything too if you ask me. Isn't that right, Billy?"

He came over, a smile on his face as he bowed his head slightly in acknowledgement of the compliment. "Glad I could be of service."

"What's a federal agent doing helping these people out?" Duncan said.

"I suppose I could say the same thing about a military scientist." He looked to Sam. "Or a CDC field agent. You didn't like the thought of being shipped off and leaving everyone here, huh? Me neither. But if you'll excuse me I have a couple of things I need to follow up on in our itinerary."

"Our itinerary? You're coming to Peru as well?"

"Wouldn't miss it for the world," he said, a wide grin on his face.

"Don't worry about him. I want to introduce you to everyone else. I'm heading down with you guys as is Cami over there—wave hi, Cami—yeah, her right there. So it'll be the five of us."

"And what exactly is the plan?" Duncan asked.

"We're going to find this woman and bring her back to the States. We have a few physicians in DC that are ready to analyze why she survived when no one else did. If we can do that, we can save a lot of lives." He looked to Duncan. "You don't have to come if you don't want to. But if you do, you gotta pay your own way. I'll be covering the ticket for Dr. Bower."

"No," Duncan said, "I don't want her in debt to you for anything. I'll pay for both our flights. Sam, I need to talk to you a sec." He took her by the arm and they stepped aside out of earshot. "This is crazy."

"Do you have a better idea?"

"Yes, let the pros handle it."

"I'm a pro. I'm a field agent. This is something I was actually planning on doing until they decided that it would be better to let everybody die."

"Sam, look at these people. They're nutballs. That girl over there can't be more than eighteen. These are the people that think the CIA killed Kennedy or that the moon landing happened at a set in Hollywood."

"That might be true, but all they want to do now is find a patient that could help us come up with a vaccine."

"We might not have needed another vaccine if these guys hadn't destroyed the shipments we got!"

"There's no proof they did that. Besides, Pushkin said it's unlikely the standard smallpox vaccine was going to do anything anyway."

"But we won't know that because they destroyed it."

"I didn't do that," Benjamin said.

Duncan turned to him. "I don't believe you."

"Believe what you want. We're all going to LA on that plane and then we have a flight chartered for Mexico. You can come if you want to. We could use your expertise. That girl that you said was eighteen is a doctor from John Hopkins who's risking her life and her job to come with us and investigate this survivor. Show a little respect before you start criticizing."

Duncan looked to the young girl. He saw the screen of the mac she was working on: it was a computer model of the smallpox virus. A program was molding and sculpting the virus into different mutations.

"She may be noble, but you're not. I know you, Ben. I know people like you. Your type. Your motives are pure and your means destructive. I'm coming, but the only reason I'm doing it is so Sam isn't alone with you."

He smiled. "The more the merrier."

CHAPTER 34

Samantha stepped on the plane and turned around to get one last look at Honolulu. Even at night it was beautiful. At one in the morning, the moon was a crescent slit in the black sky and the tips of the palm trees shimmered under its light. The night air was warm and salty and she inhaled deep lungfuls before turning and sitting down in her seat.

It was early morning in Atlanta but she knew that Pushkin tended to answer his phone at any time. She took out her phone, fully charged thanks to Benjamin's charger, and called him.

"This is Dr. Pushkin," he said on the third ring, sleep still in his voice.

"This is Samantha Bower, Doctor."

"Sam, how are you? Are you on your way back to the States with everybody else?"

She glanced around at the twenty-five or so people on the plane with her. "Yes." She wasn't quite lying. They were heading back to the States before going to Peru, as there'd be no way to get a straight flight to South America from Hawaii. "I have a favor to ask."

"Anything."

"The girl in Peru, the survivor, I may be shipping some tissue and blood samples back to you for analysis. We need to figure out what made her unique."

"I thought that operation was cancelled?" She didn't say anything. "Oh, I see. Well, I don't like doing things off the radar but this seems sufficiently warranted. Send them through the normal biohazard but have them labeled for me instead of Infectious Diseases. I'll keep my eyes open."

"Thank you. And thanks for not asking questions."

"I've been here a long time, Sam. And I'll be here long after you're gone. You're not the first field agent to go against policy. But this time I agree with you. The smallpox vaccines were ineffective. We're completely exposed to this agent and they won't even go down and interview this woman much less examine her. Just do me a favor and be careful; we don't know how the initial transmission occurred. It could've been something as simple as a mosquito. You won't know until it's too late."

"Thanks, I'll be careful."

She hung up and glanced next to her. Billy Donner sat next to her reading a copy of *Tropic of Cancer.*

"You wouldn't just lose your job for disobeying orders," she said. "They'd bring criminal charges against a law enforcement officer."

"I know. But the bureau's not as efficient as all that. I'll be back before they miss me."

She glanced back at Benjamin who was already asleep with headphones poking out of his ears. "What made a man like you put your trust in him?"

"He's sincere. That's a rare quality. And unlike most people in the government, and major corporations helping us out, he actually cares about curing this disease, not just avoiding blame."

There was a bottle of water tucked into the back of the seat in front of her and she took it out and opened it, taking a sip. "They're going to fire me for this. Pushkin's unique; they can't get rid of him. They'll put all the blame on me and I'll be the scapegoat."

"You never know. Things could go well and we could discover a vaccine. That'll probably buy you some leniency."

She chuckled. "You haven't worked for the government long, have you?"

He smiled, lowering his book. "I'm not used to bureaucracy if that's what you mean."

"I disobeyed a direct order from my boss and didn't follow the accepted procedure from the head of the department. They care more about that than any benefit they get out of it."

"Well, I won't hold it against you," he said, smiling as he brought the book back up.

The plane roared to life. It began to rumble down the strip that had been cleared and turned into a runway, and then slowed and turned the other way. It began to speed up and then lifted into the air. Samantha looked out the window and watched as the lights on the island sparkled like gems in the darkness and then began to fade. Eventually, there was only darkness beneath her as the plane leveled out, and then only the open sea. She took a deep breath and leaned back in the seat, closing her eyes and drifting off.

Sam felt a hand gently placed on her arm. She glanced down and saw the finely manicured nails of Agent Donner's hand. She looked up and saw his smiling face.

"You slept the whole flight," he said. "I didn't want to wake you."

"I haven't gotten much sleep lately."

"It sounds childish but warm milk really does work."

She unbuckled herself as Donner did the same. He stood in the aisle and offered his hand to help her up. She grabbed her gym bag from above the seats and slung it over her shoulder. They walked down the aisle and she saw Duncan up front. He smiled to her and took her bag.

"I was going to switch seats with Billy here, but you looked so comfortable I left you alone."

"I was out cold. Did you get some sleep?"

"A little."

"Let's get some breakfast somewhere."

They walked out onto the tarmac and through the airport. There didn't appear to be any other planes.

"The runway's been cleared," Agent Donner told her, "so that we could land. I'm sure we're going to have some upset people inside, so it was for the best not to let them know we were on that flight."

LAX appeared as it always had: modern and rundown at the same time. The maintenance was top notch and kept it as clean and well oiled as possible, but where a mass of human beings gathered and moved about every day, there was always decay.

Benjamin caught up to them and gave them keys to their hotel rooms at the Marriot. He and Agent Donner said they'd see them in the morning and left together in one cab as Sam and Duncan got into another.

"What's the best for breakfast around here?" Samantha asked the driver.

"Dinah's is the best I think," the driver said, his voice raspy from prolonged cigarette smoke.

"Dinah's it is."

As they pulled away and got onto the freeway, Sam leaned back into the seat and watched the multitudes of cars and SUVs passing by. She had grown so accustomed to seeing no one and nothing on the streets that at first it seemed odd to her that people would be out. She marveled at how quickly the mind adjusted to changing circumstances; it was what was responsible for our species' survival. Adaptability was more important than intelligence, than power, than connections…it made and broke men in seconds.

"You okay?" Duncan asked.

"Yeah, why?"

"You look lost in your own little world over there."

"I'm just wondering about this virus. How many more like it are out there? If this is just a random fluke of nature, there's probably more, and some of them might even be more deadly. How many outbreaks like this until our species succumbs?"

"Extinction is the most natural process on earth. It even predates our understanding of evolution."

"I think that's why climate change is such a debated issue. Some people think we're causing our own extinction and others think it's a myth. Since we haven't studied extinction as long as adaptability, it's all conjecture."

"It is and it isn't. We know about one species per day has gone extinct since life on earth began. From that we can come up with averages. For most animals, the mean timeframe before a species goes extinct is a little over four million years. But for humans and other mammals, it's about nine hundred thousand. So, I guess you could say we've already outlived our mean. Maybe it is just a matter of time until our number's up?"

She looked out the window again as the cab got off the freeway and onto the lamp-lit streets of Los Angeles. She had lived here once for a period of three years during a graduate fellowship and her mind was instantly flooded with memories of college parties and cramming for exams.

"I think it's deeper than that," she said absently. "I think mammals are perfectly capable of adapting to different environments but they still die out. I think the problem is that their behavior advances to a point that they're no longer receptive to what's happening in their environment. They lose their intuition, their imagination, and begin to rely solely on reason. When that happens, they don't respond to their environment anymore. They die."

Duncan shuddered, exaggerating it for effect. "Creepy."

He reached down and held her hand. She didn't object and turned and gave him a smile.

CHAPTER 35

Sam slept until nearly noon and when she awoke she found that Benjamin, Duncan, and Agent Donner had been waiting for her downstairs in the hotel lobby for over an hour. Duncan didn't want to wake her. Besides, their flight wasn't for another four hours and a hotel lobby was as good as any airport.

They eventually called a cab company, requested two vans, and headed back to LAX. The young doctor, Cami Mendoza, was with them as well and she mostly read on her iPad or listened to music. Sam sat next to her in the cab and noticed a tattoo of a dragon on her arm, running all the way down to the tips of her fingers.

"I like your work," Sam said.

"Oh, thanks."

"Does it mean anything?"

"I was born in the year and the month of the dragon. It's not finished yet. When it's done it's going to run over my whole body. Except my face of course."

"So, how'd you meet Benjamin?"

"At a rally actually. My daughter has autism and we began talking about that and just stayed in touch. In a few months I was working at his non-profit."

"So do you practice at all?"

"Here and there, but mostly at free clinics. I don't charge for my services anymore."

Cami put her headphones back on and they didn't speak again until they had stopped and were exiting the cab. Benjamin ran up from the other vehicle and said, "All right, so we've got a twelve-hour layover in Florida and then we head straight into Lima and take a charter flight into Iquitos. So, you know, call any jobs you need to call."

"How long are we planning on being gone?" Samantha asked, realizing she jumped into this without asking any details.

"As long as it takes I guess. Could just be four or five days."

They headed back into the airport and Sam sat next to Duncan as they flipped through a *National Geographic* he had bought at the gift shop. Her cell phone buzzed and she recognized Ralph's cell number.

"How are you, Ralph?"

"Just tell me what I heard isn't true."

"What did you hear?"

"That you're throwing your career away by following a psychopath into the jungle."

"What do you want me to do? Go back to Atlanta and do phone interviews of flu patients in Arkansas?"

"That's exactly what I want you to do."

"Ralph, you've abandoned those people. If Agent X doesn't abate on its own, the entire population of the island could be wiped out."

"You think I don't know that? You think I've actually slept these past three days and haven't been in the bathroom vomiting? I'm sick with myself, Sam. I hate this. I've seriously considered quitting, but in the end, I knew it wasn't the best thing."

"Why not? Quit and come with me."

He laughed. "Impulsivity's the kingdom of the young and I'm not young anymore. We have to be utilitarian in this; the greatest good for the greatest number."

"Why were we allowed to leave? Any one of us could be infected?"

"No one that was allowed to leave showed any symptoms of infection for longer than the incubation period." He hesitated a moment before speaking again. "Where are you right now?"

"Hopping onto a flight in LAX. Why?"

"Where are you heading after that?"

"Florida and then Peru. I should be back to work within a week. If there's work waiting for me."

He paused a moment. "It'll be waiting for you. Just be careful out there."

"I will, Ralph. Thanks."

As she hung up, Benjamin noticed that she had been speaking on the phone and he walked over.

"Who was that?"

"Ralph. Why?"

"You didn't tell him where we are, did you?"

"I told him we were boarding a plane."

"What are you so interested in that for?" Duncan said.

Benjamin said, "So, the whole island was abandoned on the off chance one person might bring the disease onto the mainland, right? How do you think it is that they've just let us fly out without so much as a doctor looking us over?"

"No one on that plane showed any signs of infection," Duncan said. "Why wouldn't they let us leave?"

Sam said, "No, he's right. They're sentencing people to death and they just let us walk away."

"I don't understand the big deal."

Benjamin said, "The big deal is that they shouldn't have just let us walk away. By right, we should be in quarantine." He looked to Sam. "Did you offer where you were or did he specifically ask?"

"He asked."

"If they wanted us in quarantine," Duncan said, "they'd just ask us to go. We'd all comply."

"Not if it was indefinite," Benjamin added.

"They wouldn't do that. That's not quarantine, that's prison."

"Let me ask you this, Dr. Adams: is there anything the government is forbidden from doing in the interest of national security? Dick Cheney, Bush, and then Obama and Holder made sure that the government has unlimited power as long as they say they're doing it for the interest of the greater good."

"Within reason. Anything else is just basement conspiracy theory."

Sam said, "Why would they book us a flight on a military charter?"

"Maybe someone was supposed to meet us when we landed that didn't show up?"

Sam stood. "Enough guesswork, let's get to our flight."

CHAPTER 36

Ralph Wilson raced through the Hollywood International Airport in Fort Lauderdale, Florida. Several military police surrounded him, their rifles held low. The airport was busy with summer travelers and they had grown infuriated at the cancellation, at least temporarily, of all incoming and outgoing flights. The military, FBI, Homeland Security, and Fort Lauderdale Police had commandeered the building and evacuated all the patrons. The airport was now only filled with men in uniforms; Ralph was the only one in a business suit.

In one sense, it sent a shiver down his spine. He had seen what occurs when people are granted too much power. But he had also seen what happens when Mother Nature gets out of control and her attacks are not contained. It was the greater danger, and had to be stopped. At any cost.

They finally came to terminal 3 and Ralph looked out the window to see a US Airways concord landing and running the course of the tarmac before turning and slowly making its way to the terminal. It was flight 1237: Samantha Bower's flight.

The decision not to quarantine them on the island was one Ralph had to fight for. Now they would be quarantined in a house on the outskirts of LA County and all their needs would be provided for. But he knew Sam and to a lesser extent Duncan Adams. Not to mention the dozens of other military and federal government employees that had been ordered quarantined. They would object and put up a fight. It was much better to simply drive them from the airport to the quarantine zone rather than have someone pull a favor with a Colonel and have all of them released.

But Sam, Duncan, Benjamin Cornell, one of his assistants, and Special Agent Donner had made it through. Donner was the one Ralph was most interested in. He didn't act like a federal agent and Ralph had known dozens of federal agents in his twenty-three years as a federal employee. Ralph still had friends at the bureau; many of his military buddies had joined the bureau after serving their stints in the Armed Forces. He called a special agent in charge out of Chicago and within minutes had Billy Donner's file emailed to him. It was identical in content to what Billy Donner had told him, except for one thing: the photograph of Special Agent William Henry Donner was not a photograph of the man Ralph had interacted with in Hawaii.

The Army's biohazard unit rounded the corner. With the space suits, thick Kevlar gloves, and plastic faceplates, they appeared like aliens casually strolling through some intergalactic spaceport. It would have made Ralph smile if they weren't about to forcefully detain one of his most dedicated employees.

The plane would be stopped outside of the terminal and the biohazard unit would go in and explain the situation to the passengers. It certainly wasn't the best way to maintain calm, but he couldn't risk any of them stepping off the plane into the airport. If the media ever found out that a possibly infected patient ever came into the airport, there'd be a shit-storm of blame-game, everyone looking to find a scapegoat, and the fault would probably land on his shoulders.

The biohazard unit walked by, one of them turning and giving a thumbs up to Ralph. He nodded in response and watched as the plane slowed and stopped at the gate. It connected to the terminal and the unit went in.

He couldn't hear anything and so his eyes were fixated on the cockpit's windows. The two pilots were speaking to each other as someone from the unit came in and spoke to them. There was some nodding and hand gestures, but the pilots didn't seem terribly surprised. After 9-11, Ralph guessed, nothing surprised them.

The bus had arrived and was pulling near the plane. It would take the passengers to the makeshift medical clinic that had been thrown together on the outskirts of town. They had built it in an abandoned factory and it would have minimal staff, but they would only spend double the incubation period sequestered. No more than twenty days. Sam, Duncan, and the rest would be heading off to the mansion Ralph had lined up for their quarantine: a six bedroom home complete with swimming pool. In time, she would forgive him and understand. Perhaps with age or a couple more promotions.

The bus came to a stop next to the plane and there were several MPs in full biohazard gear outside as the Army's biohazard unit began helping the crew disconnect from the terminal so a set of stairs could be brought to get the passengers onto the tarmac.

The passengers eventually began filing out one by one. Ralph had his eyes glued to them. The MPs had photographs of the five men and women he wanted separated from the rest. They would stop each passenger before they boarded the bus and compare the photos with the person standing in front of them.

But Ralph didn't see them yet. A man began arguing with one of the MPs and appeared to be refusing to get on the bus. He pushed one of the MPs and they froze, uncertain what to do. One of them spoke into a comm on his shoulder.

The comm on the shoulder of the sergeant standing next to Ralph crackled to life. "Sir, he's refusing to get on the bus. Please advise."

The Sergeant looked to Ralph. "What do you want me to tell him?"

"Tell him to put him in cuffs and get him on the bus, Commander. If he is infected, we have to get him quarantined as quickly as possible."

The sergeant relayed the instructions. Two MPs grabbed the man on the tarmac and spun him around as a third slapped cuffs on him. The man was fighting and yelling and kicked one of them in the shin. They took out a long plastic cord and tied his legs. They lifted and carried him, hog-tied, onto the bus. The rest of the passengers were not as difficult.

A woman stepped off the plane and climbed gingerly down the stairs. No one followed behind her.

"Where's everybody else?" Ralph said to the sergeant.

The sergeant said into his comm, "Anybody else on that plane, Griffith?"

"No, sir. That's all of 'em."

Ralph's face grew hot. He turned and began to pace. He looked back to the plane. "Sergeant, have your men go through that entire plane. Then send some men we have in LA through the airport. Notify the LAPD too and get them looking for the five people we have missing."

"You got it."

Ralph walked to the glass and watched the passengers on the bus. They appeared terrified and a woman near the front was holding a young girl that was crying. He felt a twinge of remorse in his gut, but he pushed it down and turned away from the window as he took out his cell phone, and placed a call to the FBI.

CHAPTER 37

Samantha Bower stepped off the plane onto the tarmac in the cool night air. With two layovers, the flight from Los Angeles to Florida had taken eleven hours. She looked back to the small charter plane that Agent Donner had found and paid for. It was a bucket with wings but Agent Donner had insisted they not fly commercially. Sam thought it odd. Even if Ralph meant to find and quarantine them, why would a special agent of the FBI be worried? She had seen agents stop entire airports and force all the passengers to wait until they arrived for their flight. They had power; Agent Donner had nothing to fear from a bureaucrat at the CDC.

"That was seriously cramped," Duncan said as he stepped off. "I think my ass fell asleep."

"Where'd you find that plane?" Benjamin said to Agent Donner.

"Called in a favor to a friend. It's for the best." He stretched his neck and his back and twisted his hips in a side-to-side motion. "Well, we've got an eight-hour layover. I was thinking I would go for a run and rent a hotel room for a few hours to sleep and shower if anyone would like to join me."

Cami said, "I would sell my body to anyone that could get me a shower right now."

Samantha glanced around the small, private airport and realized there were no cabs waiting here for passengers. She googled the local cab company and asked for a large van or two cabs.

"I could use a Diet Coke," she said to Duncan. "Want to come with?"

"Sure."

They left the others on the tarmac and went inside. The building was circular with windows that appeared unwashed. It was empty and the humidity and heat from outside filled the building as if the walls didn't exist.

"Do you think anything's weird about Agent Donner?" Sam said.

"Like what?"

"Why does he care if Ralph tries to quarantine him? He could get out of it."

"You don't know that. We all work for somebody. Maybe Ralph has deeper connections than we think."

They found the vending machines and Sam checked her pocket for change. She had eighty-eight cents and the bottled drinks were a dollar.

"Do you have any change?" she asked.

"What is this, 1995? Who carries around cash anymore?"

Sam sighed. She sat down on one of the seats that was bolted to the walls and put her face in her hands, rubbing her eyes before leaning back and staring at the ceiling.

"You doing okay?" Duncan asked.

"What am I doing here, Duncan? My mother's in Atlanta with Alzheimer's. I don't know how long she has left and I'm running off to the jungle with some crazy hippie."

"Hey, I'm not a hippie."

"Not you," she said with a grin. "Benjamin. I agree with you: he's clearly nuts but I really want to go down to Peru. I can't tell if it's out of altruism or just curiosity. I mean this thing came out of nowhere and nearly destroyed an entire state. Aren't you dying to find out what it is?"

"No," Duncan said, sitting in the seat next to her. "Nature's a forest of horrors. I don't need to know what new way it devised to kill me."

Benjamin and Cami came inside and collapsed onto a sofa in the corridor. They began giggling about something and Benjamin tickled her; only then did Sam realize they were in a relationship, or at least sleeping together.

"You ever been to South America?" Duncan asked.

"No, you?"

"Sort of. I went down to Mexico for a couple of years on my mission. It's like a Mormon proselytizing campaign. You go on it when you're nineteen."

"That must've been a wake-up call."

"Yeah, I didn't even know how to do my laundry and now I was pretty much on my own with just a few weeks' Spanish lessons. It was interesting, but it wasn't like here. There's no law there, not really. We saw someone flick a cigarette onto the street once and it bounced and hit the tire of this car that was parked at the curb. The driver of the car got out and he was on his cell phone. He stayed on his cell phone the whole time, even when he got the shotgun out of his trunk and shot the other guy in the chest. Never saw anybody die until then."

Samantha wanted to tell him about the first time she saw someone die, but hesitated. It was when she was seven years old. A friend of hers had been hit by a car when they were playing near the street. The body of the little boy flew up at least twenty feet and landed with a dull thud, a twisted mesh of bones and sinews and organs. Sam had been sprayed with blood and she stood frozen in the street, staring at the body.

"Ladies and gents," Agent Donner said, "our cabs are here."

They loaded up into two separate cabs, Sam riding with Duncan as the other three rode together in a separate vehicle. The cabs hopped onto a long stretch of highway. They were surrounded by everglade forest: thick vegetation with swampy land surrounding it. It looked like the kind of place someone could easily get lost in.

There were few other cars on the road as they sped down the highway and turned off an exit that appeared to just lead into the forest. But they veered left and saw a small motel tucked away in a small clearing.

"Wow," Duncan said, "I've seen less creepy motels in horror movies."

"We won't be here long."

They parked and got out of the cabs as Agent Donner paid and then went to the front desk. Sam and Cami were put into one room and Cami said something about taking a piss and ran into the bathroom, stripping down before she was even there. Samantha collapsed on the bed, and closed her eyes.

It was four hours later that Sam was woken by the sensation of her cell phone buzzing in her pocket. She clicked it off without looking at who it was. Turning to the bed next to her, she saw Cami fast asleep, nude with a blanket loosely thrown on her.

Samantha rose and headed for the shower. She was in there so long that the water began to grow cool and she turned it off and stepped out, changing into a fresh pair of jeans and a zip-up Calvin Klein hoodie. When she got out of the shower, Benjamin was in the room and Cami was dressing in shorts and sandals.

"So Billy's got someone flying us into Mexico and then we're heading down to Peru with no stops," Benjamin said, hopping on the bed and maniacally tapping his hand against the nightstand. "Should be a blast."

"Why don't we just take a commercial flight straight to Lima?" Sam asked.

"Billy thinks Ralph's trying to quarantine us and I agree with him."

Agent Donner poked his head in. "Let's go, guys. Our ride's here."

CHAPTER 38

Samantha thought they couldn't have found a worse pilot if they had put out an ad for one. He had the smell of alcohol on his breath and the cabin had the distinct odor of marijuana. The pilot concentrated only long enough to get in the air and then lit a joint and took a few puffs.

Agent Donner was sitting behind her and she turned to him and saw that he was a few words away from completing the *New York Times* crossword. "Is this plane used for drug smuggling?"

"Probably not anymore. Too many busts, too much product lost. But it most certainly was a while ago. Now they have tunnels underneath San Diego and they just bring the drugs up that way." He looked to the pilot. "Don't worry about him, though. He's got a few ghosts in his skull but he's one of the best pilots I've ever met. Well, that's not true, but he's competent enough to get us there." He returned to his crossword.

Duncan glanced to her and then the pilot as the plane dipped down. The pilot was itching his leg. He took back the controls and the plane leveled out.

"I think we'll die from him before the virus," Duncan said.

"Unless you know how to fly this thing, I think we're stuck with him."

"He looks like he's nodding off. I think I'll go keep him company."

"Good idea."

Sam watched as he went up to the cockpit and then she pulled out her iPad. She opened Facebook and ran through a few status updates. She realized she hadn't logged on since almost a month ago.

She read for over twenty minutes and as she was about to log off, her instant messenger dinged. It was Ralph Wilson.

What the hell do you think you're doing, Sam?

She hesitated, and then replied, *Still with Agent Donner and the rest. Heading to Peru as planned.*

Why weren't you on your flight to Fort Lauderdale?

Long story. She hesitated again and glanced around to see if anyone could see what she was typing. Once she felt safe no one could, she wrote, *Were you going to quarantine us?*

There was a long pause and then, *Yes.*

Why lie about it? If you would've asked me I would have gladly self-quarantined.

I didn't know that. You don't really know anyone until you encounter a crisis situation. I didn't know how you would react and whether Donner would pull rank. Cornell most certainly would have called friends and gotten my order overturned.

You didn't have to do this.

Yes I did. Where are you right now?

Left Mexico several hours ago. Somewhere over South America.

Sam, I highly recommend you turn around right now. One of you may be contagious.

No one showing any symptoms. Will keep an eye out. I don't think I could get anybody to turn around if I tried.

Understood. Have to run, someone in my office. One more thing, Agent Donner does not work for the FBI. I don't know who he is, Sam. Please be careful. I'm urging you again to take the next flight back to the States the second you get a chance. Good luck.

Wait, Ralph? You there? Ralph? You there???????

There was no response and the green icon had turned off. She switched off Facebook and glanced back to Donner who had completed his crossword and was resting his head on the seat, his eyes closed.

The plane jerked hard to the right and Sam was flung against the cabin wall. She looked to the cockpit and saw that the pilot had nodded off for a second and Duncan had grabbed the controls. The pilot was up now and apologizing.

"He's okay," Duncan said, "just a little tired is all. We'll be okay."

He looked to Sam, and blew out a nervous breath. Mouthing the words, *Pray now*, to her as the plane began its decent to a runway just outside of Lima, Peru.

CHAPTER 39

Samantha had always been interested in visiting Lima. Ever since she had studied the Inca culture and their mysterious disappearance. But she didn't get to experience Peru now other than through the window of a rickety cab, driven by a man that was drunker than their pilot. The architecture of the buildings was magnificent; the people appeared lively, the older ones wearing traditional Peruvian clothing. Handmade and colorful. The young ones dressing as any twenty-something would dress on the streets of London or New York.

But watching a city pass by through the window of a cab was the same as watching it on television. She was removed from it; an observer. She wanted to go out, eat the food, talk to the people, walk the streets. But that was impossible, Benjamin assured her. The next flight to Iquitos was leaving in less than an hour and there wouldn't be another one for five days.

They had exited the cabs at the airport and were waiting for the plane to refuel. She stepped away from the others with Duncan and they sat on worn seats and watched the tarmac of the small airport outside.

"Ralph told me something weird," she said. "He said that Billy Donner doesn't work for the FBI and he doesn't know who he is."

"Really?"

"Yeah, and I believe him."

"Well, one of the things I've found working for the military is that those secretive guys—CIA, FBI, NSA—they never say what agency they're actually with. Delta Force agents tell people they're mechanics and janitors. They use a lot of deception to make sure no one can track them. He seems like a G-man to me. Maybe he's a spook. Best cover would be law enforcement. People wouldn't ask too many questions."

The humidity and heat were nearly unbearable. Sam felt the heat coming off the walls and pouring through the windows. It felt like a sauna. She stood up and went to the bathroom. Standing over the sink, she splashed cold water on her face and down her neck, over her arms and chest. There were no paper towels so she wiped her skin with her fingers as best she could and then headed outside again. Agent Donner was standing by the windows by himself, staring out at the crystal blue sky.

"It's beautiful here," she said, coming up from behind.

"Yes," he said, not turning around. "I came out here once before, a long time ago. It hasn't changed at all. I like having that consistency. If you leave New York or DC for a decade and go back, you'd think you stepped into a new city."

She walked next to the glass, looking out at a plane that was getting ready for takeoff. "So what made you want to join the Feds?"

"Duty, I guess. If there is such a thing. Maybe it's real, or maybe it just means doing something without any rational reason behind it. I don't know. I'm too old to figure it out I guess."

"How old are you if you don't mind me asking?"

"Fifty-eight."

"What? Really? You don't look a day over forty."

"I appreciate that, but don't ever let the exterior fool you about what the landscape's like on the interior."

"So how long have you been with the FBI?"

"Nineteen years. I was law enforcement before that, and Army before that."

"What'd you do in the Army?"

"This and that. Nothing too exciting." He turned and looked at her. "Can I ask you something now?"

"Sure."

"Why are you here?"

"What do you mean?"

"Benjamin's clearly a fool and the virus is contained on an island. It's unlikely it'll get out. Why did you risk your life coming to this place just to see a woman who is rumored to have survived it?"

"Honestly, I don't know. It doesn't make sense to me either but I just had a feeling that this is where I had to be." She folded her arms, leaning against the glass of the large window. "I think about those people on the island. Seeing loved ones dying slowly with no one around to help. I can't stand it. When I close my eyes, their faces are painted on my lids."

"They did nothing to deserve that, but you did nothing to deserve the guilt you're feeling now. The virus was a force of nature, like a tornado. You couldn't control it."

"No, but I could've stayed and helped. At least I could've tried harder to stay."

"And you'd be dead just like the rest of them. Who exactly would that have helped, Dr. Bower?"

"Sam," Duncan said, "you're going to want to see this."

Samantha walked over. There was a YouTube clip playing on Duncan's cell phone. It was of a news broadcast from Los Angeles. The broadcast ran for a total of five minutes and twenty-seven seconds, but Sam only heard one line. It was a single sentence that rang in her ears and made her knees feel like they were about to buckle:

And again, for those viewers just tuning in, a case of the deadly Honolulu virus known as Agent X has been reported at Good Samaritan Hospital here in Los Angeles.

CHAPTER 40

Ralph Wilson was at LAX within six hours of hearing the news. It was a red-eye flight and he didn't arrive until 1:00 a.m. Pacific, which was 4:00 a.m. Eastern. He felt a fatigue he hadn't felt since his days as a resident at Cedars Sinai, running from room to room in the ER on thirty-six-hour shifts, hoping he wouldn't fall asleep as he sat down to do a patient intake.

He raced through the airport and opted to grab one of the cabs that were ever present outside on the curb instead of renting a car. He stepped out into the night air. It was warm and had a slight taste of exhaust in it. Two cabs were parked at the curb. One was driven by a white man, the other by a black woman. He chose the white male and sat in the back.

"Good Samaritan Hospital."

"You got it."

The cab pulled away and they began to drive. He rolled down his window, hoping for fresh air, but instead got lungfuls of exhaust and low hanging smog. He rolled the window back up.

"What you doin' out at this hour?" the cabbie said.

"What's that?"

"What you doin' out at this hour? Most guys that ride in here with suits as nice as yours don't pop in at two in the mornin'."

He shook his head as he stared out the window. "Cleaning up other people's messes. That seems to be all I do nowadays."

"Better than causin' 'em."

They rode through sections of the city that Ralph hadn't been to in decades. He had lived here once, long ago. Back when the city wasn't exploding with crime and the police were actually seen as the good guys. One thing he remembered vividly was taking walks around Echo Park every night. There would be families walking dogs, mothers pushing strollers, women jogging alone. Those things were impossible to do safely now. The city had transformed itself in such a short amount of time. Cities were like people; tragedy and heartbreak molded them. Pain molded them. Over time, they were unrecognizable.

On the corner of Wilshire several women in lingerie or fur coats with tall high heels paced along the sidewalk. They smiled to him and he smiled back. In a year, many of them would be dead or in jail. During his stay here for graduate school, he had conducted a study on the spread of disease among young prostitutes aged fifteen to twenty-five. He had bought them meals in exchange for their cooperation and most were eager to do it; their pimps only allowing enough food so they didn't starve but that they were always hungry.

He had gone back into the population in exactly one year to track the results and couldn't find a single person he had used. They were all gone, fresh new faces replacing them.

"Good Samaritan," the cabbie said.

Ralph looked up and saw that they were in front of the hospital. He dug out some cash from his wallet and handed it to the man, not bothering to count it. There was only one piece of luggage: a black doctor's bag like a physician from the 1950s would carry. He grabbed it and stepped outside.

The hospital was several stories of dull brick and appeared much like the police headquarters in the movie *Dragnet.* There were palm trees up in front and a few ambulances lined next to each other. Two of the drivers were sitting on the hood, smoking, and they stared silently as Ralph walked by and through the sliding glass doors of the ER.

The reception area wasn't staffed and he noticed a few people hanging out in a room nearby; a nurse and probably the two receptionists that should have been at the desk. Ralph waited a moment to see if they'd noticed him and then walked around the desk. There were a few charts lying out and he glanced through them quickly. He ruffled through some papers that were stacked neatly in a pile and then looked behind him to a large white board that had been made into a grid with marker.

The grid contained names and room numbers of patients. They were in blue with the names of the treating physicians and nurses in orange. Except for one. At the bottom of the list was a patient in red marker: *John Doe.* Under the diagnosis square of the grid, for patient John Doe, it simply said *Flu.*

Ralph glanced at the room number and then headed through the large double doors leading into the treatment area. There was another set of double doors and this one required swiping a key card or buzzing in. He went back out and looked at the board again before heading back and pushing a button on the intercom.

"Can I help you?"

"Yes, I'm Jake Sanders. Melissa Sanders' brother. She's in room 110."

"Okay, I'll buzz you in."

As he came into the treatment area he smiled widely at the staff and headed toward room 110. He came to 110 and looked back; the nurse at the front desk glanced at him. He smiled again and went inside.

Melissa Sanders was asleep but the light over her bed was on. Ralph reached outside and grabbed the chart that was in a holder against the wall. He flipped through it. The treating physician thought it might be Alport Syndrome, an inherited disorder that damages the vessels in the kidneys. He stared at her a moment and then stepped outside and replaced the chart. The nurse was staring at her computer. He headed down the hall.

The linoleum and harsh lighting as well as the smell of antiseptic made him miss his treating days. When he would get so tired he'd forget to eat for periods of twenty hours or more. But there was camaraderie there, a shared purpose among the staff and physicians. His days were now filled with board meetings and administrators and he sometimes longed to just hang out in a lounge and gossip.

He was at room 153 when he heard boots stomping behind him. Two security guards were running down the corridor straight toward him. He glanced into the room and saw the open window and wondered if he could make it down the street and call a cab somewhere before the police got here.

No, that was ridiculous. He had nothing to be afraid of. Under the direction of the president, the secretary of Health and Human Services was given emergency powers in dealing with a health crisis. He would just claim he was acting under those orders; the bureaucracy was so thick no one would be able to say otherwise.

He placed his bag down on the floor and kept his hands down to his sides to show them he was non-threatening, but they didn't stop running. He thought maybe they meant to tackle him but then noticed they weren't looking at him at all but past him. They sprinted past without so much as a glance.

A nurse and a CNA were running after them. Ralph managed to step in front of the CNA.

"What's going on?"

"Sir, just stay in your room please."

"My sister's a patient here. Please tell me what's happening?"

"One of our patients has escaped custody. Now please go back to your sister's room. Let us handle this."

Ralph stepped aside and let her run past. It was possible that they had a suspected criminal here and while under watch he escaped. All gunshot wounds were reported to the police and most of the gangsters in any major city knew to get treated and sneak out before the cops got there.

But he had a feeling that wasn't what this was.

Ralph watched them run down the hall and then decided to go the other way. The front doors were too heavily manned. You'd have to be a fool to run through them, and the ER was the busiest section of the hospital this time of night. The other floors, though, especially the top floors, which in any hospital usually contained the administrative offices, were nearly empty past nine. If someone were smart, they would go to the top floor and find a way to climb down.

Ralph hopped onto the nearest elevator. He pushed the button to the eighth floor. He leaned against the elevator as it rose, tilting his head back and closing his eyes. Fatigue was making his neck ache and giving him a migraine.

The elevator buzzed and the doors slid open. Ralph stepped off.

The floor was dark and only a third of the lights were on; an effort to cut costs that most hospitals were employing now. The corridor ran both to his left and right equal distances and he chose to go right. He could see his reflection in the windows at the end of the corridor. He resembled his father and it sent a chill down his spine.

He turned left and went past the restrooms and the vending machines. The floors in this hospital were massive and he thought it could take days to find someone in here.

Ralph walked another twenty minutes and then sat down near the lounge. He needed a break. A television was up on the wall with a remote on the reception desk and he grabbed it and sat back down.

He kept the volume off and flipped through the channels until he came to a fishing show. The boat was out on the Pacific somewhere—he could tell from the sapphire blue water—and the sky was cloudless. He wished he was there now, fishing and soaking up sun and thinking about…nothing. Rather than being stuck in an empty hospital doing what he was about to do.

He watched the show a long time when he heard a sound. It was muffled, coming from a far room, but it was enough. He rose and quietly followed the sound down the corridor. It was coming from a small room to his right. The lights were off. He reached in and turned them on.

A young woman sat on a gurney, her face in her hands, weeping. She gasped when the lights came on and looked up. Her eyes were rimmed red and her face was pale with splotchy patches of white. She looked healthy but malnourished. The only giveaway that something was wrong was the crusted blood that stained her teeth and the corners of her mouth.

"Please," she said, "I don't want to go back."

Ralph took a breath and sat down on the black stool against the wall. "You're the patient, right? John Doe? The one that's suspected of being infected with Agent X? Clever calling you John Doe. I could have walked past you in the hall and I wouldn't have even thought about it being a woman."

"I don't want to go back?"

"Go back where, honey?"

"Downstairs. They want to quarantine me in a room and they said I can't see my family anymore. They said they're gonna lock the doors."

"They have to. You're carrying something extremely dangerous inside you right now. The people here don't even know how dangerous it is. Otherwise, you never would have had the opportunity to get away."

"Please," she begged, "I have a fiancé. I just want to go home."

"You look healthy enough to me. Were you in Hawaii recently?"

"Yes?"

"How did you get back to the mainland?" She didn't say anything. "Don't worry, I'm not the cops. I'm a doctor."

"They were letting people in the Army off. I bought a uniform and a fake ID from this guy that was sellin' 'em and they let me get on one of the planes."

"How many other people bought uniforms and IDs?"

"I don't know. There were three other people with me. I don't know how many others."

Ralph nodded, melancholy on his face. "The will to survive. It never ceases to amaze me." He reached into his bag and came out with a syringe and bottle with a white label. He stuck the needle through the rubber top of the bottle and pulled up an amber fluid.

"What's that?" the girl said.

"It's to help you relax. You're frantic. Stress aggravates your condition."

"I don't want it."

Ralph took a cotton ball out of the bag along with a Band-Aid and then approached her.

"I said I don't want it."

"You need it."

"No I don't. Get away from me."

"Listen to me," Ralph said, showing her his palms in a placating gesture. "If you don't get this shot and sleep through the night, you will overwork your endocrine and cardiovascular systems. It could literally give you a stroke. We've seen it in other patients with your condition. I'm just going to give you the shot and then let the staff know where you are. They'll take care of you. As soon as you're better, they'll release you. I'll see what I can do about your fiancé coming to visit you here."

She didn't speak or move. Her lip quivered a little and Ralph didn't push it. He stood silently until she was ready.

"What's in it?"

"It's Mebaral. A sedative. You'll feel like you're slipping into a warm bath. It'll be euphoric at first and then you'll sleep like you've never slept before."

She looked away a moment, and then held out her arm.

Ralph came over and wiped an area just underneath her bicep with the cotton ball. She didn't notice that he hadn't used any antiseptic to clean the area; he wasn't worried about her getting an infection.

He injected her and then withdrew, gently caressing her forearm, and he laid her back on the gurney and sat next to her. He held her hand; her breathing was slow and growing labored.

"I feel weird."

"I know," he said.

"Wait…wait…I don't like this. I don't like this, Doctor. Please stop it. It feels like my head is burning."

"It is. It's potassium. It's slowly suffocating you and soon your heart will stop. People will think it was a natural death, probably brought on by Agent X."

"No," she said, her eyelids dipping and then opening again. "No. Ple…please."

"I'm sorry. There's no other way."

"No," she said, attempting to cry. "No no…please."

"I'm sorry," he said, gripping her hand tighter.

She wept for a few moments and he didn't interrupt her. She looked up at him, their eyes locking. Ralph wanted to look away, but didn't. There was a measure of respect involved.

"I have to tell you somethin'," she said, her breathing growing difficult. "About the other people."

"What is it?" She mumbled something. "I didn't understand you." There was more mumbling. Ralph hoped he hadn't moved too soon; perhaps she had information that could help him track down the three others that had snuck off the island with her.

He leaned down close to her, staring into her eyes. They were blue, but he saw that they were growing dim and wondered if it was life leaving her body or the disease eating away at her. The edges of the whites of her eyes were dark black; blood was seeping into them. Soon, she would be blind.

"What is it, honey?"

It happened too fast for him to notice. She seemed meek, mild mannered. Weakened from the disease and unable to defend herself. He hadn't seen her coming.

He reached up and touched his face. The thick glob of black spit, mingled with her blood and mucus, dripped through his fingers. He jumped off the gurney as the girl laughed.

Ralph ran to the bathroom and ran the hot water. He splashed his face as much as he could, knowing the ooze had gotten into his eyes and onto his lips. The water burned him but he didn't stop. He took soap and scrubbed his face until it was raw. Rummaging through the contents of a shelf, he found packaged iodine sponges and wiped his face before repeating the hot water and soap.

He wasn't sure how long or how many times he repeated this but it must have been several dozen because his face felt like it had been stuck in a furnace. He stood over the sink, panting, looking at his eyes in the mirror. Had it gone into his mouth? Or had it hit his forehead and dribbled down, missing the orifices of his face and just dripping off his lips?

He stepped out into the room. The woman lay still on the gurney. He walked over to her. Her eyes still had life in them, but she wasn't breathing. It'd be six minutes until brain death. He wanted to reach out and slap her across the face. Instead, he sat down again next to her, and held her hand.

A few minutes later, he saw the light in her eyes fade and he closed her lids and said a prayer. He rose and took his bag and left the room, turning the lights off behind him.

CHAPTER 41

When Sam had thought of Iquitos, Peru, she had seen degraded huts about to fall onto the muddied floors they covered, swarms of mosquitos, meat hanging to dry on long ropes between trees. Instead, she saw a perfectly modest city with paved roads, plenty of apartment buildings, and red Spanish-tile churches and government buildings that could have been found in many European countries.

The plane landed on a small airstrip outside the city and she watched the massive green trees and lush grasslands that lay before her. There was another side to the city; shantytowns where the poor were huddled in the huts she had imagined. Some of the children were wearing little more than shorts, their feet hardened like clay from not possessing any shoes. As the rented cars with the young drivers pulled to a stop and they climbed aboard, Sam stared at the hovels. She could see families inside them, and not just nuclear families. Probably uncles, aunts, cousins, and grandparents. Many of the huts didn't look like they were any larger than studio apartments.

She rode with Duncan and Agent Donner and they wound through the city streets, avoiding bicyclists and rickshaws and the occasional donkey hauling coffee beans or rice. They drove for what seemed like an hour and Agent Donner spoke to the driver in Spanish. The driver, suddenly, looked like he had seen a ghost.

"What'd you say?" Duncan asked.

"I told him that he shouldn't push his hours up or we won't use him again."

Samantha said, "That's all?"

"That's all. Why?"

"He looks frightened."

"They rely heavily on the tourists. They don't want to piss anybody off and have me leave bad reviews all over the place."

From there, it only took five minutes to get to the hotel. It was a baby-blue structure of three stories and they parked at the curb. The driver hopped out first and collected their bags, taking them inside. Agent Donner got out and stretched his back, inhaling a deep breath of the city air.

"You know," he said, "even ten years ago the air here was crisp and refreshing. Like the air at the top of a mountain. It tastes like exhaust now. It's a shame our species had to ruin that. We'll miss it when it's gone, I think." He looked to a small café across the street. "I'm going to grab some lunch. Anyone care to join me?"

"I'm starving," Duncan said. He turned to Sam. "You in?"

"No, I'm exhausted. I need to get some shut-eye."

"Suit yourself. Come by if you change your mind."

The two men walked across the street as Sam watched. Agent Donner never let his back relax; it was always straight, held stiff as if he were waiting for an inspection. She got the feeling that he was a man that never lost control.

She walked inside the hotel. She was going to ask the desk clerk in her broken Spanish where her room was. But he already held out a key that said 121 on it and she smiled and said, "Gracias," before heading down the hallway.

Sam found room 121 and unlocked the door. A couple was in the room, laughing. They were dressing and it was such a surprise Sam didn't say anything. They quickly put on their clothes and snuck past her, apologizing. She glanced to the bed and saw that it was messy.

She walked in and sat down on the couch, asleep before she could think about whether they had used the couch as well.

Duncan sat across from Agent Donner at a table that was set outside on a veranda. There were a few other people there, mostly tourists, and they sipped coffee and beer and ate snacks rather than large meals.

Agent Donner ate an odd smelling beef stew and drank something that smelled like paint thinner. Duncan watched him a while and Donner said, "What?" without looking up from his food.

"Nothing. I've just never seen someone eat something that smelled so bad with that much gusto."

"This is nothing. In Ghana, there's a large rodent that I still don't know the name of. They barely cook it over a large spit and then slice off pieces, fur and all, and if you don't eat it with them, because food is so scarce and they're extending their hospitality, they'll never talk to you again."

"What were you doing in Ghana?"

"Research."

"On what?"

"Their water supply. Water's privatized over there and warlords own it. You think Microsoft or Standard Oil were monopolies? You should see a methed-up warlord with a machete try to keep his market share."

Duncan took a sip of coffee. It was so strong it made his nostrils burn. "You seem to have travelled a lot. Didn't know the FBI paid for so many flights."

"New world now. We're not the former accountants in black suits anymore."

"How long was your training in Quantico for?"

Duncan watched as Agent Donner wiped his lips with a napkin and then looked him in the eyes. "Twenty-one weeks. Why do you ask?"

"Just curious. Seems like an interesting job to me. So what'd you do after Quantico?"

"I was in violent crime and then computer forensics before being transferred to terrorism after 9-11. If you're so curious, you should apply. The bureau could always use good scientists."

"No, I can barely stomach working for the government as it is. Don't know how I'd feel if I actually impacted people's lives."

Agent Donner took a long sip of water and then placed the glass down as if to signal that he was done with the conversation. He looked at Duncan, their eyes locking. A grin came over his face. "We should go. You need some rest before we go trekking through the jungle together."

CHAPTER 42

Sam woke sometime in the evening to a knock at her door. For a moment, she wasn't sure where she was, the surroundings completely alien, and then she heard Duncan's voice on the other side of the door.

"You awake, Sam?"

"One sec," she said. She made her way to the door, stretching her neck, which had tightened up like ball of rubber bands. It shot pain through her head and she rolled it in a circle before opening.

"Hey," Duncan said, "you slept a while."

"What time is it?"

"Almost seven. You ready to go?"

"Where?"

"To the hospital. Benjamin called ahead and set everything up."

Sam stretched again and then went to find her shoes. Duncan hung by the door, staring off into space.

"Is this how you pictured life as a scientist would be?" he said.

"I see myself as a doctor, not a scientist."

"Not me. Maybe that's why I feel so out of place here. I should be in the lab with Pushkin, running cultures."

"Then why'd you come?"

"For you."

They exchanged glances as she laced up her shoes and followed him out the door.

Outside the heat was causing waves to come up off the ground and the stink of sweat and exhaust filled the air, broken occasionally by a soft breeze that would fill the nostrils with the scent of jungle vines and grass.

Sam went to the edge of the road, as there was no sidewalk. A few merchants approached her, hawking cheap homemade goods, and she politely turned them down. Eventually a car came for them and Duncan, Sam, and Agent Donner, who had just run out of the building in time to meet them, climbed aboard.

"Ben and Cami are already down there," Agent Donner said.

"Holly's not contagious," Duncan said, "but I had Ben bring some gear for us. I think we should treat her as potentially infectious."

As the car got moving, Sam opened her iPad and began writing a document. It was a makeshift journal; just something to use to help jog her memory later on if she should need it. If this girl did provide something useful, maybe the journal could later become an article in the *New England Journal of Medicine.*

They reached the hospital and got out. It wasn't much more than five stories of what appeared like an office building but there were ambulances coming and going and she saw doctors in white coats smoking outside with nurses. They followed several people inside the double glass doors and Agent Donner spoke with someone at the desk before they climbed onto the elevator.

"They don't have her in isolation anymore," he said. "She's just on the third floor in a room."

"Why is she still here?" Sam asked.

"No idea. I assume observation. But from what Benjamin told me she's recovered completely."

They stepped off onto the third floor and it was nearly empty. A few gurneys were being pushed around, medical staff were speaking in hushed tones in the hallway, but there wasn't the flurry of patients she expected in a moderately-sized city in South America.

They walked to the end of the hallway and saw Benjamin speaking on his cell phone. He seemed agitated and was pacing back and forth in the hallway. He saw them, ended his conversation, and put the phone away.

"You guys," he said, "it's not pretty."

"What do you mean?" Sam said.

"You'll have to see it for yourself. I'm just warning you. Your gear's right there in that suitcase."

They took out their suits, Kevlar gloves, booties, and clear plastic facemasks. After they suited up Sam was the first to open the door and step inside.

The first thing she noticed was Cami in a chair by the bed. She wasn't suited and was just sitting in shorts and a tank-top with her legs crossed near Holly Fenstermac.

Holly's hands were what she noticed next. They appeared as if they had been boiled in hot oil. They had large swelling balls of skin and fluid over them and Sam thought of the old scripture for Job, cast with boils for a bet between God and Satan, innocent and undeserving of such a fate.

Sam's eyes followed the hands up the arms, which were filled with the same boils. Though she knew they only looked like boils. They were fluid-filled blisters and they took up every inch of skin. She had seen them in some of the patients in Honolulu, and in textbooks for smallpox.

Her face was covered with so many blisters you could only see the general shape. Her lips were swollen shut and even her eyes were covered in maculopapular rashes and the beginnings of blisters.

Cami was speaking softly to the woman, but it didn't appear that she was responsive.

"Is she conscious?" Sam asked, barely able to get the words out.

"No," Cami said. "I've been speaking to her for over an hour and she hasn't responded."

"I've never…I've never seen—"

"I know," Cami said. "I haven't seen it this bad either. I can't even imagine the pain she's going through. The blisters on her corneas have blinded her and the ones in her ear canals are making it difficult for her to hear. One of the doctors told us she only responds to touch, but that hasn't worked either."

Duncan came close to the patient and examined her eyes. He stepped back and looked at Sam. "I wouldn't want survival like this," he whispered, just in case the patient could hear.

"Me neither."

"Come on. Let's go."

As Sam turned to leave, a noise startled her. It sounded like an animal's hiss and she realized it was the patient. Cami leaned in close.

"I'm here for you," Cami said. "My name is Dr. Mendoza. I'm here for you."

The patient opened her eyes. The eyes themselves were overtaken with deep scarring from the blisters and it appeared as if they were covered in dried and cracking skin. Her head tilted and she began to speak in an almost inaudible volume.

Cami would whisper, "Yes," or "No," every once in a while but for the most part let Holly speak. After about half a minute, Holly tilted her head up again, glanced once to Samantha, and then closed her eyes.

"What did she say?" Agent Donner asked.

Cami wiped the tears away from her eyes. "She said she wants to be buried in the States. She's from California and she wants to be buried there next to her mother. We need to make sure that can happen."

"What else?" Agent Donner said. Sam assumed he was thinking what everyone else in the room was thinking; there was no way they would let her body return to the States.

"She said something about a canister. Some canister they found on their tour and that's how they got sick."

"She didn't say any of them were bit by an animal?" Duncan said.

"No, she said it was a canister. They found it and that's when Michael got sick."

Agent Donner said, "Where is the canister now?"

"They gave it to someone in a village, a little boy."

"What village?"

"I don't know."

"Ask her."

Cami looked to Agent Donner. "No. Let her sleep."

"She's slept enough, Dr. Mendoza. Ask her what village. You can ask more gently than I can. If I have to wake her up, she won't enjoy it."

Cami stared at him a moment and looked like she was about to say something, but didn't. Instead, she leaned down next to the patient's ear and whispered something. The patient whispered something back but it was inaudible to Sam.

"She says it was a Pisac village on the route they took. She gave it to a little boy there."

Agent Donner immediately left the room. Sam didn't follow. She stood quietly and stared at the woman lying in the gurney, half alive and half dead, blind and going deaf. Soon the world would be nothing to her but darkness and pain.

"We can't leave her like this," Sam said.

Cami nodded. "I know. Please leave."

"I can help."

"No, just leave. I brought us down here. I talked Ben into coming. She can't suffer like this. This is something I have to do. Please just leave, Dr. Bower."

Sam waited a moment longer, and then turned to leave the room. Duncan held her by the arm. She wasn't sure if it was to help her or himself.

CHAPTER 43

Dr. Gerald Amoy looked down at the streets of Honolulu. Streets he had once loved and known like the inside of his home. He grew up running around on these very streets with a gang—not much more than just some neighborhood kids calling themselves a gang. They would steal candy bars and throw water balloons off buildings. Later, in their teenage years, they would break into cars and sell marijuana at school. As far as he knew, he was the only one of his childhood friends that hadn't been to jail.

"Doctor?"

He turned and saw a nurse, Heather Yang, standing there in blue scrubs. She had volunteered to stay at the hospital and help those that needed help; one of only twelve out of a staff of hundreds.

"Yes?"

"Our runner came back from the urgent care clinic. They're out of antibiotics as well. They did have a few boxes of gauze and rubber gloves but I think we were good on those."

"Okay," he said, sighing. "What about the pharmacies?"

"I've heard they were cleared out a long time ago."

"They might not have taken the antibiotics."

"Maybe. I don't think your average dopehead knows the difference. They probably took everything to sort it out later."

"Send someone around anyway."

"You got it."

“And Heather? It’s coming to the point where we’re not doing anything but keeping these people comfortable. I don’t need you here for that. You should go home.”

She looked to the floor. “Tim died two weeks ago.”

Amoy didn’t say anything at first. It was something he had heard so much of that he’d grown numb to it. But he knew that some sort of condolences were the proper response and so he said, “I’m sorry. I didn’t know.”

She nodded, fighting the tears that were rolling down her cheeks. “This takes my mind off it. I’d like to stay if that’s okay.”

“Of course. Please let the rest of the staff know that they can leave at any time.”

When she left, Amoy collapsed into the chair at his desk. He was exhausted; his back and neck felt like they’d been pumped full of acid. His head ached constantly and if he didn’t try to take catnaps every couple of hours he’d develop a migraine. He looked out the window again and wondered if he should have left when he had the chance.

Some of his friends had left on yachts to port in harbors that would keep their departure quiet. He knew many people had taken boats to the nearest island, Molokai. Many were inexperienced seamen and had no doubt been stranded or drowned. It was thirty-two miles of treacherous water. An annual race had developed there. World Class yacht masters came from all over to compete there, knowing the reputation of the waters as some of the most treacherous in this hemisphere.

Of course, the only people with boats were those of means, which meant that only the poor were absolutely stuck on the island. He wondered if it had always worked this way throughout history.

There was commotion outside. He looked down and saw a group of men trying to tear down the barrier that had been built at the entrance of the hospital. At first it was to keep people in and make sure the patients didn't get out to infect others. But more and more, it was becoming a barrier to keep people out that were looking to raid the hospital's supplies.

He ran downstairs to find the nurses gathered around the front entrance. Heather was standing with her hands on her hips, staring at the front doors.

"There's a lot of 'em this time," she said.

"Has anyone told them we don't have anything?"

"They're starving. I don't think they're going to care."

Amoy ran down the hall to check on the patients. Three days ago there had been over sixty in the ER. Now there were less than twenty. One of the major concerns had been what to do with the bodies. They didn't want to leave them outside as he wasn't entirely certain this virus wasn't airborne, so instead they piled them up on the fifth floor, hoping that the height would contain the smell. It didn't.

He found Doug, their only security officer, asleep on a gurney.

"Doug, wake up. They're back."

He roused himself awake and swung his legs over the gurney. He rubbed the sleep out of his eyes before standing.

"Yeah, so?"

"There're a lot this time."

Doug stepped out of the room and went down the hall, Amoy behind him. They came to the front entrance where they all stood around, staring at the doors as if an alien were about to land on earth and they were to be the first contact they would have.

"Fuck me," Doug said. "How many a 'em are there?" He turned to Amoy. "I only got six rounds and a Taser."

Amoy stared at the doors a long time. The furniture they had piled in front of the doors was slowly decreasing as the men outside patiently worked to clear a path.

"I'll be right back," Amoy said.

He ran upstairs and to the second floor. He went to a window facing down on the street and looked down.

"We don't have anything here," Amoy shouted to the men. "There's nothing for you here."

One of the men, a white male with tattoos over his bald head and no shirt on, wiped his brow with the back of his arm. He looked to Amoy and said, "Well that ain't true now. You got yourself a few honeys in there. They be worth something."

Amoy felt a chill down his spine. "They've stayed here to help the sick at the risk of their own lives. Leave them alone."

"Don't worry, we'll take good care a 'em. They gonna get lots a lovin' from the homies."

Amoy stepped away from the window. He stood there silently; his arms limp by his side. All he wanted to do was sit down, so he did. There was a chair behind the desk and he sat and put his feet up, his arms on his chest. There were at least thirty men out there.

He sat staring at the ceiling a long time and began dozing off. After what seemed like an eternity, he heard yelling and screaming and the sounds of shoes running on linoleum downstairs.

Shots began to be fired.

He counted them. One…two…three…four…then there was silence. He heard a woman's scream and then the laughter of men. He felt no emotion at all, only a dull ache in the pit of his stomach, but warm tears flowed down his cheeks. He stood up and headed for the stairs.

He walked up three more flights of stairs and went to the end of the hallway on the fifth floor. Another set of stairs led to the roof and he took them.

The sunshine was bright and warm. A breeze was blowing and it was the type of breeze that under normal circumstances he might have noticed. It carried the salty scent of the ocean and cooled his face, which felt hot though he hadn't been outside all day.

Amoy walked to the edge of the roof and climbed the stone barrier. He looked down to the men that were still outside, and the few that were coming out. He thought they looked like bugs scrambling around and it gave him the adolescent pleasure of feeling bigger and stronger than those around him. He smiled.

And then, he jumped.

CHAPTER 44

Samantha followed Benjamin Cornell, who was led by a guide they'd hired in Iquitos, into the deadly green maze that was the Amazon Rainforest. Ben had translated as the guide explained that, encompassing 1.7 billion acres, the Amazon was the planet's largest eco-region on land and contains—it's believed—more unknown species of insect, bird, rodent, and small mammal than there are catalogued and identified species currently known to science. Wet, tropical rainforests are the richest biomes of life, and the Amazon is king among them all. Sam, who had previously known this, had always wanted to visit the forest.

The bulk of the forest is found in Brazil with only a small fraction found in Peru. But that small portion is rough and uninhabitable for those not accustomed to its harsh climate, its deadly insects, and the constant threat of exposure. The days swell to temperatures over 130°F and the nights, though they have the potential to not be much cooler, can dip to temperatures requiring winter clothing and sleeping bags, depending on the season.

Now that Samantha was here, she couldn't remember why she had wanted to come.

Her mind travelled off and she thought about the last conversation she'd had back in town yesterday. It was with Ralph and they'd spoken over a landline at the hotel.

He sounded weak, as if he hadn't gotten any sleep the few days before they'd talked. He coughed incessantly, every few sentences, but when Sam would press him on it all he'd say was, "I'm fine, I'm fine," and then move on to a different topic.

"I'll be back in eight days," Samantha had assured him. "Four in the forest and four to get back to Atlanta. Hopefully there'll still be a job waiting for me."

"Always, my dear," he said wistfully. "Always."

They'd said goodbye and Ralph told her that he'd like to speak with her again after they found whatever it was they thought they were looking for. But he'd said that in case they didn't speak again, he wanted her to know that careers in the government didn't last.

"You'll love the CDC," he'd said, "but she won't love you."

He sighed and said goodbye and Samantha had sat for nearly five minutes afterward, pondering why he would have ended the conversation the way he had.

Sam stopped and took a sip out of a Nalgene bottle that was attached to a backpack that carried her supplies. Villages along the way would offer food and shelter for next to nothing, but just in case, their guide had told them, it was best to bring your own camping gear. You never knew who would offend one of the local Indians and cause the group to be denied entry to the village for the night.

Duncan, Cami, and Agent Donner were behind her. All of them, panting and sweating and red-faced, had to stop every mile or so for a sip of water. The humidity soaked their clothes and made them feel sticky and wet; like they'd taken a bath in cola. The heat cooked it onto their skin so that it would begin to itch. The guide told them if they didn't stop and rest to air themselves out, the skin that was covered by clothing could peel.

"You doin' okay?" Duncan looked at Sam and wiped his forehead with a bandana.

"Yeah," she said, taking another sip of water. "How far you think we've gone?"

"Twenty miles maybe, give or take a few. I have a pedometer on my iPod but that ran out of juice. Anybody's cell working?"

They all checked; none of them were getting reception.

Benjamin yelled out behind him, "Don't slow down. We've got a village about ten miles from here. We can make it before nightfall if we hurry."

They continued the slow, grinding work of putting one foot in front of the other as their feet swelled in their boots and the last drops of moisture leaked from their skin. Sam kept her head low but would occasionally glance up at the beautiful scenery around her. It appeared like something out of an Ansel Adams photo. It was haunting and beautiful simultaneously, and somehow, perhaps subconsciously, it frightened her. The fear of the unknown. Deep in this jungle were things that lay undiscovered, just waiting for a living organism to pass by.

The day grew hotter and the insects seemed to get worse. They were a constant blanket around her, their buzzing growing unbearable in her ears. They went for the moist parts of her face: her nostrils, eyes, mouth. And they were unrelenting. She would bat several of them away only to have double that amount swarm in to take their place.

Soon her Nalgene bottle was empty and she began getting pasty-mouthed. It amazed her how quickly dehydration set in. When her lids closed they felt like sandpaper against her eyeballs and the warm breeze that was blowing gently through the rainforest wasn't helping.

The terrain grew rough for a while, turning uphill on a steep slope, but it soon declined and she leaned back and relaxed her thigh muscles, letting gravity do the work.

"There's a bug out here," Duncan said from behind her, out of breath and panting, "that stings you on your lips or in your eyes. But it's not a sting, it's an injection. It lays its eggs inside you and you won't even know until you get a big bump that eventually hatches."

"Thanks," Sam said.

Sam counted three and a half hours before the dense vegetation began to clear and they were in a valley. She could see huts in the distance and as they drew closer she could make out children playing in front of the village, goats tied to stakes, a couple of donkeys, and the glistening brown figures of the villagers. They dressed modestly compared to what she expected; the women's breasts were exposed but other than that, they covered up everything that would have been covered back home. Some of the men wore sneakers and T-shirts. The Nike slogans and 80s mantras on the T-shirts—thrift store donations all of them—looked out of place in the serene and majestic background of this lush wilderness.

The guide began speaking with a group of men that had come out to meet them. Sam noticed that two of the men were carrying rifles, a gift from the modern world. No doubt along with cigarettes and alcohol and chewing tobacco. Indigenous tribes rarely adopted anything good from civilization; there was no money in teaching them about books and computers. Instead, Coca-Cola and Marlboro were the greeters at the door.

The guide turned and spoke to Benjamin in hushed tones before Benjamin turned to the others.

"Okay," he said. "He says we can stay here for fifty cents apiece. That includes dinner tonight and breakfast tomorrow."

"That's nothing," Cami said. "I think we should pay them more. Dinner by itself'll be worth more than that."

"No," Agent Donner said, "we can't let them think we have money to burn. They'll rob us and dump our bodies in the river for the piranhas. In case you haven't noticed, there's no police out here."

"He's right, Cam," Benjamin said. "These people are noble 'cause they live off the land, but they don't think the same way we do. They only see survival."

"Noble my ass," Duncan said, motioning with his chin toward the village.

They turned to see what he was looking at. A man was strangling a woman while she fought against him with everything she had. As she fell to the ground, he began to kick her in the head before some of the elders ran over to restrain him. No one helped the woman up.

Sam sprinted over as Benjamin yelled, "No, don't get involved."

The woman was bloodied and the strangulation marks around her neck were bright red. Her nose was bleeding profusely and Sam held her hands open, hoping she understood that she was not here to harm. She took a first aid kit out of her pack and used guaze to control the bleeding, tilting the woman's head back and squeezing the nostrils shut. When the bleeding had stopped, Sam checked her other wounds. A bruise on her eye was causing it to swell shut but she had no ice to give her.

"Are you okay? Bueno?" she said, realizing that the odds of her speaking Spanish were no better than her speaking English.

The woman rose without a word and began walking away before disappearing into one of the huts.

"What was that about?" Duncan asked.

Benjamin asked the guide and replied, "He says the woman had disobeyed her husband."

"Disobeyed how?"

Benjamin asked and then translated, "He doesn't know."

Sam rose and turned to see the group of men leering at her, venom in their eyes. The man that had beaten the woman was waving his hands at her, clearly furious and causing a scene, like he wanted to come over and do the same to her. Just in case, Duncan walked over to her and put his hand on her arm.

"Funny thing about being out in the jungle," she said to him. "People seem to forget their civility."

"It's not that, Sam. I think this might be what we naturally are without God."

"Guys," Benjamin shouted, "let's get our huts set up. They're having dinner soon and if we miss it, there won't be any leftovers."

Sam took a deep breath and began walking with Duncan to rejoin the group. She glanced back once to the hut the woman had disappeared into. There was a small child at the door, peering out and she smiled at him. He turned and went back inside.

CHAPTER 45

The hut was small and hot and the floors were just swept dirt but Samantha didn't see any spiders or vermin. It was surprisingly clean considering that it had been made out of jungle plants and mud. There was one cot in the corner and another by the entrance. A small tray with a pitcher of water and a bowl was on one side of the hut and the only light came from the entrance which was nothing more than a flap of cloth covering only a portion of a large hole in the hut.

Dinner had consisted of a chicken that the natives had killed, plucked, and gutted right in front of their guests, throwing their entrails to a few of the village dogs that were roaming around. The chicken was then cut up, thrown in a boiling pot with herbs, potatoes, roots, and a little pink flower that Sam had been told was used for sweetening. The stew was served in bowls made of large leaves and a type of beer was served with it. Sam chose to drink water from a well the village used and Duncan joined her as the rest of them got drunk and ate several bowls of the stew.

As night fell, she rose to go back to her hut and Duncan followed her, proclaiming that he wanted to make sure she was all right. They saw Agent Donner sitting on a carved-out log, sipping beer. He smiled to them and his teeth appeared little and abnormally white in the moonlight.

"How was the feast?" he said.

"You didn't eat?" Sam said.

"I wasn't hungry. I'll have some rice later." He took a long drink of beer. "You know, the village we're going to, I did some reading up. They have a weekly, well I don't even know what you'd call it, an orgy I guess. They get absolutely thoroughly drunk and begin having sex with each other; married or not. Then the men choose fighting partners and usually somebody gets badly hurt if not killed. I've never actually seen one. Should be wild."

"How have you been out here before?" Duncan asked. "This is the middle of BFE. How'd you get out here?"

Donner smiled as he took another drink. "I've been around."

Sam stared at him and they exchanged glances.

"Well you'll have to excuse me, Agent Donner," she said. "I'm pretty tired."

"Of course. Don't let me stop you. Good night."

"Good night."

She walked around him as she went to her hut, Duncan following right behind her. As she was about to go inside and say good night to him as well, he grabbed her by the waist and kissed her warmly on the mouth.

"Sorry," he said when they had separated, "I've been wanting to do that for a while."

She smiled playfully. "Good night, Duncan."

"Good night, Dr. Bower."

She went inside and took off her boots. Duncan was still standing outside but had turned around, looking like a sentry at a post. He was genuinely concerned about her, probably because she was the only white woman in the entire village and they didn't know whether that was prized or not. She smiled again to herself as she lay down, falling asleep to the drunken chatter that was taking place outside.

CHAPTER 46

The morning came with nothing but heat and the stink of moisture soaking into the hut. It was perfectly quiet outside except for the chirp of crickets though the sun was already up. Sam rose and brushed her teeth, using a little water out of her bottle, and pulled her hair back with a rubber band.

The village was empty; a smoldering fire and empty bowls that had contained their potent beer the only evidence that people lived here.

She walked over to the adjacent hut and peeked in. Duncan slept next to Benjamin. There was a third sleeping bag and she was unsure who it belonged to. She heard some banging nearby, like someone was knocking on a metal door, and she walked in that direction to see Agent Donner bent over a pan that was slowly heating up over a fire.

"Eggs?" he said.

"Sure." She sat down against a tree, the shade covering her entire body as she stretched out her legs in the soft dirt. "Have you had any contact with the bureau?"

"No. Why do you ask?"

"I thought you guys always had to be checking in."

"No, they trust us. More or less."

They were silent a long time and he looked over to her, a grin on his face.

"You look like you have something to ask me, Dr. Bower. So just ask."

"You're not FBI. I've dealt with dozens of agents. You don't walk like them, you don't talk like them and you certainly don't act like them. I've never heard of a federal agent abandoning an assignment and chasing some crazed hippie into the jungle."

"Maybe I'm after the crazed hippie? Maybe my assignment is to follow him wherever he goes?"

"Bull. You have no jurisdiction here. You couldn't effectuate an arrest if you wanted to. He would call the police and you might be the one arrested. You wouldn't have let him out of the country if he's what you were after."

He chuckled softly to himself as he flipped some sunny-side up eggs upside down in the pan. "You are clever, aren't you, Samantha? You must get that from your mother. She was an artist, wasn't she? And your father was brilliant too if I recall. It must be really difficult to watch one die and the other's brain get eaten away a little bit every day."

She stared at him a few seconds and said, "How do you know about my mother?"

"Leslie? I know a lot about Leslie. I even saw some of her paintings. She had talent. If she'd have been some drug addict freak instead of a normal housewife the art community might've taken her in as one of their own."

"Who are you?"

"I, Dr. Bower, am a man who maintains balance in all the things." He took out some olive oil from a small container and poured a little more in the pan before taking out the eggs and placing them on a paper plate. He took a slice of bread out of some tin foil, put it on the plate, and placed it in front of Samantha before cracking another two eggs and putting them in the pan.

"What do you mean balance?"

"Well, Duncan there is a Mormon. Have you ever read the Book of Mormon?"

"No."

"Fascinating read. I'm not Mormon, mind you. But it was fascinating nonetheless. Many see it as a spiritual guidebook, but that's not what I saw. I saw a chronicle of war. It's filled with cannibalism, rape, murder, genocide…its essence is that without faith in God, that is our natural state. In Honolulu, for example, the strong are devouring the weak right now. That is what happens without balance. Civilization needs people that can bring balance. That can keep us from the destruction predicted in the Book of Mormon."

"Are you CIA?"

He laughed. "CIA? No, I am definitely not CIA. They devoted decades and hundreds of millions of dollars to fighting the Soviets and they didn't know the Berlin Wall was coming down until the bricks were hitting them on the head. The CIA has failed at every mission they have ever had and you know what their cover is? That we don't hear about their successes, only their failures. Can you believe that nonsense? If their failures can leak, surely their successes would too. But we haven't heard of them because there haven't been any.

"The KGB won their war. They had covert operatives in every branch of government, especially the CIA. They beat the CIA in the spy game, but then lost the politics game. Balance, you see. The Communists pushed too hard and it swung the other way. It's people like me that cause that swing to begin."

Sam watched as he finished cooking his eggs and then threw dirt on the fire. He sat down, pulled out some bread, and dug into his breakfast. "I really wish I had some Tabasco sauce," he said.

"I think you should leave," Samantha said. "Leave now and I won't tell everyone what you just said."

"Oh? And what did I just say? A lecture on balance? And perhaps I should remind you that there are no police within a hundred miles of where we are and you are the only white woman in probably triple that distance. Without me here, these Indians would keep you as their sex slave until they drunkenly raped you to death one night. Then, I don't know, they'd probably cannibalize you I guess. I've heard that was their custom for intruders for centuries before the Peruvian government outlawed it. But then when has the law ever stopped anything?"

"Why are you here, Agent Donn—" Before she finished her sentence she saw the look of amusement on his face. "Of course, your name's not Billy Donner. What are you doing here?"

Duncan walked up from behind them. "Hey," he said to her. "You guys got eggs? Got any left?"

"Of course."

Sam watched as he took out the pan and began to make more eggs. She stood up and walked away, Duncan asking her what was wrong as she brushed past him without a word.

She got far enough away that she couldn't hear what they were talking about and then wondered whether she should go back. Instead, she went to find Benjamin.

She came to the hut and saw him standing outside in his boxer shorts, speaking with the guide. He was scratching his underarms and he glanced to her and stopped. When they had finished speaking, he walked over.

"We got news," Benjamin said, "a town two days from here. There's a rumor that the population was wiped out by a sickness. It's where that canister that Holly mentioned might be."

"We need to talk about Donner."

"What about him?"

"He's not FBI."

"Shit, you just figure that out now?"

"You knew?"

"Hell yeah I knew. What federal agent would quit his job to follow my ass around? But the fucker's good at just about everything. He repaired this old truck the organization had that mechanics didn't think would work anymore. He got Cami a fake passport too."

"What did she need that for?"

"She's illegal. She's not a doctor in the States; she's a doctor in Mexico. Or was, until she helped out a journalist that the cartels tried to kill. They went after her and she ran and kept running until she got to the States."

Sam shook her head. "He's dangerous."

"He's weird, I'll give you that, but I don't know about dangerous. Best I can tell, he's ex-military or something. Probably just looking for a cause and happened to find ours."

"No, he's too smart for that."

"Oh, so now you have to be dumb to believe in what I've dedicated my life to?"

"That's not how I meant it."

"Well, whatever, look, I've known him longer than I've known you so you can chill out or take off. I don't really care. We're heading out to the village. If you're coming, you've gotta pack up now. If not, I'll ask one of the folks in the village to take you back next time they go into town. Might be a while, though."

He turned and walked away, leaving her standing there. She glanced back to Duncan who was sitting against the same tree she had been and eating eggs with Donner. She caught movement off to her right and saw one of the villagers glaring at her. It was a middle-aged man with darkly tanned skin and missing teeth. He was looking at her with madness in his eyes and she knew, just knew, what he was planning to do to her the second he had the opportunity. It was the man that had beaten the woman the previous day.

She thought about it a few moments, and then went inside her hut to pack.

CHAPTER 47

There was really no trail as Samantha was winding her way up the mountain, behind all the others and far behind the guide and Benjamin, who were pumping their arms like distance runners and trudging up the slope. It was a five-hour journey to the village they were heading to but the five hours turned to two days because of the terrain. In many areas, you had to walk so slowly that if you didn't keep your eyes on the ground, you couldn't be sure you were actually moving.

The humidity would go from completely dry to soaking wet in a matter of minutes and they were having to constantly stop and rest under the shade of a tree or next to a cool stream. They could hear the mighty river in the distance now but the guide assured them they weren't near it.

Duncan looked back to her and smiled, slowing his pace to allow her to catch up. She had told him earlier about the conversation with Donner and he shrugged his shoulders and just said, "Since when are they ever honest with us?"

At this point everyone was exhausted and dehydrated. Even to Sam the question of who Donner really was and who he worked for seemed to fade in the distance. He was certainly government and he was certainly some type of law enforcement; that would have to be enough.

They made it to the top of either a large hill or a small mountain and they rested on some boulders, the tree-top view before them a sea of green against the backdrop of a sparkling blue sky.

Sam took out a breakfast bar and ate half, washing it down with half a bottle of water. They didn't speak much and that was fine with her. She removed her pack, feeling the sweet release of lightening weight, and the tightness in her muscles instantly began to disappear. She felt like she could sleep right now, like she could close her eyes and lie down on the rock behind her and not wake up for years. Her stomach was queasy and had been for two days. She was concerned that she may have picked up a trematode worm from the water supply or the food. Iodine pills could only do so much.

"All right," the guide said in his heavily accented English, "it's not far."

They continued down the path as Sam re-strapped her pack. It wouldn't have been as bad if it was just clothing, food, and water, but she also carried biohazard gear and several laboratory kits to run preliminary tests in the field. Porters had offered their services in town for less than five dollars a day and she wished now she'd taken them up on it.

The sun kept beating down on them but mercifully they declined in slope and were eventually on flat ground; the jungle canopy above them shielding most of the sizzling rays that were slowly cooking them.

They hiked until night fell and they set up their tents near what could be considered a path but was little more than a worn trail where animals and people had gone down before. A stream flowed near them but the guide warned that camping next to a water source was a good way to get killed—either by native Indians or the jaguars whose roars were ever-present in the darkness.

The morning came and Sam placed Duncan's pack on him and he did the same for her. He looked to her and brushed aside a strand of hair that was in her eyes.

"We need to have another dinner when we get back to the States," he said.

"We will."

They began the day's long trek before the sun was even up but soon the rejuvenation of sleep was gone and the same exhaustion of yesterday was there.

Sam kept checking her watch incessantly. She tried to fight it, but every few minutes her eyes would wander down to her wrist seemingly on their own. She counted three hours of torturous jungle hiking before they came to a small clearing and the guide stopped and began speaking with Benjamin. He nodded several times and then came back to speak with the group.

"Well," he said when everyone was gathered, "the village is just up ahead past that patch of trees. What do you guys want to do?"

"I'll go," Duncan said, placing down his pack.

"Me too," Sam said. She glanced at Cami to see if she wanted to come but she had already sat down cross-legged on the dirt, leaning against her pack.

"Okay," Benjamin said, "you guys check it out and tell us when we can head up."

It took nearly twenty minutes for both Sam and Duncan to suit up in the yellow biohazard suits they had brought with them. The suits were thinner than those found at USAMRIID or the CDC, but they had two underlayers and thick plastic helmets that had been designed for the handlers responsible for testing chemical weapons.

They walked past the group of trees and saw the outline of huts in the distance. The suits kept the heat and their sweat contained, but abandoning their heavy packs was well worth the trade.

They didn't speak as they neared the village. Duncan was readying sample casings, checking and re-checking the thin glass tubes to make sure any samples he took wouldn't expose everyone else to what was inside.

"I don't know if I love this or hate it," Sam said.

"Hate it. Definitely hate it."

The first thing Sam noticed as they neared the village was a lack of inhabitants, and then the vegetation that engulfed the structures. It eerily reminded her of some of the buildings in Honolulu once maintenance had been halted.

The path they were on led them to the center of the huts. There weren't more than ten of them. It appeared less like a village and more like the encampment of a breakaway family. There were posts around each hut like there had been in the village they'd been to before, posts meant to tie up wildlife, but nothing was tied to them now, the tethers lying empty on the dirt. There was no breeze, just an unsettling motionlessness. In the distance Sam could still hear the river.

"Well," Duncan said, "I guess the first hut's as good as any other."

CHAPTER 48

Ralph Wilson sat on the edge of his bed and vomited into a bucket. When he was through, he lay flat on his back, in a coughing fit so violent he was afraid it would tear his esophagus.

The coughing settled after half a minute and he breathed as deeply as he could and stared at his ceiling. He reached over and rubbed his hand over the empty space next to him, the mattress still dipping where his wife used to lie. Every morning he woke up and thought of her and every morning the pain would be so deep it would feel like hot needles in his guts.

But not today. Today, he was actually glad his wife wasn't here.

He sat up, pushing against the bed with his arms, and swung his legs over the side. His chest felt compacted and it was like he was breathing through water. He sat motionless a while, enjoying the lightheadedness that came with a brain that was starved of oxygen and slowly dying.

He knew what he needed: immediate thoracentesis to remove the fluid that was pooling inside and around his lungs, a blood transfusion, pain medication, preferably Demerol, and supplemental oxygen.

But he also knew that all these had been applied to the patients in Honolulu, and it had only delayed their pain. Perhaps it had even extended their lives by a couple of days, but no more.

He stood up and reached for the crutches he kept by his bedside and rose to his feet, his stomach spasming and causing a coughing fit that spewed blood over his carpet. When he was done, he wiped his lips and chin with the back of his arm before hobbling out of the room.

He headed down to the basement by way of the kitchen. His cell phone was on the table and he glanced at it and then stopped and turned around to retrieve it. He sat down at his table with a grunt, pain shooting through him as if rats were eating his bones and spitting them out in his veins. Every inch of his body was in agony. His eyes were on fire; his heart pounded so hard in his chest he felt it in his throat; his joints felt like they could tear with just the slightest movement. He leaned back in the chair and tried to remain as motionless as possible, but the pain didn't recede.

He picked up his phone and dialed a number. It went to voicemail.

"Sam…I just…I don't know what I'm calling for. I don't know what happened. This all went so bad I can't even remember when it was good." He paused. "Sam, I killed someone. A young woman that was infected with the virus in Los Angeles. She was going to infect other people…I did it for the greater good. That's our job. That's what we signed up for."

Ralph began to cry. He let himself float away on a wave of emotion and when he was through he noticed the message had ended and he redialed.

"I killed her, Sam. And I deserve to go to hell for it. Please let them know. Her family will have a suit against the CDC and the US government; they deserve some sort of compensation. I don't…I don't even know if she had children. If you talk…just tell them that I'm sorry. I'm so sorry. Goodbye, Dr. Bower."

He hung up the phone and threw it on the table, getting back to his feet and hobbling down the steps to the basement. He fumbled in the dark until his hand hit a thin metal cord and he pulled it and the lightbulb flicked on. The light revealed several canisters of gasoline and lighter fluid along with stacks of matches. He tossed his crutches.

The jarring movement of pouring gasoline over the basement and the wooden beams that supported the main floor caused him to begin coughing and this time he couldn't stop. The blood kept spewing and he noticed that his vision blurred. When he reached up and wiped his eyes his fingers came away stained a dark red.

He kept pouring as he kept coughing and bleeding. Eventually, he couldn't see. The blood was pouring so quickly, he couldn't wipe it away fast enough. His heart was pounding from the exercise and it was causing the blood to shoot out like a fountain. He was eventually left looking at the ceiling but he didn't remember collapsing.

He tried to stand but found his legs weren't responding. His head was throbbing so badly he thought that he had gone blind but realized it was just the pain, searing his vision with white hot flashes. He glanced to the matches on a metal worktable. He could no longer stand or didn't have the will to so he just rolled over and rolled over again until he felt the metal leg of the table against his ribs. He took a moment to rest and then reached up, gripping the side of the table, and pulled himself up enough to grab a set of matches before falling back down again.

He was blind now, the blood filling his eyes and not draining. He felt the matches with his fingertips, the grainy surface of the strike pad, the smooth wood of the match. He held them a long time, inhaling the fumes of gasoline that made him feel like he could faint and fall into a deep sleep at any moment.

He struck the match, and threw it on the floor, the crackle of flames immediately filling his basement.

CHAPTER 49

Samantha walked into the first hut through the open doorway. It smelled…like nothing. Dirt perhaps. It was bare except for the everyday items found in any household: dishes, quilts, sandals by the entrance, decorations up on the walls. There was a bed with a quilt over it laid flat. It was just a slab of stone with a few furs and she went and removed the quilt.

"You see something?" Duncan asked, coming up behind her.

"No."

"I don't see anything either. Let's go."

They exited the hut and made their way to the next one. There was nothing there. They searched two more and then two more, each one barer than the last. In the center of the village was a large pit that looked like it had been used for fires. It was the village's meeting place, Sam guessed. Serving the same function as the forums in Rome and the capitol buildings, or maybe the shopping malls, in modern cities.

"I think there must've been a mass exodus," she said. "Everyone took off in a real hurry."

"If Agent X infected this village, there should be bones."

"They probably buried them in the jungle and the animals got them after that. I don't think there's much wasted here."

Duncan glanced around. "We haven't checked out those huts over there. Let's hit them and then head back."

They went to the first hut and found it just as bare, but the second hut had bowls with food in them lying out on the floor. The food was rotted, maggots finishing off the remnants. There was a quill of arrows in one corner. Sam ran her hand over them; they were sharp and made of smooth iron with jagged edges that made them more difficult to pull out of flesh once they'd entered.

In another corner was a pile of clay dishes. The dishes were old and cracked and heaped on top of each other. Sam was about to turn away and head out of the hut when she noticed something silver in the pile of clay. She reached down to the dishes and carefully removed a few of them. Underneath was a metal canister. It was about a foot in length with a secure black top that had been opened. The thick, black, plastic bottom had grooves cut into it.

"Duncan, get over here."

He came up behind her and peeked over her shoulder. "Holy shit."

"It's a viral container."

"Holy shit."

"What? What's wrong?"

"Hold on." He reached down and though he had on two layers of gloves, he used one of the dishes to flip the canister over. "That's not just a viral container. That's a military viral container. We use the same ones at USAMRIID."

"The Russians use the same too. I'm sure the North Koreans and Iranians would as well."

"Only one way to tell. On the very bottom we print a series of alphanumeric code. The Russians don't do that. Neither does anyone else I've seen."

He hesitated. Holding the dish in his hand, he didn't make a move toward the canister and neither did Sam. Time seemed to slow and Sam thought she was holding her breath but couldn't be sure. Finally, he flipped the canister the other way, turning the bottom toward them.

There were three lines of code.

"I was really hoping you wouldn't see that," a voice said behind them.

They turned. Standing at the entrance of the hut was Donner. His arms were on either side of the entrance and in his right hand Sam could see a gun.

"What is this?" Sam said. "This is American. What the hell's going on?"

"Balance, Dr. Bower. I told you once. It's all about balance."

Duncan scoffed. "Our enemies have this weapon so our allies should too, is that it?"

He shrugged. "Or maybe our allies have this weapon and our enemies should too. Balance runs both ways. Do you know what happens when one civilization dominates the world for too long? Decadence, corruption…evil. Sodom and Gomorrah, Babylon, Egypt, Persia, Rome, the French, British, Germans, Russians, and now us. We've learned our lesson. We need balance. It is the only thing in history that matters."

Duncan turned and picked up the canister. "Just take it and leave."

"I think we're past that, Dr. Adams."

Duncan looked down to the canister and then threw it at Donner. After the throw he rushed him but Donner was too fast. He punched at the canister sending it to the ground and lifted his firearm, getting off two rounds that slammed into Duncan and sent him flying off his feet.

"No!" Sam screamed.

She ran at Donner as Duncan got back to his feet. Donner fired off a round and missed as Sam threw her entire weight into him. He easily twisted to the side and sent her flying off her feet and onto her back. He smirked as he raised his weapon to fire.

Duncan slammed the canister into the back of Donner's head. He toppled over and Duncan jumped for the gun in his hand. The two men started wrestling on the ground, each dazed and bleeding.

"Run!" Duncan screamed. "Run, go!"

Samantha got to her feet and sprinted out of the hut. She stopped at the entrance, unsure whether she should leave Duncan. She decided she couldn't do it and started to run back as Donner elbowed Duncan in the jaw, knocking him unconscious with one blow. Sam froze as Donner pulled up the gun and fired two rounds, the slugs embedding first in the dirt and then in the hut behind her. She screamed and ran, heading to where she had left Benjamin and Cami.

She ripped off her suit and faceguard, tearing off her gloves and throwing them. She sprinted so fast she hit something that was sticking out of the ground and fell flat on her face. She sat up, glancing back at what had caught her foot. It was long and off white with a bulbous end and a thin middle. She thought perhaps it was a root and then recognition rang in her mind: it was a human femur bone.

Sam was up on her feet again and running before she had time to process what she had seen. She ran until her legs burned and realized she had already passed where they had left Benjamin and Cami. She stopped and looked behind her. There was nothing but jungle.

She jogged back a few paces and saw something in the road about ten feet up. It looked like some garbage drifting out from the bushes. As she got closer she saw the brown leather boots and the white socks that went up past the ankles.

Reaching the spot, Sam bent over the body. It was Benjamin. He had a black wound in his eye; a large hole where his eyeball had been. The round hadn't exited and she checked his pulse, but it was too late. He had bled to death just moments ago. She quickly scoured the bushes and vine and weeds for Cami's body. But she didn't see anything.

There was a buzzing sound by her ear and she thought it was an insect. She glanced up to see Donner down the road firing at her. Another round whizzed by her head, closer this time, and she screamed. She turned and started running again.

CHAPTER 50

Samantha ran for over an hour. By the time she stopped her lungs burned and acid rose in her throat. She fell to her knees, her hands buried in the soft dirt, gasping for air. She knew it wasn't a good position for deep, heavily oxygenated breaths so she slowly rose and held her arms above her head, stretching out her lungs as far as she could.

It took almost ten minutes for her heart rate to slow to the point where she felt comfortable walking and she held her hands to her hips and looked around. There wasn't a single thing she recognized and she didn't know whether it was because she hadn't paid attention as they came up this road or because she was somewhere new. Either way, from the position of the sun, far west on the horizon, she could tell it was late afternoon. Night would fall soon and unless she could make it to a town she would be camping out here. Aside from the local tribes who might view her as an invader, she would be exposed to jaguars, snakes, venomous insects, and poisonous fire ants. Without something to keep her off the ground and a fire, she might not make it through the night. She checked her cell phone; no reception.

There was only one thing to do: she had to go back to the infected village. She had to check on Duncan and find their other cell phones. If she could find Cami they would have a much better chance of survival. Donner would be on the road. She glanced to both sides and chose east, going off the road about twenty feet. Enough that she could see her tracks but could duck under the jungle's vegetation if she had to.

She took a deep breath and started walking.

Every few minutes she looked back over her shoulder and looked down the road. She would stop and listen to the jungle but it was such an alien environment she didn't know what she was listening for. Someone could be walking right behind her but the noise of the insects and animals and river drowned everything else out.

Though the shrubbery wasn't thick it varied from razor sharp to blunt and sticky. It tore at her clothes and the exposed skin on her ankles and arms. She tried to distract her mind from the itchy, burning pain by thinking about home and what she would do first thing when she got back. She thought about her relationship with Duncan and whether…

The thought of Duncan pounded in her head. She shouldn't have left him. But what could she have done?

She thought of this and other things; her career, her relationship to Ralph, anything that would take her mind off the idea of reaching down and tearing at her flesh to relieve the pain.

By the time she looked up she was in familiar surroundings; the clearing right before the village where she had left Benjamin and Cami. The sun was setting but it was still light and she crouched down and watched the sunbeams glisten off the leaves and grass.

She wasn't sure how long she stayed there or what she was even looking for, but after a lengthy time she felt comfortable enough to get up and start making her way into the village.

It was as quiet and empty as it had been before. As she walked toward the hut she had left Duncan in, she kicked herself for not checking Benjamin for his cell phone as hers would soon be out of power.

The hut was right in front of her and she froze. She wasn't sure how long she stood there, but when she did move her heart was beating so fast she felt like it might tear out of her chest.

Samantha made her way to the hut and looked in. Duncan sat up, holding leaves to his shoulder just above the acromion bone. She ran in and threw her arms around him.

"Easy easy easy," he said, grimacing from the pain. "I'm okay. I'm okay."

"I'm sorry," she said, tears welling up in her eyes as she cupped his face in her hands. "I'm so sorry. I never should've left you."

"It's okay. It's okay. We're okay now." He pulled himself up a little stiffer, glancing down to the wound and then back up at her. "I need stitches, Sam. In Benjamin's bag I had a med kit. Can you get it?"

"Yeah, wait here," she said, wiping the tears away from her face and taking a deep breath.

"Wait, where's Billy? What happened?"

"I don't know. He came after me."

"Forget the med kit, we should get outta here. He'll be back."

She helped him to his feet and wrapped his arm around her neck. He didn't need stitches, Sam knew. She could see that the wound was only lightly bleeding now but he appeared ghostly white and was trembling; he was bleeding internally. Something had been nicked or punctured.

She stepped out of the hut and was startled by an image next to her. She saw Cami standing next to the hut, her face red and caked in sweat. Before Sam could say anything, Cami raised a small, black Beretta handgun and placed it against Sam's temple.

"What the hell are you doing?" Duncan said.

"Both of you back in the hut, now."

"Cami—"

"Right now or I finish the job."

They stepped back a few paces as she entered the hut with them. Sam noticed the quill of arrows and walked in front of it.

Cami kept the firearm away from her body and up at shoulder height, not low. Sam leaned against a wall of the hut and kept Duncan's weight on her.

"He'll be back soon," Cami said. "We're all just gonna wait right here."

"Who are you?" Sam said.

"You don't need to know."

Duncan said, "There's no need for this. Just let us go. We won't tell anybody anything. We don't know anything. We don't even know your real names."

"And you guys will just go back and not tell anyone that your own country gave a biological weapon to our enemies? You'll be able to keep your mouths shut, huh? You must have some serious self-control 'cause I couldn't do that."

"Cami, he's going to die if we don't get him to a hospital."

"He's going to die anyway."

"Fine, but he won't die here because of me. I'm taking him to a hospital." She took a few steps toward the door and Cami put the gun to her forehead.

"Then I guess you die with him," Cami said.

"You first."

Sam swung out with the arrow she was holding behind Duncan's back. It jammed into Cami's neck up to the shaft. Sam grabbed the gun and lowered it to the ground as Cami screeched. Sam ripped out the arrow, tearing away a large chunk of flesh, and lifted it above her head. She swung down and slammed the arrowhead into Cami's eye. It went through it like a knife into a tomato and the blood began to pour as Sam took the firearm and stepped away.

Cami fell to her knees, screaming as she frantically pulled at the arrow, causing more pain as it tugged at the flesh and arteries. Sam aimed the weapon at the back of her head. One shot to the back of the head was instant death, but she couldn't do it. She lowered the weapon.

Duncan had fallen on the ground and Sam rushed over to help him up and out of the hut, the screaming from inside fading in the distance as they hobbled down the road.

CHAPTER 51

They had walked through the night and it wasn't until dawn the next day that a few of the Penco tribe happened upon them. They didn't speak a word of English or Spanish but they understood that Duncan was severely injured and they led them back to a village that had a landline. Within two hours, a Jeep had arrived to take them to an awaiting plane and a hospital forty-five minutes from there.

She stayed with Duncan in the hospital. Partially, it was her affection for him, but it was also the fact that they didn't use sterile surgical equipment and the ceiling in the operating room was caked with dry blood. She scrubbed in and stood by his side as they removed the slug from his shoulder.

The recovery was short and they were on a Boeing 747 within three days, heading to Mexico, then LAX, then their separate ways. Duncan insisted on buying a ticket on her flight but she assured him she was fine and that they both had business to take care of before meeting up. He didn't seem convinced and bought the ticket anyway, but Sam persuaded him to reserve his own flight back to Maryland.

Duncan promised to come down to Atlanta as soon as he had recovered and she promised to come up as soon as everything was settled with the CDC. There would be massive reports to file, investigations, and possibly even some interviews with law enforcement. As she walked down to her gate, she turned and saw him standing against the wall, watching her. She would have preferred if he came with her; she didn't feel like being alone right now, but she wanted to be pragmatic.

As her plane descended into the airport in Atlanta, she felt a powerful sense of welcoming. Atlanta wasn't her hometown and she had few memories there, but there's just something about landing in the city you live in that calms you and fills you with optimism.

After landing and heading out to the curb for a taxi, her first call was to Ralph, but he didn't pick up; her second to her direct supervisor to apprise her of what had happened. They agreed that they would call the FBI tomorrow morning for a full briefing on Agent Billy Donner. But Sam had been through this before. Without any information to guide them, a report would be drafted and then filed away in an open case drawer somewhere, left untouched for years, even decades, until some agent with time on his hands decided to take a look at it. If lucky, because a federal employee was involved, the bureau might assign a special agent to follow up. Perhaps even send him to Honolulu.

The cab driver had to wake her as she got to her house. She went to pay and realized she didn't have cash. She told him to wait and ran inside to find her money. Sam kept some cash in a drawer in the kitchen and she took a fifty and ran back outside to pay the cabbie.

The night air was hot and the moon was out but it was partially hidden by the few clouds that were dotting the night sky. She walked down her porch steps and stared at the stars as she came to the driver side window.

"How much was the fare again?" she asked. The driver didn't respond. She bent down, closer to the window. "Excuse, how much was the fare?"

As she reached in to get his attention, she noticed the trickle of blood from behind his ear that was soaking the collar of his shirt. His eyes were glazed over and his head tilted just enough to the right that she couldn't have noticed it at first.

She felt soft cloth around her neck and then it tightened like a vice. It tightened so violently that she was lifted off her feet and her air was cut off instantly. She began to gag, and drool began to slop from her mouth.

"You know," Robert Greyjoy whispered in her ear. "It would've been far easier for you in the jungle. One quick shot and it would've ended. Now, I'm going to take my time."

He began dragging her into the home, her feet kicking the pavement as she tried to scream but nothing escaped her throat. She was dragged up her porch steps and into the house as he kicked the door shut behind them.

He threw her into the living room. As she lay on the floor, he lunged and kicked her in the ribs. She spun over with a groan, the air knocked out of her, as he smashed down on her hand with the heel of his shoe.

Robert paced a few seconds and then stomped on her ribs, and then on her Achilles tendon, sending a shockwave of pain up and down her body. He kicked her again and again in the head and ribs and chest until she lay flat on her back, silent, the blood pooling around her and her vision spinning. He stomped on her stomach and when she didn't move because of how numb her body had become, he stopped and stood over her.

"She was the only person in the world that I gave a shit about. The only one that actually knew who I really was. And you took that away from me. Do you know what that feels like? To be absolutely alone in the world? I was alone my entire life and for a brief period I thought, maybe, there was something else. Now I know there's not. You've shown me something, Dr. Bower. You've shown me that the universe is the cold, dark place I always thought it was. And I hate you for it. I hate you more than I've ever hated anything in my life." She mumbled something and Robert leaned down over her. "Was that begging that I just heard?"

"No," she said. "Turn around."

Robert looked up just as the 9mm Smith & Wesson fired. The round entered his cheek and exited out the back of his head, spattering brain matter, blood, and bits of skull over the carpet and wall. The corpse fell back over Sam, but she didn't have the strength to heave it off her.

Duncan leaned down and lifted the corpse, moving it to the side. He helped Sam to her feet, putting her arm around his neck as they began to walk out of the house.

"You came for me," she said, her voice hardly a whisper.

He looked to her, placing a soft kiss on her cheek. "There's nowhere else I want to be."

The numbers flashed on the computer monitor as General Lancaster sat in the executive chair in his office at the Pentagon. Numbers meant little to him, and yet for many people, those numbers were horror. They were the death of a husband or father or mother or child. He watched as they flickered higher and higher, nearly hypnotized. A knock at his office door snapped him out of his trance. Taking a sip from his coffee mug, he pressed a button on his keyboard and the screen turned to a still image of an American flag.

"Come in."

A tall man in a military uniform walked in. His chest looked like colorful Lego pieces had been attached. Lancaster always wished they had another system to show rank, especially since other groups had commandeered the rainbow.

The man sat down across from him, folding his hands across his lap.

"Well?" Lancaster said.

"It's not good."

"How bad?"

"California's lost. We have managed to stop anyone from leaving. All the freeways and bridges have been closed, planes grounded, no one in or out."

Lancaster exhaled. "Any other known cases?"

The man shook his head. "Thought we had one in Japan, but it turned out to be something else. Oahu and California seem to be it."

"What about South America?"

"Everyone's dead that was infected, best we can tell. Haven't gotten any new reports."

Lancaster nodded. "Withdraw all the troops from California. Have them stationed on the methods of exit."

"What about the deserts? They're huge, someone could just walk to Nevada."

"California is now foreign territory and needs to be treated as such, understood?"

"You…you saying you want us to open fire on our own citizens?"

"You think I like this decision, Marty? Give me another viable alternative, I'm all ears…nothing? I didn't think so. Get the order out among the population. Anyone trying to leave will be gunned down. I want chopper patrols, men on the ground, Humvee's, you give me everything you got."

"If you say so. But someone infected with this thing probably couldn't walk very far anyway."

"We're not risking it. This thing stops here. If we need to, we'll build a damn wall."

The man shrugged. "You're the boss," he said, rising. As he was leaving, he turned and looked at Lancaster. "We're just leaving them to die, aren't we?"

"No, we're leaving them so the rest of us can live."

The man nodded, and walked out the door.

PESTILENCE, Book Two of the Plague Trilogy, at Amazon.com

AUTHOR'S REQUEST

If you enjoyed this book, please leave a review on Amazon. Good reviews not only encourage authors to write more, they improve our writing. Shakespeare rewrote sections of his plays based on audience reaction and modern authors should take a note from the Bard.

So please leave a review and know that this author appreciates each and every one of you!

ABOUT THE AUTHOR

Victor Methos is the bestselling author of THE WHITE ANGEL MURDER and DIARY OF AN ASSASSIN. His works have appeared in magazines and literary journals across the United States and United Kingdom. He is currently on a quest to climb the "Seven Summits," the highest points on earth, and to attain his certification as a deep-sea submersible pilot. He can be reached through his blog at www.methosreview.blogspot.com

51243594R00192

Made in the USA
San Bernardino, CA
31 August 2019